ANGEL WRATH

By
J.E. Taylor

J.E. TAYLOR
SUPERNATURAL SUSPENSE
& DARK FANTASY AUTHOR

ANGEL WRATH

On the outside it looks like my life has returned to normal.

I have Valerie, my soul mate, by my side in wedded bliss. But darkness overshadows my happily-ever-after. My guilt for sending my father to an eternity of torture at Lucifer's hands is a pain I cannot escape.

When Valerie and I return from our honeymoon, a note from the king of hell greets me, outlining in sickening detail his plans for the rest of those I hold dear.

With everyone I love on the devil's hit list, it's time I start living up to the bargains I made in Heaven. I need to close Hell's gates. All of them. But for every portal I close, its one less available for my father's escape.

Chapter 1

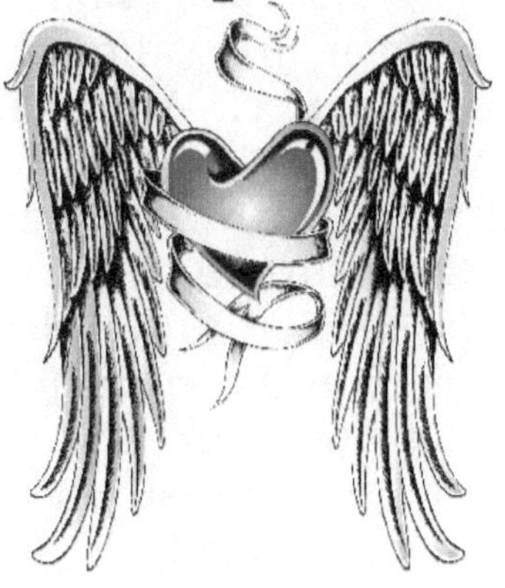

I SHIFTED MY WEIGHT, doing my best to conceal the nerves biting at my skin. The warm fall day didn't help with the light sweat seeping through my shirt and into the black fabric of the tuxedo. I scanned the small crowd settling into the chairs arranged overlooking York Harbor and smiled at the familiar faces.

I would have only recognized a handful of these people last year, but after my adventure to heaven and back, my memories returned along with the truth of what I really was. A trinity, infused with angel grace.

I glanced at my watch. The ceremony was supposed to have started five minutes ago.

Tom's hand landed on my shoulder, and I met his gaze.

"Raven was a little late to our wedding, too. Remember?"

I nodded, but it didn't really settle me. I wouldn't relax until Valerie was in my sights. It wasn't so much wedding jitters as that old paranoia that accosted me any time she wasn't with me. I'd learned to deal with it, just like I'd learned to deal with my asinine stutter. At least it wasn't as prevalent as it was when I came out of the coma, but it remained like an unwelcome reminder that I was still vulnerable to human frailty.

The violins started the wedding march, and people stood, blocking my view. I held my breath, waiting for her to appear at the end of the makeshift aisle. When she stepped into view, the familiar tingle that locked my chest took over and I had to force myself to breathe. She was beyond stunning.

"Wow," I whispered, and she lit up. Even at a distance, she knew my thoughts stalled, and I knew she had the same reaction seeing me in the finely tailored Armani.

She glanced at Damian, his arm ensnaring hers as he walked her down the aisle. He stopped in front of me, leveling the look I knew came with a warning. If I ever hurt her, I'd have to answer to him.

I gave him a slight nod of thanks and he passed her hand into mine.

My gaze locked with hers and I didn't even hear the preacher's opening greeting; I was so focused on the slow storm swirl in her lightly frosted eyes. This was the first time I ever remember seeing her with makeup and it was subtle enough to draw out the vibrancy within her irises, completely mesmerizing me to the point nothing else made a difference. I wanted to pull her into my arms and kiss her glossy lips, wondering if that shine had a sweet taste to go along with it.

Her dimples appeared, and she broke eye contact, bringing me back into the here and now.

The preacher looked at me, raising his eyebrow expectantly.

"Hmm?" I hadn't heard a word since she stepped into view.

"Are you ready to proceed?"

My cheeks heated, and I slid my glance to her. "Yes, sir."

She pressed her lips together in a smirk. *You didn't hear a thing he said, did you?* Her thought crept into my head.

Not a fucking thing. I sent the thought back and grinned, looking out over the ocean for a minute before focusing on the minister. *You are that stunning.* I glanced at her and the rose hue in her cheeks was more than just powdered blush. Her sweet dimples appeared, and I had to take a deep breath.

"If anyone here can show just cause why these two should not be joined in holy matrimony, speak now or forever hold your peace."

Silence settled, and I squeezed her hand. She squeezed back, and the minister waited another ten seconds before he glanced at the two of us.

"Please, join hands," he said.

I turned toward Valerie, taking both her hands in mine, painfully aware that I had to focus, and not zone out on the thoughts parading through my head of what I wanted to do with her on our wedding night.

"Christopher James Ryan, do you intend to take this woman, whose hands you hold, to be your lawfully wedded wife? And do you pledge before God and man to love, honor, and protect her through sunshine and shadow alike, keeping yourself unto her alone until death shall separate you?"

"I do," I said without prompting.

"Valerie Elizabeth Denongalis, do you intend to take this man, whose hands you hold, to be your lawfully wedded husband? and do you pledge before God and man to be to him a loving and true wife, through sunshine and shadow alike, keeping yourself unto him alone, until death shall separate you?"

"I do," she answered, and her eyes sparkled like a rainbow.

"Christopher and Valerie have written their vows," he said, and gave me a nod.

I licked my lips and took a breath, praying my stutter wouldn't ruin the moment. My gaze met hers and she squeezed my hands, making me smile.

"Valerie, you know me better than anyone else in this world, and somehow you still manage to love me. You are my best friend and one true love. Getting to this point hasn't been easy for either of us, but all the trials were worth it to be standing here today. I'd gladly walk through the fires of hell for you." I unclasped my hand and cupped her cheek, wiping the single tear with my thumb. "You are more precious than anything the kingdom of heaven has to offer," I said and paused with my gaze locked on hers. "I love you with my whole heart and beyond the depths of my soul, and I promise with everything I am, to love and honor you, faith...fully, for all time."

Her lips twitched into a smile at my stutter. I resisted the urge to pull her closer and deliver the kiss I'd been itching to give her since she took the spot next to me.

"Chris," she began, and her voice cracked. She cleared her throat and lick her lips. "I never used to believe soul mates existed, and then I met you. The feeling hit me the moment we made eye contact. It was so immediate and powerful—far deeper and inexplicably beyond any calculation of time and place. You described it perfectly that night with two words that I won't repeat here." Her cheeks turned crimson, and I knew exactly what two words she meant.

"You completely stole my heart with your awkward attempt at wooing me."

God bless her, she even added the right Irish inflection as she mimicked the way Raven first said those words and it earned her a soft chuckle from most of the guests. She grinned and glanced over her shoulder at Raven before meeting my gaze again.

"You're right, we've encountered a lot of bumps in the road to get to today, but there isn't anyone I'd rather take this journey with. I promise to stand by you through hellfire and brimstone, to soar with you on life's highs. I promise to help shoulder our challenges because I believe there is nothing we cannot face if we stand together. And above all else, I promise you my love, through all eternity, because one lifetime with you could never be enough."

My eyes misted, and I blinked back the tears that had blurred my vision at the bull's-eye of her words. I mouthed the words 'I love you' before I focused back on the minister and the ring ceremony.

I slid the ring on her finger, reciting the words the minister prompted, and she did the same.

"Ladies and gentlemen, I give you Mr. and Mrs. Christopher Ryan. You may kiss your bride," the minister said.

I pulled her into my arms, kissing her like it was our first kiss. Soft at first, but the strawberry wine gloss on her lips fueled my desire, and I ran my hand into her finely coifed hair, dipping her as the kiss deepened. The guests started whooping, and I stood her back up, releasing the kiss and turning toward the audience that I had momentarily forgotten existed.

"Party time, Mrs. Ryan," I whispered with a grin, and we headed toward the Reading Room where we were planning on drinking, dining and dancing the night away.

I glanced at Valerie as we organized into a reception line.

"How the hell did I get so lucky?" I whispered, and she beamed. "If I forget to tell you later, you look beautiful tonight."

"So do you," she whispered.

We strolled down the curved stairwell onto the outside deck overlooking York Harbor. The sunset painted the sky a rainbow of colors that blended with the autumn leaves and I couldn't have envisioned a more perfect evening.

We stood in the reception line greeting guests. The first one through was my grandfather. I hadn't seen him since before my accident and he looked even frailer than when we buried my grandmother five years before.

"Papa, this is Valerie. Valerie, this is my grandfather, Russ Campbell," I said, and she extended her hand, unsure of whether a hug was appropriate, especially since the man was in a wheelchair. He waved her hand away and pushed himself to his feet, offering her a hug instead.

"Pleased to meet you," he said, and lowered back into the chair, bringing his gaze to mine. "Your mother would be so proud of you," he added, and patted my hand before the nurse wheeled him into the reception hall.

"How old is he," Valerie whispered, and I shrugged, trying to calculate his age in my head.

"Close to one hundred," I said, still watching my grandfather as he directed his nurse to the bar. I smiled and turned my gaze to the next guest, and my smile froze.

Sandy's hazel eyes met mine. I had sent the invite to Dan and LeAnn as a courtesy, but I never thought they'd show, never mind bring Sandy along.

I recovered and turned toward Valerie, suddenly uncomfortable with the less than thrilled expression on her face. It took her a moment longer to replace the shock with a smile.

"It's good to see you again," Valerie said, in that fake saccharine voice that pulled a smirk to my lips.

"Likewise," Sandy said, but the flare of jealousy that tightened the corners of her lips betrayed her actual feelings on the matter. She gave me a peck on the cheek. "I'm glad you're happy," she whispered, and wandered away.

I turned to the next person in line and met Dan's hard gaze. LeAnn stood next to him, and her features were more genuine.

"Dan and LeAnn Connor," I said to Valerie, and she nodded, flashing her winning smile in their direction.

"It's a pleasure meeting you," she said.

"The pleasure's ours," Daniel replied and placed a kiss on the back of her hand. "This is my wife, LeAnn," he added, as they moved down the line.

Tom met my gaze as soon as they passed him, and his eyebrow rose.

I didn't think they'd actually show. I sent the thought and his smirk appeared.

"You really sent her an invitation?" Valerie whispered in my ear as soon as they stepped out of hearing range.

I met her glare and gave a single shoulder shrug before focusing on the next guest. I knew I'd pay for that later, but for now, she put the dazzling smile back in place and we both turned to another blast from my past.

"Ted, how the hell are you?" I grinned.

"I'm good. You remember Heather," he said, motioning to his wife.

"I certainly do. This is my bride, Valerie. Val, this is Ted and Heather Beaumont, good friends of Steve and Jen's."

"Nice to meet you," she said, and opted for hugs instead of the overly formal handshake. She had our memories, so she knew they went way back with Steve. They were one of the few real friends Steve had. They'd come by with their kids almost every summer since Steve took us in, and I smiled beyond Heather at Sydney and Andrew Beaumont who had accompanied their parents, with dates of their own.

A group of Valerie's friends approached us after the Beaumont's cleared out and she was kind enough to do introductions.

"So, this is coma-boy," said one of the women with whom Valerie did her first- and second-year residency. Her gaze slid up and down my form, and then returned to Valerie with a nod of approval.

"Nice to meet you, too," I said, and unfortunately, my sarcasm bled through in my tone.

"I'm sorry, but the last time I saw you, you were covered with tubes and wires." She offered a wry smile and extended her hand. "I'm Claire," she added.

I shook her hand and gave Valerie a raised eyebrow as Claire continued into the reception.

"She's a neurosurgeon," Valerie said, like that explained the weird, direct, non-personality.

The next two people in line brought a smile. "Mrs. Kincaid," I said.

"I've told you a million times, please call me Carolyn," she said, and pulled me into a hug. "Congratulations!" she added, and then focused on Valerie with a grin.

"Valerie, this is Carolyn Kincaid and her husband Randy," I did introductions and then added, "Randy manages our portfolio."

Randy took her hand and kissed it in the same manner as Daniel had, but his was more sincere. "Pleasure to meet the woman who finally pinned this guy down," he said, hooking his thumb in my direction.

"Nice to meet you," Valerie said, grinning.

The next few folks to pass through the reception line included our lawyer, Lynn Trueman, and Steve's old boss, Ron Cleary. Beyond them stood Captain O'Keefe, of the York Police Department.

Captain O'Keefe stepped up and offered his hand. "Congratulations, kid."

"Thanks, Captain," I said. "I'd like you to meet my wife, Valerie. Val, this is the captain of the York Police Department. He hauled my ass in so many times when I was younger, it wasn't funny."

He chuckled. "Your husband and his brother were a little wild in their youth."

Valerie grinned. "I'll bet," she said and added, "Thank you for sharing this day with us."

He wandered off and a few other stragglers from my high school days came through the line. And then it was time for the rest of us to head in and grab something to eat before the real festivities began.

"You invited Sandy," Valerie said, when we were the last two on the terrace.

I met her sharp stare. "I invited the family. I never in my wildest dreams thought she'd show up with them."

"Jesus, Chris," she said, and turned away from the building. "It's supposed to be our day," she added, crossing her arms.

I glanced up at the windows and there was the subject of our conversation just staring at the two of us. Her expression was one of longing and I turned away, irritated that my ex had the audacity to show up at my wedding. I invited her parents because of the family history and their connection with Steve. He had asked if I minded, and honestly, they were a big part of our lives for many years, so I didn't think it through.

"It is our day." I focused back on Valerie, stepping beside her and slinging my arm over her shoulder. My motive was two-fold: one to comfort my wife, and the other to bring home to my ex that there was absolutely nothing there. "I'm married to the most wonderful woman in the world, and I couldn't care less about who else is here, beyond the wedding party."

Her gaze slid to mine. "Liar," she breathed, and I rolled my eyes.

"Okay, I'm not thrilled, either," I admitted and a smirk appeared. "But here's the deal. I just promised my heart to you, in front of everyone. I meant every word of my vows. You're it, whether or not you believe me."

While my biggest insecurity was having Valerie out of my sight, hers was my ex and the fifteen-year history we had shared before it fell to pieces. I had valid concerns, but hers were just asinine.

"Why would you even send them an invitation?" she pushed.

"Because Eric was Steve's partner and Dan is his father," I said, even though she knew that. "Steve asked me if I minded having them on the list." I took her hand. "Eric is the reason I exist," I added, and she softened. "So..." I trailed off and shrugged.

"I get it." She sighed and squeezed my hand. "But you'd better not dance with her," she muttered and started in, dragging me with her.

Chapter 2

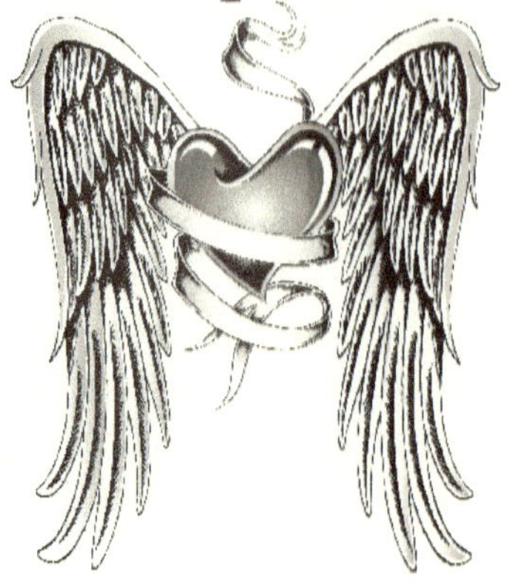

THE DINNER AT THE reception hall was to die for, and everyone raved about it. I led Valerie out onto the floor and the band began the haunting melody she loved so much. Granted, Hallelujah wasn't exactly a love song, but it had meaning for both of us, and she wanted to hear me sing on her wedding day.

I crooned as I spun her around, my voice lifting over the instruments and caressing the crowd as much as it did Valerie. She just stared at me with rapture, and I grinned as the last note trailed away.

"How's that Mrs. Ryan?" I whispered in her ear.

"Perfect," she grinned, and nibbled on my neck. She led me off the floor and pecked me on the lips. "I'll be right back," she said, and pointed toward the bathroom. Raven followed her to help with the dress and I sighed when she stepped out of view.

"Care to dance?"

I turned, meeting Sandy's gaze, and shifted. Valerie's warning had been clear. She didn't want me touching Sandy tonight in any manner. But now that I was cornered, I traded a glance with Tom and he nodded to the dance floor, knowing I couldn't gracefully decline the offer without offending her. Besides, it was a dance beat and not a slow song.

"Sure," I said and as we stepped onto the dance floor, the fast beat transitioned to a slow song and I paused, glancing toward the restrooms.

"She isn't jealous of me. Is she?" Sandy asked, drawing my attention.

I sighed. "Just a little," I said. "Can you blame her?"

Sandy raised an eyebrow. "Does she have something to be jealous about?" She wrapped her arms around my neck, tilting her head and licking her lips in that come-hither way that used to get me, but it only irritated me now. She stepped close, swaying her hips against me with the slow cadence of the music.

I unwrapped her arms from my neck and took her hand in mine, opting for a more formal position with my hand at her waist and space between us. If I was going to dance with the girl, I'd damned well make sure only a limited portion of our bodies touched. I didn't want her getting the wrong idea, especially since this really was a bid to get under my skin.

"No, she doesn't," I said, answering her question. "She's just always been intimidated by the fact we were together for so long." I shrugged and glanced beyond her. Valerie hadn't come out yet and my nerves bundled in my stomach. I bit my lip, contemplating the time that had gone by since she disappeared into the ladies' room.

"What's wrong?" Sandy asked, pulling my gaze back to her. She knew my tells, and I debated just keeping quiet, but her eyebrows arched, prompting me silently.

"I don't like it when Val is out of my sight," I said.

"Why?" she asked, her voice filled with coy reserve.

"Demons," I said and her face blanched, bringing back unwanted memories. "They haven't hit in a while, and I wouldn't put it past the devil to fuck up my wedding day."

"You know, I had years of therapy for what you did to Josh," she said, and I couldn't help but laugh.

"I know," I said, still smiling. "I'm sorry for leaving such a mess."

"You killed my boyfriend," she said, and her features hardened.

"I killed a demon that was trying to kill you," I replied, meeting her gaze. "Unfortunately, that demon was wearing your boyfriend."

"You did that two places at one-time thing, too. When the hell did you start that?"

"When Valerie and I traded memories," I said. "She got the healing mojo, and I got everything else."

Sandy's gaze jumped to Steve and then back to me. "I thought Steve had that."

"A lot of shit went down after I walked in on you, but the bottom line is really simple. Val and I have everything, just like my mom and dad did."

She slowed to a stop and just stared at me. She knew the story of my parents from Eric, our half-brother. Eric had said a million times my parents were meant to be together. That they balanced each other out. That it was written in the stars.

Sadness engulfed me because now they weren't together. Mom was in Heaven and my father was in hell, and there wasn't a damned thing I could do about it.

"We were never meant to be, Sandy."

Hurt flared in her eyes, and she stepped back just as Valerie came into view. I didn't look up at my wife. Instead, I kept Sandy's gaze.

"You kept me sane at a time in my life when things could have pushed me over the edge, and I'm grateful to you for that, but Valerie is the one I was always meant to be with," I added, and shrugged. "I have a feeling if she had come along when we were together, it wouldn't have made a difference. I'd still be standing here today with her... not you."

Tears filled Sandy's eyes, and she spun away, bolting off the dance floor and passing where Valerie stood without a glance.

I met my wife's gaze as she crossed to me. She stepped into my waiting arms.

"I thought..." she started, her breath tickling my ear.

"She asked me to dance," I said, stopping the rest of her admonishment.

She pulled away and met my gaze. "You didn't need to make her cry," she said, and for the first time since we met, there was pity reflected in her eyes where Sandy was concerned.

"I told her the truth. In the nicest possible way I know how."

"It was still a crushing blow," she said, but her eyes softened.

"Not insecure anymore?" I asked, tilting my head.

She slowly shook her head. I had left my mind open to her during the entire conversation and she was privy to the sincerity of the words I spoke.

"It's about damned time," I smiled and caught a gentle kiss.

"Now we just need to work on you," she said, when our lips parted.

I let out a small laugh. "That will not be as easy. Not until we close every portal and I know that bastard can't get topside," I said. I glanced around at the people dancing and mingling in the other room, and then back at her. "I'm actually surprised he didn't somehow crash this event," I added, and met her gaze.

The mere mention of Lucifer, even if I didn't use his name, brought a shadow to her eyes. She still battled the image of me hurting her and I knew if I ever got the drop on him, I'd pummel his ass until he was worse than I was the first time we squared off.

Chapter 3

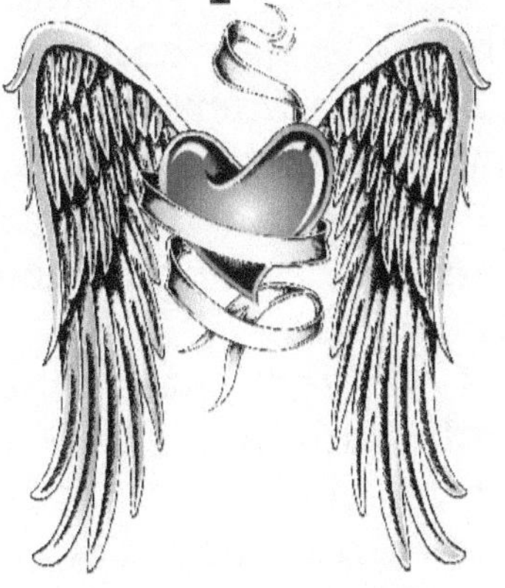

THE HOTEL DOOR CLOSED, and I turned, staring at my bride. I stepped toward her, licking my lips with anticipation. I'm not sure whether it was the hungry look in my eyes or the way I stalked toward her, but her face paled and I stopped. My eyes widened at the hints of the fear triggered in her. It had been almost a year since I saw her flinch at my approach, and it was not welcome on our wedding night.

I pressed my lips against the curses that wanted to spill forth, and she gave me a strained smile. The fact Lucifer cast a gray net over this day pissed me off to no end, but I attempted to shelve that anger and focus on Valerie.

"I'm sorry," I said.

She laughed, but her eyes sparkled with a layer of tears. "You just..."

"Reminded you of him." I tore off the cummerbund I was wearing, turning toward the bathroom before I lashed out in some other way.

"Chris," she whispered.

I came to a halt at the doorway. A deep cleansing breath and a slow count to three loosened the tension in my shoulders and I turned toward her. "You just look so goddamned beautiful tonight." I tried to explain the appearance of the hungry animal in me. The one Lucifer had used to poison her memories.

Every time I lapsed into that mindset, she freaked out and tonight I had to swallow the budding fury and forget about it. If I didn't, he'd drive a wedge between us again.

"Come, take a bath with me." I pointed at the huge whirlpool tub in the bathroom suite.

She crossed to my side and her eyebrows arched at the bathroom accommodations we had and the large tub that looked out on our private balcony and the ocean view beyond.

"A bubble bath?"

I smiled at the intrigue in her voice and nodded. "Anything you want."

The darkness between us passed, and I saw the Valerie I dearly loved in the smile forming on her lips. Her eyes danced with renewed mischief, and I grinned, waving her into the room ahead of me.

She stopped in front of me and pulled her hair to the side, revealing the intricate lace buttons lining the back. "Do you mind?"

I debated on just pulling it apart and letting the buttons sail everywhere, but she sent a cocked eyebrow in my direction.

"There's a zipper," she said and smirked.

"Oh." That sucker was hidden behind the lace, and as soon as I unclasped the top hooks, the zipper was easily accessed. I pulled it down slowly, each tooth clicking, and I smiled at her beautiful honey-tanned back. The view pulled me in, and I planted kisses along the pathway my hands took to peel the wedding dress from her shoulders.

She shivered under each swipe of my tongue, and I circled around to the front, pulling her to me in a kiss that swept us both away. When her dress dropped to the ground, she pulled away from my mouth and gingerly stepped out of the silky fabric.

"What are you doing?" I asked when she leaned down and picked up the dress.

"I'm not leaving this on the bathroom floor. Are you nuts?"

I guess a man really doesn't get the attachment a woman has to her wedding dress. She was handling it as gently as one would handle a china doll and all I could do was think of the ways to get her beautiful body out of the dress. She glanced over her shoulder at my train of thought.

"It's a five-thousand-dollar dress," she said like that explained it.

"And?"

She rolled her eyes at me. "It's my wedding dress. I'm never going to wear it again," she stressed the word wedding, and I gave her a smirk. "But if we ever have a little girl, she might want to wear it."

"We can afford for our daughter to get whatever she wants. Even a diamond studded dress."

She carefully laid the dress over the chair and returned to my side. "You mean I could have had a dress designed with diamonds instead of Swarovski crystals?"

I chuckled. "Yep. But I doubt it would have outshone you."

Dimples appeared. "That was pretty corny," she giggled, and unbuttoned my shirt. I went to help her, and she knocked my hands away. "I got this."

"By all means." I let her undress me. Each stitch of clothing dropped to the floor, and she stepped back, studying me. She still had her undergarments on, and I stood with just the black dress socks still adorning my feet.

I lifted my hands to the silky fabric of her corset, and she stopped me with a shake of her head. Again, I had to control my reaction until I met her gaze. The grin on her face told me this was her game tonight. Her tease; and it would put me into orbit.

When she stepped out of the floor length slip, I scanned her, my gaze locking on the hints of blue steel connecting her garter belt to her stockings. Handcuffs. Blue steel handcuffs. My gaze jumped back to hers and I laughed.

"Something blue?"

"Yes," she replied, and unhooked the first pair, dangling it from her finger.

I reached down to strip my socks, and she shook her head.

"Get into the tub," she added, the commanding tone of her voice arched my eyebrow.

This was her way of dealing with the atrocities Lucifer rained on her.

Control.

Without it, she flinched, and I had long since given up in that department. It was the only way we were able to get past what he did; the only way she trusted me in the bedroom. Since Lucifer defiled her, she had gone farther into the kink zone, insisting on all the control. I knew the drill well enough by now, but I had hoped tonight would be different.

Sighing, I stepped into the tub, and took a seat with the ocean view greeting me. Warm steel clasped around my wrist with a bite, and I glance up at her. She pulled my hand toward the fixed handrails on the tile outside the tub. The click of the other end split the silence and along with it came that seductive dominatrix smile that always worried me.

I dropped my gaze to the other pair on her hip and noticed the engraved sigils. In the back of my mind, I cursed Lucifer for the damage he had done to her, and when my gaze traveled back to hers, I saw the hardness move in.

She snapped the other cuff on my free wrist, pulling it to the opposite handrail. The position I was left in wasn't all that comfortable, but that was part of her game. Secretly, whether or not I wanted to admit it, the juxtaposition of the pain and pleasure was hotter than hell.

The smile returned as she stepped into the dry tub and pulled my covered foot to her stomach. The slow peel of my sock and the way she was standing stirred the heat in my stomach and I smiled back at her. She did the same with my other sock, sending it into the same careless arc that the first had taken.

I was naked and at her mercy, just the way she liked me. I hadn't tied her down since after Tom killed Raven's father, and right now, the memory of our bondage escapades ran through my head. I could have easily broken the cuffs, but I knew the power it instilled, and Valerie needed that more than I did.

To my surprise, she stepped out of the tub, cranking the hot water on full blast. The heat was immediate, unlike our slow furnace at home, and when she leaned down and closed the drain, my gaze jumped to hers.

"Are you trying to scald me?" I asked, pulling my feet away from the water.

Her reaction was almost enough for me to unclasp the handcuffs. She just smiled. Her gaze traveled to the shelf lining the wall where an ice bucket holding a chilled bottle of champagne sat, along with a plate of strawberries and cream. Her silence and the creeping water made me shift. I could easily break free any time I wanted or add the cold water to the river of heat filling the tub, but if I intervened with her private fantasy, it would end up in an argument.

I didn't want an argument tonight. I just wanted to make love to my wife.

The heightened color in her cheeks told me she was enjoying my discomfort and if I played along, I would be rewarded. I turned away and closed my eyes, gritting my teeth against the burn as the water climbed onto my toes. Valerie sprinkled an elixir in the water and the soft scent of lavender filled the room, along with the steam.

"Fuck. That's hot," I whispered through clenched teeth and opened my eyes. Bubbles had grown from the concoction she poured in the water, and I glanced at her. "Too hot," I said and willed the cold dial to turn, diluting the heat from scalding to something manageable.

Her pouty lips thinned with aggravation.

"It's not like the water at home," I said, glaring at her. "This is near boiling."

"Wus," she muttered, but she stepped closer, dipping her finger in the brew surrounding me. She yanked it back and her eyes widened. "Oh, shit, babe, I am so sorry," she said and reached for the cold water.

"I already adjusted it a little," I said, and her hand stopped, testing the water under the cooler spout.

"Really, I didn't mean to burn your ass," she said, sliding her gaze toward me and I grinned.

"No?"

She huffed a small laugh and shook her head.

"Ah. You just meant to ride me until I drown in these bubbles?" I cocked my eyebrow as the suds rose to my chin. The water had already risen above my lap and was approaching the halfway-full mark.

Her laughter rang out, and she stripped the rest of her clothing, turned the faucet off, and stepped into the water with me. I got a quick view of her slender form before she kneeled into the suds, straddling me. She leaned in, planting her palms on my chest and caught a soft kiss before she flipped the whirlpool jets on.

The results were hilarious.

Bubbles expanded at a rate neither of us was prepared for, spilling over the sides of the tub and onto the tile floor. Her eyes went wide, and she started giggling as the soft lavender-scented spheres overcame both of us. I just leaned my head back and laughed while she fumbled with the controls. Her first attempt to turn it off did the opposite; it turned the jets on full blast. They felt good against my back, but they reproduced bubbles faster than an atomic blast. By the time she found the off button, we were both laughing so hard the water was already sloshing under the thick bubble layer.

Valerie cleared a path from her to me, and still laughing, she kissed me. The kiss lingered under the laugh and then it transformed time and space, sucking the air from my lungs as our tongues intertwined. Even the soft crinkle of popping bubbles dulled to a distant white noise, and I longed to wrap my arms around her.

When she pulled back, I opened my eyes and met her gaze.

"I want to hold you," I said, diverting from her usual game.

A shadow passed over her features. "Chris," she sighed. Her fingers lightly traced the tattoo on my chest. Uriel's mark. My reminder of my time in heaven. Her gaze lifted to mine.

"I need to hold you," I whispered, breaking the rules she dictated. I still hadn't willed my wrists free, so she knew I was asking her permission. It was a psychological game, a step toward further healing, and I knew I might tip the balance, but I really didn't care.

"I want to hold my wife tonight, while we make love," I said, this time with more strength behind it. "Please," I added, and for the first time in years, I saw the same need in her. When she nodded, the double click of the cuffs releasing drifted through the bubbles.

I resisted the urge to wrap my arms around her and pull her to my lips; instead, I cupped her cheeks and met her halfway. This kiss was filled with her hesitations and fueled by her passions; it was just as polar as the pleasure-pain realm of being locked in chains while she toyed with me.

My hands drifted. One slid around her waist and the other caressed her breast. She stiffened, and I realized my hand covered her heart. Instead of reacting, I continued my gentle kneading, rolling her nipple between my fingers while our tongues danced.

She pulled away.

"It's okay. I will not hurt you," I said, meeting her gaze. She had that deer in the headlights look like she expected my hand to form a claw and tear through her skin. I kept on playing with her breast, offering her what I hoped was a reassuring smile until the tension in her face relaxed a fraction.

I licked my lips and pulled on her lower back, bringing her wet nipple to my mouth. Tasting her on my terms was better than stepping into the soothing, warm sea in heaven and her hands laced through my hair.

She sighed my name, and I moved to her other breast, alternating between gently sucking and rolling my tongue over the hard nipple. I took advantage of her bliss and moved my hand between her thighs.

Again, she stiffened and pulled away. I remained quiet, just staring into her eyes while I circled her clit with my thumb. I had won two psychological wars tonight, and I was going for the trifecta.

"I love you, Mrs. Ryan," I whispered, and tears sprang to her eyes.

The battle between fear and pleasure raged within her, and she kept my gaze. I made no other moves, but I also didn't stop my gentle fondling. I wanted her. All of her, not just the wild control monger. I needed to break down Lucifer's last strangle hold.

The soft purr that came from her throat took her by surprise and I couldn't help but lick my lips and send her a small smile. I tried not to grin. That would send her running for the cuffs, but the sparkle in her eyes set me on fire. I closed my eyes and sighed, forcing control over the wants flitting through my head.

"God, Valerie," I whispered and opened my eyes, meeting her stormy irises. I wanted to ask her to just let go and let me love her, but I left the thoughts behind the blockade I'd built in my mind. Most of the bubbles had fizzled and the effect she had on me was now obvious.

I don't think she realized it, but her hips were moving in slow circles, heightening the color in her cheeks and the hardness of her nipples. Her breath rasped in her throat as her body began accepting the pleasure and rejecting the fear.

She grabbed my hand, grinding into me, and her eyes squeezed closed. I understood and slid my finger inside her with care, despite her frantic efforts. My thumb still worked her the way she liked, and she clenched around my fingers, her moan filling the caverns of my soul as she came for me, spouting my name to the heavens.

The moment my hand pulled away, my cock filled her, and I pulled her close, crushing her lips. Her legs wrapped around me, and our sinuous motion rocked warm waves against us. Her hands threaded through my hair, and she moaned in my mouth, her body shaking with another orgasm.

I wrapped my arms around her and climbed to my feet. The kiss didn't stop when I stepped from the tub, nor did it while I crossed to the bed with her. When we were laid out on the soft linens and I was circling my hips with hers, I broke the kiss and stared down into her eyes, pushing the strands of wet hair away from her face.

"God, how I love you," I whispered, searching her soul for any shred of fear.

She smiled and pulled me back to her lips. I hadn't indulged in this bliss in over two years, and I lost track of time, moving slowly with her, letting my climax build until it burned, while she jumped hurdles like a champion show horse.

When I finally let go, I swear my heart stopped with the force of it.

I propped myself on my elbows and nuzzled my head on her shoulder. "I love you, lady," I whispered, my voice shaky with exertion.

"I love you, Christopher James Ryan," she said and planted a kiss on my shoulder.

I forced myself up from her soft shoulder and stared down into her stormy eyes. "I think the bath is probably cold."

"I'm not sure there's any water left in the bathtub."

I chuckled. "Would you like to resume that bath now?" I asked, rephrasing the question.

"Handcuffs and all?" she asked, and her eyebrow rose with the question.

"If that's what m'lady wants," I said, grinning.

"M'lady wants you at her mercy now," she said, and I rolled off her and headed into the bathroom. I stopped at the door, and she came up behind me, peeking over my shoulder.

A little giggle erupted, and I glanced over my shoulder at her. "Remind me to leave a hell of a tip for the maid before we leave, okay?"

"Okay," she swatted my bare behind and without direction, I stepped into the lukewarm water that barely covered my ankles.

I offered her my wrists and this time, there wasn't the angry flare in her eyes as she bound me in place, and the water she added wasn't enough to scald. This time, she also didn't add bubble bath, instead she engaged the jets and began her quest to slowly drive me insane with her hands and mouth and body.

After she had her way with me, we snuggled in the warm jets with glasses of champagne, and I fed her strawberries as we watched the moon's progress over the water.

"I think we finally beat him," she said, after the comfortable silence settled between us.

My heart soared.

Chapter 4

W E WALKED PAST THE security lines and Valerie cocked her head at me.

"Private jet," I said, and winked. I had been successful at keeping the honeymoon destination a secret and with the private plane; it would remain so until we landed, unless she took a peek in the pilot's mind. I had packed for the two of us and figured if I missed anything, we could pick it up in Honolulu before we headed out to Turtle Bay.

I navigated her through the terminal into the VIP lounge where we waited for Ted Beaumont to arrive. His family was staying with Steve and Jen down at the lake while Ted flew us to Hawaii. His sleekest private jet sat on the tarmac, and I couldn't wait for Valerie to see the flight accommodations we had. I knew the flight plan and the stop in San Diego was only for gassing the plane up for the last leg of the trip.

I arranged for a limo to drive us to the resort, and from there we'd have two weeks of honeymoon bliss in an ocean-side cottage.

I would have opted for longer, but I had already committed to a show at Carnegie Hall the week after we returned. I almost canceled my singing gig after Damian sprang an unwanted surprise on me at my bachelor party. He didn't know if the portal at the warehouse in New York was actually closed. I almost clocked him when he sprang that doozie on me, and it was enough to want to extend our island adventure just to avoid that fresh hell, but Valerie didn't want to leave her patients for more than two weeks.

Damian had pulled me aside and wanted me to make a side trip while I was in the city. I balked and asked what the hell he actually did that day besides making the building a pile of rubble. He mumbled something about angel fire and said I was the only one who seemed to have that talent down.

That was another piece of information I have successfully kept from Valerie. I wasn't sure I was going to share that planned adventure with her or not. I would rather have her safe in Maine than standing by my side at the place that nearly destroyed both of us. Besides, if it wasn't closed, I knew shutting the portal would tear my insides to shreds. Guilt was a funny thing, even with the promises I'd made in heaven. The fact my father was rotting in hell conflicted with the desire to close the devil's topside access because that meant one less avenue my father could use to escape.

"Are you okay?" Valerie asked, catching a whiff of the sadness that had crept into my heart.

"Yeah. I just wish my parents had been there to see us get married." I pulled her hand to my lips.

"I'm sure you feel the same," I added, knowing her family had been snuffed by Lucifer, as well.

She pressed her lips together, offering a tight smile of agreement. "Where are we going?" she asked after a few beats of silence.

I opened my mouth and then closed it, narrowing my eyes at her. "Oh, no you don't." She'd almost tricked me into spilling the surprise, and I shook my head. "Are you coming down to the Carnegie Hall show?" I asked, switching topics on her.

She chewed on her lip, moving her gaze away, toward the window. "I'm not sure. It depends what Martha puts on my schedule," she replied. "I'd like to, but it's usually my on-call day and I don't think it's fair if I bag out after taking almost three weeks off."

I gave her a small nod. She had taken the week before the wedding off, as well, and I saw her point. In some ways, it was a relief, but not having her with me would really up the ante where my anxiety was concerned. "Would you mind staying with Damian and Naomi while I'm gone?"

"Not at all. It'll give me a chance to share the wedding pictures with Naomi, as well as whatever we take on our honeymoon. Plus, I always love spending time with the kids."

I exhaled, relaxing a fraction. I would miss her in New York, but at least I could make sure she was safe, and she didn't question my motives. She knew how unhinged I got when she's out of sight.

"Are you staying with Steve and Jen?"

"Yes. Jen is excited about singing with me again." I stretched, yawning, and she chuckled.

"Aw, did I tire you out last night?"

I laughed and nodded, draping my arm over her shoulder. "You completely crushed any hope of me having energy this morning," I answered. "And I couldn't be happier." I planted a kiss on her cheek.

"Hey there, Mr. and Mrs. Ryan," Ted said, as he approached in his formal pilot uniform.

I grinned and stood, taking his outstretched hand. "Hi, Ted. You didn't have to get all formal on us," I said, waving to his get up.

"It's part of the job." He winked and grabbed one of our rolling suitcases, leading us out on the tarmac.

"Valerie has been trying to get me to slip on our destination for weeks." I said as we climbed the stairs into the plane.

Ted glanced over his shoulder, raising a brow at her. "Sneaky guy, isn't he?"

"Yes." Valerie laughed, and her eyes narrowed in concentration.

"Don't even think about it," I whispered in her ear, already knowing she was trying to pick his brain.

All attempts at getting the information from Ted stopped the minute we stepped inside the jet's cabin. I vaguely remember the last trip to Atlanta when I was eight and I thought that plane was posh, but this one took the cake. There was a giant screen television on the wall that separated the cabin from the captain's deck. A couch and two captain's chairs were situated mid-cabin, then there was a round dining table with two chairs that was set with a magnificent breakfast. A small kitchenette stood opposite the table and the cabinets were stocked with snacks. The refrigerator held both wine and sodas, as well.

"There's more beyond that door," Ted said, and turned toward the cockpit. He stashed our luggage in the closet as we started toward the door beyond the kitchenette.

I opened the door and stopped. I'm sure my jaw hung open, but beyond the cozy living room area sat a plush bedroom.

"Chris?" Valerie asked from behind me, and I opened the door all the way, standing to the side so she could see the private jet bedroom.

I was impressed, but she, she was floored. "This is more beautiful than the hotel room," she said, stepping inside. Her eyes didn't know where to go to first.

I smiled and crossed to the doorway beyond the bed, assuming it was the bathroom. I was right, but it wasn't like any plane bathroom I ever saw. The only thing missing was a whirlpool tub, and it would have been just as nice as our bridal suite room last night.

"I trust this is acceptable?" Ted asked from the doorway.

I laughed and nodded. "Way more than just acceptable. This is superb. When did you get this?"

Ted grinned. "I acquired this puppy about six months ago. Business has been good, so, when this was listed, I looked into it." He shrugged. "It was too good to pass up."

"This must have set you back a bit," I said. Just on the first survey of the interior, I would have guessed this ran near twenty to thirty million.

"It'll pay for itself within a few years," he said with a smile.

"Business is that good?" I asked, shocked at the cost of recovery time.

His smile deepened. "Yep. Especially with clients like your family." He pointed at me and headed back toward the cockpit. "We'll be up in a few minutes, so settle in up in the front and I'll let you know when you can indulge."

This was the one thing Steve always splurged on, and I think Tom and I were just so used to the convenience that it never occurred to us to take a commercial flight. Besides, commercial airlines were just so crowded and unreliable these days and Ted's company was always available, even at the drop of a hat.

I escorted Valerie to the captain's chairs, grabbing a piece of fruit from the table as we passed. She did the same, and we hooked the lap belts in place, waiting for our flight to be given the go ahead. I wondered if the cockpit was as nice as the rest of this plane. The last one was comfortable, but then again, I was eight.

"You've been in the cockpit?" Valerie asked, and I smiled, waiting for her to find the memory. When she did, she cocked her head and glanced around. "This plane is a lot nicer," she commented and met my glance.

"Yes, it is." I threaded my fingers through hers, and she brought my hand to her lips.

Instead of just kissing the back of my hand, like I assumed she would, she sucked my finger, pulling it out slowly in an insinuation of what she wanted to do once we were at cruising altitude.

"You don't want to see the cockpit?" I couldn't keep a straight face.

"Do we have time?" she asked, and I looked up at the ceiling, calculating the time to destination.

"I think so," I said, bringing my gaze back to her with a grin.

"Where are we going?" she asked as the plane taxied.

"Somewhere over the rainbow," I sang, and she yanked her hand from mine, swatting my arm in frustration.

"You're an ass," she muttered and crossed her arms.

"You like my fine ass," I said, and stretched my legs out in the open space, snuggling into the seat.

"Yeah, well, just because I married your fine ass doesn't mean I like it at the moment," she said, smirking.

The light-hearted spirit remained as the engines increased and the plane took off in an arc into the sky. As soon as we smoothed out, I unbuckled and took a seat at the table. Valerie spun the chair toward me with a creased brow.

"It's a private jet. They don't have a seatbelt sign," I said. "Come have breakfast." I pointed to the opposite chair and lifted the glass cover from the small grooves holding the plate in place. The berry filled crepes tasted like a small slice of heaven and I had to give it to Ted. He sure knew how to pamper his clientele.

"Oh, my god, these are fantastic," Valerie said around her first bite.

Neither of us had eaten breakfast this morning. We woke up later than either of us had wanted, and I had to push the speed limit to get to Logan on time, so this gourmet meal was well received by both of us, and we devoured the food.

I folded my napkin and regarded the sprinkle of confectionary sugar on Valerie's lips. I leaned over the table and licked the sweet confection before I trapped her in a soft kiss. I pulled away and planted my butt back in the seat, just taking all this in.

Through her eyes, this was quite the extravagance, but for me, it was just another plane ride. I guess this was one of the spoils of the rich that I took for granted.

"You aren't taking me to a deserted island that you happen to own, right?" she asked, prying again.

I chuckled. "I don't own an island," I said. "But Tom and I do have a place on the French Riviera and a cottage in the Caribbean."

"Really?"

"Yep, but we aren't going to either of those places," I replied.

"Did you grab my passport?" she asked, and I smiled.

"Of course," I said, and although I really didn't need it, having it threw her off the mark.

She chewed on her lip. "The French Riviera?"

"Yes. It's actually a rental property now. Same with the cottage on Grand Cayman."

"So, you have to rent it?"

I chuckled and raised an eyebrow. "You want to become a jet-setter?"

Blush bloomed in her cheeks, and she wiped her mouth, placing the napkin over her empty plate. "No," she said, but her statement lacked conviction.

Before I could razz her on her newfound travel bug, the cockpit door opened. Ted smiled as he stepped through the door.

"I see you didn't waste any time on those," he said, nodding toward our empty plates.

"They were fantastic," Valerie said, as she swiveled in her seat.

"Heather made them," he said, beaming. "We figured you two were the best guinea pigs to try her recipes."

"Do you mind if I look at the setup up there?" I asked, pointing toward the cockpit.

"Not at all," he said and cleared the plates.

"You're our steward?" I asked, a little surprised. Usually, we had a perky stewardess besides the pilot on board.

"Doing double duty. I could only shuffle a co-pilot for this jaunt," he said and shrugged. "Thus, the pre-set meal." He stowed the plates in a dish rack under the counter. "And the opportunity to make use of Heather's culinary talents."

"Thanks," I said, suddenly uncomfortable that I put him in the tight scheduling spot.

"Don't sweat it, CJ," he said, as he ran a cloth over the table and smiled at the two of us. "I would expect from this point forward, if you need something, you'll give us a buzz," he said, and sent a wink in my direction.

My cheeks heated, and I glanced at Valerie before I nodded. He fully expected us to make use of the bedroom during the flight.

"We will stop to refuel in about four hours," he said, glancing at his watch and then at the two of us. "Is there anything else I can get you?"

"I'm sure we can figure things out," I said and stood. "But first, I want to see the cockpit."

Valerie's surprised expression caught the corner of my eye as I passed, and I stopped. "Do you want to see?"

She scrambled out of the seat, her face lighting up at the unique opportunity and we followed Ted beyond the living space into the extra-large cockpit. Besides the comfortable leather seats and modern flight panel, they had their own bathroom, which looked more like the bathrooms on commercial flights than the extravagant bathroom we had at our disposal. They also had a small fridge, microwave and coffeemaker, so they didn't have to invade the customer space to hydrate or relieve themselves.

It was just as sweet as the rest of the plane. "Nice," I said scanning the room one more time. "Hey, Jeff," I said to the familiar co-pilot.

"Hello, Mr. Ryan," he said, in that formal way that always made me uncomfortable.

"This is my wife, Valerie. Val, this is Jeff, one of Ted's pilots."

"It is a pleasure to meet you, Mrs. Ryan," he said, and gave her a nod.

"Nice to meet you, too," Valerie said. She was still in awe of the expanse of sky surrounding them, but she offered a glance and a smile before her eyes drifted back to the spectacular scene.

With that, I wrapped my arm around her waist and escorted her back to our oasis in the sky. I gave Ted a nod, and he shut the door behind us, getting back to the business of flying the plane.

"I hate to admit it, but I could get used to this," Valerie said, as we crossed into the bedroom quarters.

I closed the door and turned toward her, aware that I held the hungry look that triggered her fear, but this time, I figured we'd already pushed the boundaries and succeeded. I wanted to dominate today, but without the bonds. There was one more memory that I needed to cleanse and now was the perfect opportunity.

I stalked towards her and this time when she stiffened; I didn't stop until my arms captured her, pulling her against my body. Her breath caught in her throat and her panicked eyes widened. Without words, I crushed her lips under mine, taking control for the first time since before I returned from the dead.

"I'm going to take you to heaven," I whispered against her lips.

I'm not sure if it was my words, or the insistence in my mind that made her mouth part, giving my tongue access to intertwine with hers. The kiss, as always, stopped time and space and when we broke free from each other, she just stared into my eyes.

"Chris," she started, and I shook my head, stopping her.

"Today is my day," I said, staring her down in an attempt to break that last barrier. Her hesitation burned, but this time, I wasn't backing down. Instead, I dipped my mouth to her neck, taking the time to nip the skin before I traced a line with my tongue from her collarbone to behind her ear. Her skin broke out in gooseflesh when I nipped at her earlobe. "I want to make you wetter than Niagara Falls before I make love to you."

Her skin paled, and I grinned, slowly untying the ties that held her pretty sundress in place. The dress fell to the ground around her feet, and she still hadn't moved. I stripped my shirt, tossing it over my shoulders in a grand spectacle.

"Baby, get ready to join the mile high club," I added, and dropped my shorts.

She blinked at me as I stepped close, staring down at her upturned face.

"It's time for me to kill the last strangle hold he has on you."

She stepped away from me, right onto the mattress, and I followed, knowing I held that predatory demeanor that scared the shit out of her. She scrambled backwards, farther onto the bed, and I crawled over her, keeping up with her mad dash before she hit the headboard with nowhere else to go.

Color bloomed in her cheeks, and before she could do any damage, I dropped my weight on her, pinning her to the bed, and I kissed her again. She resisted at first and then her arms wrapped around me, pulling the kiss from feral to burning hot.

Her chest heaved under me, and I broke away from her grasp, reversing my path, using my mouth to heighten her pleasure. It seemed like forever since I'd explored her with my mouth and my hands together. Despite the tension in her muscles, I continued my southerly route, taking my time on her breasts and her stomach, meeting her gaze every now and then and flashing a smile of satisfaction at the fact the conflict in her eyes was transitioning to the deep want I felt every time we touched.

The moment my mouth settled between her legs, her entire body stiffened, and the fear flared in her eyes. I slowly licked her and met her gaze. "Complete mind fuck," I whispered and something about that phrase settled her fear. She actually smiled at me and the triumph that ripped through me was surreal. Almost as surreal as the orgasm I brought her to moments later.

Niagara Falls. Yep, I achieved my goal and when I finally slid inside her writhing form; it was better than anything I'd imagined over the past two years. Making love to my wife and seeing her find her sense of abandon again was soul affirming.

Chapter 5

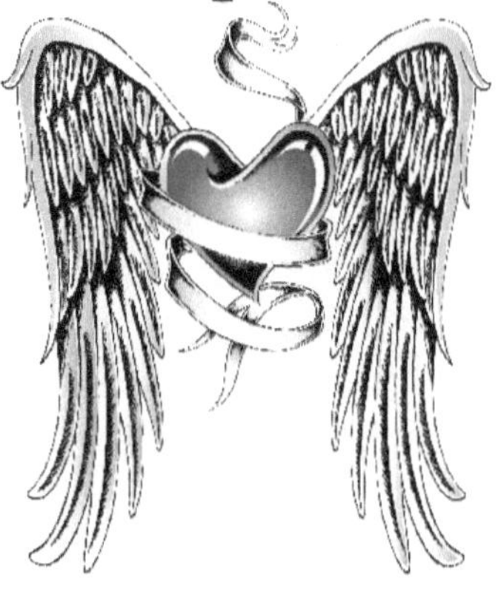

"YOU WEREN'T A MEMBER of the mile high club before this, right?" she asked, turning her head toward me as we lay side by side, spent, on the lush satin fabric.

I grinned and slid my gaze to hers. She already knew the answer, but I still shook my head. "No. You're it, babe."

She let out a soft chuckle. "I really want to tie you up now," she said, and I sent her a raised eyebrow.

"I don't know if I have the energy for that," I said, and she rolled on top of me, grabbed my wrists, and pinned them next to my head.

"Well, find some," she whispered, and nipped at my throat. I smiled up at her. "Where are we going?" she asked.

"You'll love it," I said.

"How do you know?"

"Because it's on your list of things to see before you die."

She let go of my wrists and sat up, her mind wrestling with all the places she wanted to go. There were at least a dozen options, and she puckered her lips in that way that made me want to crush them under mine.

I ran my hands over the smooth skin of her thighs while she ticked off the locations in her mind.

"New Zealand?" she asked first.

"You really think we'd only take two weeks to go halfway around the world?"

She bit her lip, staring into my eyes, and I couldn't help the smirk that surfaced. Her dimples appeared briefly, and then she cocked her head to the side. Without asking another question, she leaned down and trailed kisses from my throat to my cock.

The tease was on, and I grinned, putting my hands behind my head as she slid her lips over my tip. I came to life in her mouth, and with her slow stroke, my eyes rolled back. After a while, I had to restrain myself from grabbing hold of her head and moving at the pace I wanted. The slow burn she was producing catapulted me into the realm of insanity.

"Shit, Val." I squeezed a handful of the back of my hair to keep my hands in place.

"Tell me where we're going and I'll go faster," she whispered. Her hot breath sent a shiver through me.

I met her gaze and clenched both my teeth, and my mind, not allowing our destination to slip past either. With a shake of my head, she went back to her little game.

"You know, I'm not tied up," I said to her in a low, gruff tone that made her smile.

She didn't miss a beat either. Just kept doing that slow swallow that brought me to the edge. She stopped and blew a stream of air on my wet skin, setting me back a few notches.

"If you move, I'll bite," she whispered, and I stared at her.

I dropped my head back on the pillow, wondering just how long I was going to hold out. If I told her where we were going, I'd get a hell of a reward, but it would spoil the surprise. If I moved to speed this up, she'd bite, and that thought sent a shiver through me, chilling the need to take over.

Her mouth started the slow, insane pace all over again.

"Holy fuck, girl," I breathed out the words, forcing my arms to stay in place, wishing I was tied up because it would be easier fighting the bindings than my own internal fire.

My eyes rolled, and every cell clenched. My head tilted back, and I groaned. Every inch of my body ached for release, and she knew it.

"Where?"

"To the fucking moon and back," I whispered, and I didn't give a damn anymore. My hands moved into her hair, and I held her in place, willing her to finish what she started.

It only took three more strokes before I exploded like Mount Vesuvius, and Valerie swallowed every drop. When I finally released her, she sent the most infuriating glare in my direction.

I sat up, despite my trembling muscles, and took her face between my palms. "You know I love you."

She rolled her eyes. "You're not going to tell me where we are going, are you?"

I couldn't help but laugh. "No. I'm not."

"Royal pain in my ass." She climbed out of the bed, heading into the bathroom to freshen up. I glanced at the clock, calculating the time, before following her into the shower.

Warm water cascaded over us, and we washed without toying around. I was exhausted and needed either a nap or some more food and I could tell from the sluggish movements of my wife, she was in the same boat as I was.

I stepped out of the shower first and wrapped one of the plush towels around my waist before starting the search for our clothing. The clothes were flung in different directions, and I gathered all of them, dumping the pile on the chair before pulling my boxers on. With her underwear in hand, I stepped to the bathroom door just in time to see a towel wrap around her gorgeous body, blocking my interested view.

Dangling her undergarment on my index finger, I smiled. "Sustenance or sleep?" I asked. I knew which one took priority in my mind and I yawned, voicing my preference by my actions alone.

"Sleep." She slid her underwear on before towel drying her hair.

We fell into bed, and I pulled her into me. I don't even remember my eyes closing.

My father's scream of pain ripped through me, and I sat up, panting. My eyes darted around the unfamiliar space and my heart clamored in my chest. It took me a few moments to get my bearings.

The roar of the engines broke through the cobwebs, and I closed my eyes, forcing my breath to slow down. Valerie remained softly snoring by my side. "Plane," I whispered and rubbed my face, blinking at the surroundings again.

I wondered if I'd actually heard my father, or if it was just a nightmare. Either way, the guilt crept in, biting and relentless. Instead of lying back down, I slid out of bed and headed into the bathroom to wash the bitterness out of my mouth. I ran wet hands through my hair, trying to tame the wild bedhead I sported before I slipped on my clothing and headed to the front of the plane to find out where we were.

I slowed to a stop at the new food spread on the table. Ted had already set our lunches, and I crossed to the window. Nothing but blue sea met my gaze and my eyebrows rose. We must have slept through the landing, refueling, and take-off in San Diego.

Tearing my gaze away from what I assumed was the vast Pacific, I knocked on the cockpit door.

The door opened and Ted tried to suppress a knowing grin, but he didn't do a very good job of it. His silent assumptions were pretty much on target, and I shifted under a wave of discomfort. Even though Ted had known me since I was a little kid, his silent high five still made me feel like I had done something sneaky. Heat filled my cheeks, and I dropped my gaze.

"Where are we?" I asked, doing my best to ignore the urge to apologize for my behavior.

Ted gave my shoulder a pat, and I met his amused gaze.

"You're married now, son. It's okay," he said, addressing my discomfort before he cleared his throat and adopted a more professional demeanor. "We are a couple of hours out from our destination. I set up your lunch a little while ago, so relax and enjoy the rest of the flight."

"Thank you," I said, and he gave me a nod before his gaze moved toward the bedroom. I turned and Valerie stood in the entry. Her hand combed hair and rosy cheeks made me smile.

"I'll let you know when we're on our landing approach." Ted closed the door, leaving me with my curious wife.

"Where are we?" she asked, rubbing her eyes and covering a yawn.

"Over an ocean," I said, being cryptically generic on purpose.

Her lips thinned, and she crossed her arms. "Which ocean?"

"A big one." I grinned and walked to her, planting a kiss that lingered. "Come on, let's eat," I said, and pulled her towards the table.

The minute her gaze landed on the food, her mind switched gears, focusing on staunching her sudden hunger pangs. She took a seat and lifted the glass cover, revealing the succulent steak salad presented below. I grabbed a couple of waters from the refrigerator and followed her lead. Within minutes, both our plates were picked clean.

Valerie snickered as she opened her water. "I guess we both worked up an appetite."

"No kidding," I said, and chugged my water. "Want to watch a movie?" I asked once I finished draining the water bottle.

"We have time?"

"Yep," I answered and stood, stretching my tired muscles.

"How long were we asleep?"

She was fishing, and I shrugged. If my math was correct, we had to have been asleep for close to four hours, which equated to a little more than half the trip. Our sexual romp was a solid hour and a half, if not longer, so we had just enough time to fit in a two-hour movie before we landed in paradise.

"What if I want to watch War and Peace?" She slung her arm over the back of the chair, cocking her head in that challenging way.

"Then you'd be shit out of luck," I said.

"So, we aren't traveling to the other side of the globe," she said, and the slow grin spread.

"You have no clue how long we slept," I pointed out, and replaced the glass cover so it wouldn't fall if we hit turbulence or when we landed. She did the same, and we moved to the captain's chairs facing the television screen.

"What about Lord of the Rings Trilogy?" she asked, and I rolled my eyes, turning my gaze towards her.

"How about something a little lighter?" I wasn't in the mood for battles between good and evil. We already lived that on a daily basis.

"Like what?"

"I don't know," I shrugged. "Something funny?" I handed her the remote when the movie choices appeared.

She scrolled down the list, landing on *The Avengers* and shot me an arched brow. She knew the Marvel franchise had some of my favorites, but I was looking for more of a comedy, even though this one supplied some decent laughs.

"Lighter," I said, and she continued scrolling.

She leaned forward and pressed play before I could see what she landed on. When the opening credits rolled, I glanced at her.

"Reese Witherspoon?" I asked, and she nodded. "You picked a chick flick?"

"It's funny. You'll see," she said, and I settled into the chair, crossing my arms.

Even though my skeptical radar was pinging, I tried not to pass judgment too fast. "What is it?" I sighed.

"This Means War," she answered at the same moment the title appeared on screen.

The opening scene showed promise and I uncrossed my arms, taking her hand in mine. When the final credits rolled, I pulled her closer, planting a kiss. "That wasn't bad," I said when our lips parted. "But I'd still categorize it as a chick flick," I added with a smile.

"You wanted light and funny." She shrugged.

"And you delivered."

She grinned. I didn't have time to explore the spark behind that grin because Ted poked his head out from the cockpit.

"We're beginning our descent," he said, and Valerie's gaze jumped to the windows before the door even closed.

She started to get up, and I clamped down on her hand.

"Seatbelt," I said and tried not to smile at the aggravation etched in the creases around her mouth. "You only have a couple of more minutes, and then you will know our honeymoon destination."

She rolled her eyes and sighed, clasping the belt together, succumbing to the reality that I was able to keep this a secret right to the last second.

I didn't offer the promise that she'll love it. Instead, I just glanced out the windows as the scenery changed from the ocean to lush greens, and as we descended, the cityscape of Honolulu filled the windows.

Of course, Valerie didn't recognize the city, but she had enough of a view to know it fell into the tropical category. The bump of the landing gear followed, and before we came to a full stop, she was out of the chair and leaning on the couch overlooking the airport.

Her building excitement made me smile, and she turned towards me.

"Hawaii?"

I smiled and raised my eyebrows, cocking my head. "It is on your list, right?"

She actually squealed and my grin widened.

"Waikiki?"

I shook my head and her smile faded as she bit her lip, trying to guess where I would hole us up for two weeks.

"So, what do you have planned? Two weeks in a beach bungalow?"

I grinned. "While I would love exploring—you, for two weeks—I thought we'd like to do a little exploring outside of the bedroom," I said, and sent a wink in her direction. "I scheduled a few... excursions."

"Why is it you can make anything sound dirty?" she asked, putting her hands on her hips.

I chuckled and rolled my eyes. "Because I've mastered the art of making a stutter sound cool."

She burst out laughing.

The engines powered down and Ted opened the door, collecting our baggage from the closet. When we climbed down the stairs to the tarmac, a Bentley limousine waited along with a driver. Ted handed the driver our bags and turned to me, extending his hand.

"Two weeks?"

"Ayup." I smiled. "Thanks for the smooth flight and stellar accommodations," I said and shook his hand. "See you in two weeks."

I helped Valerie into the back of the Bentley, and she grinned at the single rose laid across the seat and the bottle of champagne chilling next to two crystal flutes.

"Nice touch," she smiled up at me and slid to the other side of the car while our luggage was stowed in the trunk.

I took a seat next to her and gave her a peck on the cheek before pouring her a glass of champagne. The driver gave me a nod and closed the door, encasing us in a luxurious wrapper for the hour-long scenic ride up Oahu's eastern shore.

I tapped my glass against hers. "Welcome to paradise, Mrs. Ryan."

"Hopeless," she whispered, and I grinned.

"I told you; I wanted the fairy tale."

"You are so much sappier than I am." Her light laugh filled the car, and she sipped the bubbly before focusing on the world around us. The lush green mountainside swallowed us before relinquishing the car to the populated center of Kaneohe. The driver took us up the coast highways, giving us breathtaking views of the Pacific and the pristine shoreline beaches.

Her eyebrows rose as we pulled off the highway and followed the signs toward Turtle Bay; the excitement in her eyes sparked.

"The north shore?"

I grinned. "Killer surfing." The waves that I saw rolling in on the eastern shore put the ones I rode on York Beach to shame, and I couldn't wait to give these a go.

Concern passed her features, and I rolled my eyes.

"I want to take on Waimea Bay, even though it's a little early for the big winter waves."

Her lower lip disappeared between her teeth.

"Honey, I'll be fine. Besides, it's only one day. I have us booked for horseback riding, snorkeling, helicopter tours, dinner cruises and a couple of spa days, too."

"Spa days?"

"Yes. I figure after a day of activity; we might want a massage."

"I really thought you'd just want to hang out in bed for two weeks."

I chuckled and rolled the glass stem between my fingers. The car slowed to a stop next to one of the luxury cabanas and I met her gaze. "Hold that thought," I said as the driver stepped out and opened my door. I peeled off a couple of one-hundred-dollar bills and handed them to the driver before helping Valerie out of the car.

A bellhop took our bags and handed me the keys after opening the door. The suite was perfect; with a king-sized bed, a small sitting area that lead right out to the small patio, and the beach beyond the small grass yard. I had made sure we were in the most remote of the cottage clusters and that the other three rooms were unoccupied for the duration of our stay. We could even cottage hop between the four rooms if we so chose, but I didn't want to bring that up just yet. Not with her wide-eyed stare at the nicest of the four rooms laid out in front of her.

A candlelight dinner waited for us on the terrace just like I had planned, and Valerie turned towards me, waving her hand at the butler waiting for us to take a seat.

"Wow. You pulled out all the stops," she said, and leaned up to give me a kiss. "I'll be right out." Valerie disappeared into the bathroom, and I handed the bellhop a one-hundred-dollar bill.

He stared at it for a moment, and then his gaze jumped to mine. "I'm sorry, sir, but I don't have change," he said, his cheeks filling with blush while his mind categorized the tip as a mistake and not intentional.

"That's for you," I said with a smile, closely watching his eyes blink rapidly and his jaw pop open for a moment.

"You realize this is a one-hundred-dollar bill," he said, just to make sure I knew.

"Yes. I'm well aware," I answered. He blinked and then pressed his lips together against a grin.

"Thank you, sir," he said and slipped out the front door, closing it behind him.

I chuckled at his reaction, enjoying the shock as well as the conflict of emotions the bellhop displayed. In that respect, I was a lot like my father. My smile faded as my dad crossed my mind. A weight pressed on my chest, and I turned my gaze to the glorious sunset, wishing he wasn't in a place where he'd never see beauty like this again.

Valerie stepped out of the bathroom, her face newly washed and her hair combed back into place. Her gentle kiss on my cheek reminded me of everything he sacrificed. Sensing my melancholy, she wrapped her arms around me in that way that made me forget where I was, and my hands found her waist. Her stormy eyes drew me in, and I smiled.

"Thank you," I whispered, and she turned her head toward the waiting meal. Mai Tais and Mahi Mahi graced the table, and I pulled out her chair for her, giving her the full ocean view.

The butler filled each water glass and then disappeared, leaving us to dine in peace.

"You were going to tell me why we aren't spending two weeks in this room?" she asked, her lips toying with a smile.

I laughed and heat filled my cheeks. "Honestly?"

She nodded and dug into the meal.

"I didn't want to be tied to a bed for two weeks," I muttered under my breath, focusing on my food instead of her reaction. When I booked the trip, she hadn't gotten over her need to dominate and I was dead set against living that way for the duration of our honeymoon.

Her hands froze in place, and I chanced raising my eyes. I expected a glare, but not the cautious study she was performing on my profile.

"I, uh, I thought you liked that," she said, and I sighed.

"Yes, and no." I focused on my meal while I tried to put the conflict into words. She waited a moment before resuming eating.

The silent clank of silverware against china filled the space between us and I looked out at the water before setting my fork and knife down.

"It was exciting when we first tried it out, but after I came back..." I trailed off at the hurt blooming in her eyes. "It was the only way to get past our, um, issues." I shrugged. "And I loved you enough to suck it up until you got past it."

She just stared, her mind reeling from the revelation.

"Come on, you knew it wasn't comfortable for me," I said, leaning back in the chair. "A couple of times you purposely hurt me, like your subconscious was acting out against my image."

"I most certainly did not," she muttered, and wiped her mouth.

"Uh, yeah, you did." I picked up my drink and drained it, thinking back to the time she dislocated my shoulder and another time when she tried metal wire. My pain seemed to fuel her, giving her some underlying sense of satisfaction that was far more visceral than the sexual release.

Valerie met my gaze, and she bit her lip. "I'm sorry," she said, and hung her head.

I set my glass on the table and reached for her, cupping her chin in my hand and tilting her head towards me. I waited until she met my stare.

"No apologies nec...essary," I pushed out the words, annoyed the stutter showed up now. "You did what you had to do to get past it." I caressed her cheek with my thumb before I dropped my hand back on the table.

"I just..." she trailed off and glanced at the beauty surrounding us.

"I know," I said, pulling her gaze back. "And I'll still let you from time to time, but it won't be the norm, okay?"

"I'm not sure I could reciprocate," she mumbled.

"We pushed some boundaries already. We could try that out, as well," I asked and cursed the hopeful lilt of my voice. The time I tied her to my bedposts was still fresh in my mind, even though it was over two years ago. The power trip was just as satisfying as the sex.

Of course, Lucifer used that to his advantage when he stole my form, and the damage he did was so deep in Valerie that I think if I tried tying her in place, I might end up pushing us back to square one.

Her sharp laugh cut the conversation off just as much as her glare.

"It was worth a try," I said, and the inappropriate grin surfaced. "Besides, I like the feel of your hands on me." I backtracked, trying to bring us back from the darkness of our past.

"I forgot how good yours felt on me," she said, and the grays and blues in her eyes swirled. Her cheeks reddened at the thoughts streaming through her head of last night and today.

I pulled her to my lips, tasting her and letting our tongues intertwine in the slow dance of seduction. A throat cleared, and we jerked away from each other, our gazes jumping to the butler who had returned with dessert.

He cleared our plates and set down the crème brûlée encased in an almond brittle cup in front of each of us. The bed of fresh berries under it made for just the right color palette. Before he left, he handed me the room charge, and I scribbled my name and room number and handed it back along with another one-hundred-dollar tip.

"Thank you, sir, madam, have a nice evening." And with that, he disappeared with dinner dishes balanced on a tray.

"If you plan on eating like this every day, I'm going to be eight hundred pounds by the time we get home," Valerie said. When she took the first bite of the dessert, she closed her eyes. "My god, this is delicious."

I couldn't have said it any better and focused on inhaling every bite.

"Want to go for a walk on the beach or..." I glanced over at the bed before returning my gaze to hers.

I thought, by the soft smile that appeared, she was going to say we needed to break in the bed. "Walk," she replied, and a mischievous light danced in her eyes.

Disappointment flushed through me, and she grinned.

"We have all the time in the world for that," she whispered and kissed my cheek as she stood. Valerie walked down the steps onto the grass and crossed to the small incline leading to the sand.

"God, I hope so," I said but a nagging feeling disrupted the peaceful setting. My fun and games would end the moment I stepped back in York and started closing the portals in earnest. I stood and crossed to her, trying to shed my sense of foreboding.

Chapter 6

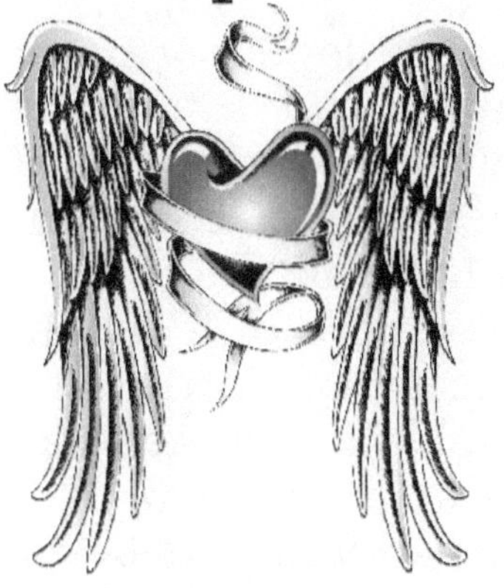

I SAT ON THE beach in awe of the ocean's power. The cadence of the waves lulled me into a state of relaxation that even the massage we had couldn't give me. Valerie lay on her stomach next to me, reading a book on her kindle. The surfboard I rented sat unused on the sand. I grabbed the ankle tie and clasped the Velcro together on my leg before leaning over and kissing Valerie's shoulder.

"It's time for me to tackle that," I said, nodding toward the ocean.

She glanced at the fifteen-foot waves and then at me. "You're crazy, you know that?"

I grinned and hopped to my feet. "I've only seen this kind of surf during a hurricane in York, and these aren't even as big as they get." I tried to convey the excitement zinging through my muscles, but she had never surfed and didn't know the feeling of flirting with the ocean the way a surfer does. It's an extension of our soul, and there was no way to describe that to her.

"Be careful," she called after me, and I glanced back with a shrug.

Respectful of the forces of nature in play was a more appropriate mind set. The volume of each crashing wave was ten times that of what we had in Southern Maine, and it pounded along with my heart. Man, did I feel alive.

The rush was more of a buildup than the zipline we had done earlier in the week and the water here didn't numb on contact like Maine. It was more like bathwater, and I waded in and climbed onto my board, paddling out beyond the breakers. The idea of sharks never phased me like it did some people, and perhaps that's because I could project a protective net predators couldn't penetrate.

The freedom I felt when I hopped up on the board and rode that wave, cresting and cutting through the water, made me forget all the shit I had been through. The only other time I lost myself like this was when Valerie and I kissed.

I even caught the smile on Valerie's lips after the first few sets and when I finally cruised into shore and walked up to her, she stood on her tiptoes and planted a kiss.

"You're amazing," she whispered in my ear.

I grinned. "I'll show you amazing when we get back."

She bit her lip, sucking it in her mouth in that way that made me want to strip her right now. "I think I've had a little too much sun today," she said and smiled. "And I'd like to see your definition of amazing."

"You'll have to hold that thought a little longer. We've got a sunset horseback ride tonight."

"Really?" She perked up, and I laughed.

"Yeah. I thought it would be kind of cool," I said and kissed her cheek. "I'll be right back; I need to return this." I tapped the board and headed toward the surf shop on the edge of the beach.

By the time I finished settling up with the rental shop, Valerie was waiting by the door with all our stuff. We took a seat on one of the benches in the parking lot, waiting for the car service I contracted to take us wherever we wanted during the two weeks. I had texted when I returned the surfboard, knowing it would be a little while for the driver to get from Turtle Bay down to Waimea Bay.

"Do we have to go back home?" Valerie asked, and I glanced at her with a smile.

"We could always stay here. Live a simple island life," I said. Of course, my idea of simple would be an ocean view paradise with a private beach and she knew it. It wouldn't be a little shack by any means.

I saw the draw in her eyes, the possibilities and then her thoughts went to her patients, and she sighed. People counted on her, and to just up and disappear wasn't in her nature.

"You'd miss your family," she said.

"Yeah. So would you," I added and got a nod of affirmation. She had gotten very close with Raven. Closer than she was with Naomi, and I think it had to do with the abuse Raven encountered at her father's hands. Between Raven and Jennifer, it was clear you can shed your past if you put your mind to it.

The car drove to a stop in front of us and the driver stepped out, opening the back door for us with flair.

"Enough sun today, Mr. Ryan?"

"Yes, Akamu. My wife has more of a tendency to burn than I do." I smiled, peeking at the hint of pink cropping up on her shoulders. "Thank you for getting here so quickly."

He gave me a nod, and I slid into the car before he closed the door. The sun danced on the water as we rode east, and I couldn't help the thought creep. All that talk about family as we were leaving made my mind wander.

"What if I can save him?" I glanced at Valerie.

She met my gaze and said nothing. This was a conversation we'd visited a couple of times since my father's sacrifice and she was dead set against me going up against Lucifer, and even more leery of me trying to put together a rescue mission.

"You know how I feel."

"I know. But the question still stands. What if I can?"

"What if you try and end up getting killed?"

It was her normal argument. The one that always burned, because if I failed and died, my father would be pissed. I had to live with the guilt of his sacrifice, and the knowledge that if I disappoint him or screw up, his sacrifice was for nothing. It sucked.

I hung my head a moment, resting my elbows on my knees in the spacious limousine. Her hand landed on my back and her gentle scratching was meant to console, but it didn't. There wasn't anything anyone could do to take this away. The only thing that would clear my conscience was saving him from hell.

Chapter 7

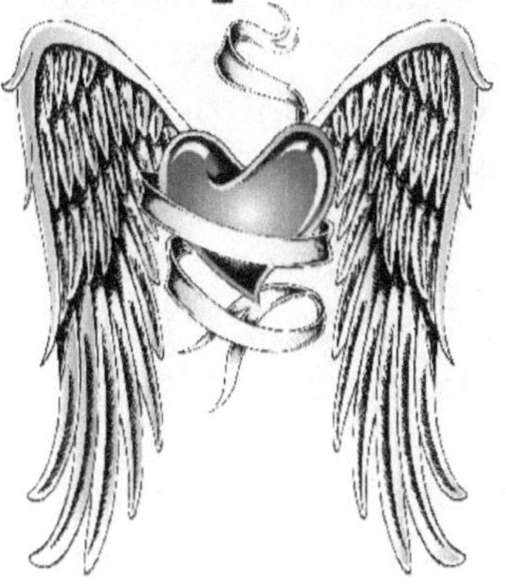

AKAMU HELD THE DOOR to our cottage open while we carted our beach crap inside. The sun was still high enough in the sky to create odd shadows on the walls, and Valerie dumped her stuff on a chair near the sliding screens before pushing them all the way open.

"Will you need me again this evening?" Akamu asked, and I focused on him.

"No, I think..."

His face turned pale and his eyes nearly bugged out of his head. The saliva in my mouth dried and my head whipped in Valerie's direction in time to see a clawed hand swinging toward her back.

With no thought, I stuck my hand out like I was stopping traffic and sent a blast of power at the thing. It flew into the far wall with a yelp. I held it still.

Valerie spun at the sound, and she stumbled backwards, away from the thing. Neither of us had any words to describe this thing, but Akamu did.

"Kupua," he gasped, and my head turned back in his direction while I held the thing in place.

"What?" I snapped, and his gaze jumped to mine. Akamu's audible gulp might have been funny if the thing wasn't pressing against my invisible hold.

He waved his hand nervously at the thing snarling against the wall. "Kupua... monster," he said, his voice shaking just as much as the rest of him.

I gave a nod and focused back on the thing that would have sliced Valerie if his claws ever reached her. I crossed, putting myself between it and her, studying the Kapua. Its pale features reminded me of a vampire, but it had an elongated snout with what looked like shark's teeth. Multiple rows of razor-sharp teeth snarled in my direction and my gaze dropped to the clawed hands.

"You certainly are an ugly motherfucker," I said and met its hollow-eyed gaze.

Akamu still stood plastered to the wall by the door. His broken thought process almost pulled a chuckle from me. He was terrified beyond the ability to move, but I couldn't worry about him at the moment.

"What the hell is it?" Valerie said from behind me, as she peeked over my shoulder.

"Akamu says it's a Kapua."

"What the fuck?" she asked, and I couldn't help the bark of a laugh that escaped.

"Lucifer has plans for you," it breathed, filling the room with the rank stench of the dead.

"Tell me some...thing I don't know."

"Your father broke much faster than Lucifer expected," he snarled. "And now he is coming for you," he added with a grin.

Movement flashed in the corner of my eye and before I could react, I was tackled onto my side. Whatever hit me was up on their feet faster than my blink and my concentration broke, releasing the other snarling beast I held to the wall. The one that attacked me had now cornered Valerie.

This time I didn't fuck around. The pulse of power escaped, toasting the one attacking my wife and I turned toward the other in time to see its pre-launch. Silver flashed through the air, and I blinked as a knife embedded in its throat.

The roar shook the walls, and the thing stumbled toward me. Another power burst turned the beast into dust and the blade clattered to the ground. I glanced toward the door as the first tingle of shock bit through me. Akamu stood with his pant leg pulled up to reveal an empty leather ankle holster.

He met my gaze before his wide eyes glanced at Valerie.

"Are you okay, Mrs. Ryan?" he asked. This time his voice was surer than before.

"Yeah," she said.

I climbed to my feet and hot liquid drizzled down my leg. For a minute I thought I had lost control of my bladder, which, considering the quick turn of events, wouldn't be that farfetched. However, that thought vanished the minute I looked down.

Red saturated my shorts, and shreds of skin hung from my side. The fucker cut me.

"God damn it. I just bought these swim trunks," I muttered and looked at Valerie. My eyebrows arched when she didn't immediately step to my side. Her gaze bounced to our chauffer, and I laughed. "He saw me turn those things to dust. I think we're past the 'shit, we can't show what we've got' stage."

She let out a nervous laugh and stepped to my side, planting the healing kiss. I clenched my teeth against the onslaught of pain as Akamu crossed to his knife. He picked it up, pointing it at us as my side healed from the inside out.

"Fuck, that hurts," I growled, and my fists curled in response. Closing my eyes, the sting of skin thatching together filled my senses, fusing until there was no evidence of having been nearly skewered. When I opened my eyes, I addressed the elephant in the room.

"We're human," I hissed out, meeting his frightened stare.

"No human can do what you two can," he said, his tone just as accusing as I expected.

I sighed and nodded toward the knife. "Where'd you learn to throw like that?"

"What are you?" he said, his voice growing to the pitch of panic.

I grabbed the towel off the chair, wiped the blood off my side, and held the stained cloth out to him. "Have it tested if you want."

The knife dropped a few centimeters, and he stared at the bloody towel, his face a mask of mistrust.

"Real...ly, we're just flesh and blood like you," I said, putting my hand up as the stutter arbitrarily hijacked my speech pattern.

"Who are you?" he asked, his inflection incredulous, but he lowered the knife.

"CJ Ryan," I said, using the name splashed over every news station on the east coast, but I highly doubted my rise to stardom in the singing realm made it this far west.

He shrugged, but my name tickled something in his brain, and he looked at the ground, at the blood drying on the tiles in the bright sunshine. His brow creased, and he looked up.

"The singer? The one who was in a coma for a couple of years?"

I nodded. I guess my story really did go national.

The knife arm lowered to his side and his mind started racing with questions. "I, I didn't put it together," he mumbled and shifted his weight. "Did the coma..." he trailed off and waved the knife at me.

I laughed. "Uh, no. I was born with this, whatever." I waved at the dusty air.

The events of the past few minutes hit him all at once, and his arms shook. When the knife clattered to the ground, I reached to steady him, but his eyes had already rolled into that of a faint. I stopped him before he face planted the floor. After getting his limp body into the chair, I turned toward Valerie.

"The barrier's up. Don't let him leave or he'll fry. I'm taking a quick shower, then I'll clean up that." I pointed to the bloody floor, and she nodded, still looking like the last few minutes hadn't settled in yet.

I needed a moment because the words that shit said had already embedded themselves under my skin and the drying blood started itching. The trail of red blended with the dark stone in the shower stall, and for the first time since I came back from the dead, my demons overwhelmed me.

Breathing became difficult against the imaginary strap tightening across my chest. Tears burned, and I squeezed my eyes closed against the onslaught, letting the shower spray mix with the hot saline leaking from the corner of my eyes. My ragged breath trembled with each silent sob. I couldn't seem to find a voice for the pain.

The bathroom door opened, and I shook the devastation away, sniffling and washing my face under the water.

"You okay?" Valerie's soft voice rose above the steam, and I glanced back at her, meeting her inquisitive gaze.

I thought I had blocked her from my thoughts, but the concern in her was as palpable as my pain. I nodded anyway, and shot her a smile, or at least what I hoped was a smile. I wasn't sure I pulled it off when her gaze lingered.

"Akamu is awake," she said. "And I wiped up the mess as best I could with our beach towels."

"You didn't have to do that," I said and shut the valve off. I wrapped a bath towel around my waist and sighed. "Grab me a pair of shorts?" I asked.

She disappeared, and I ran a comb through my wet hair. Going through the motions brought some sanity back and the strap around my chest released, allowing me to draw in a breath without force. I moved my gaze from my reflection to the door when she stepped in and handed me my clothes.

"He's getting antsy."

"I'll be right out," I snapped, and nearly tore the clothes from her grip.

Her sudden flinch and step back told me just how harshly my spoken response had been. Before I could say I was sorry, her jaw tightened, and she spun away, slamming the door on my attempt to get her attention.

I gathered the bloody swim trunks and deposited it in the garbage before stepping into the main room. "Val, why don't you go clean up while Akamu and I talk," I said, forcing my voice to come out soft and calm.

I waited while she gathered her things, and the moment she closed the bathroom door; I turned to Akamu. His complexion was near green, and I crossed to the refrigerator, pulling out a ginger ale. He pressed himself farther into the chair as I approached.

I offered the soda to him, and his gaze bounced between the cool can and me until he finally snatched it from my hand. His dagger sat on his lap, and I studied the ornate carvings on the handle and the more subtle designs on the blade.

"Can I see?" I pointed to the knife and his eyebrows rose.

I think he forgot he had his talisman, but when his gaze dropped, some of the fear radiating from him also dropped a notch. In the few seconds he stared at the blade, the true nature of the knife transferred.

"If I wasn't human, I wouldn't be able to hold it?" I asked, and his eyes moved to mine.

"No," he said with more confidence than he felt, and he stared at me when I put my hand out. "It will kill you."

I laughed. "You think?"

My sarcasm didn't impress him, and he shrugged. "It's your funeral," he said and offered the knife to me hilt first. He fully expected something to happen when my skin touched the knife because he flinched and moved back in the seat.

I wrapped my hand around the silver, studying the swirls carved into the blade before I inspected the handle. "What do these mean?" I asked, curious by the artifact I held.

"They are sigils," he muttered, clearly confused. "Symbols meant to protect the holder and destroy the monster."

"I know what sigils are," I said, raising my gaze to his.

"What are you?" he asked again, and awe bled through in his tone.

"I'm just a man," I said, not really interested in explaining the complexity of my heritage and the reason I'm special. It's not something I took pride in, not since I found out some of it came from my connection to Lucifer.

"Right," he said, drawing out the word, and I looked up from my study of the knife.

"I just happen to have a few... gifts that are a bit... abnormal," I said, choosing my words carefully. "And it's obviously not common knowledge," I added, handing the knife back to him before I crossed to the stocked bar and pulled out the whiskey. I needed a shot of something to calm my raw nerves and after I poured a glass for myself, I held up the bottle, extending a silent offer.

He shook his head. "I'm supposed to be driving, remember?"

I smiled. "We're booked on the sunset horseback ride." I wasn't willing to let these fuckers ruin the last half of my honeymoon. "If you want to crash in one of the bungalows, you can. I have all four of them and we won't need you until tomorrow, anyway."

"Are you out of your fucking mind?" His hand flew to his mouth, covering the words as soon as they escaped, and his cheeks bloomed red at the less than professional slip.

I chuckled and raised an eyebrow. "There are a few people who would agree that I was," I said, and a smile appeared as soon as his hand dropped away from his face.

"I meant going out," he clarified. "With those things hunting you." His hand fluttered toward the ocean.

"Did you want a drink?" I asked, and he shifted, looking at the floor before he sighed.

"I'm not old enough," he muttered. I knew he was younger, but I didn't realize he was underage.

"Okay." I threw back the shot, relishing the burn as it slid down my throat and my teeth clenched at the explosion the alcohol created in my stomach before it settled, sending warmth radiating out through to my fingertips. "Yes, we're going out," I said after the last shudder and crossed to the chair facing Akamu. "You have questions."

He laughed and put the knife on the table next to him before running both hands through his hair. "Questions. Okay. How come they are after you?" he asked, meeting my gaze.

"It's complicated." He didn't like my answer and his lips pressed together, stifling the rude remark filtering in his head. "How do you know about these things?" I asked.

"Hawaiian traditions. Myths. Word of mouth." He crossed his arms and leaned back. The mental commentary clued me in to more than just his words. His family had some history, thus the knife was handed down for generations.

"What about the knife?" I asked, prying in a way I really shouldn't have. The kid wasn't aware I could read minds, and in that respect, he had a hell of a disadvantage.

"My grandfather gave it to me when he told me the story of the different Kupua." He traded the soda can with the knife, twirling it slowly in his hand. "It protects its owner." The way his gaze drifted from the blade to me sent a shiver down my spine.

"And kills inhuman things," I added.

"Usually," he said and huffed a laugh. He still didn't believe I was a mere mortal.

"Can it hurt angels?" I asked, garnishing arched brows and a shrug from Akamu. I fell back to a conversation I had with Valerie about how clueless the general population was to the beings sharing our planet. "Never mind the angel question." I waved it away. "Have you ever seen those things before?"

"No. But my grandfather has," he said. "But I really thought he was wacked when he told me about them."

I couldn't help the chuckle. "When I was twenty, I had my first experience with true monsters, and it freaked the living shit out of me." I glanced at the bathroom door and then back to Akamu. "She doesn't even know how much finding out these things exist fucked me up." I said, just above a whisper.

Akamu chuckled and glanced around the room. "I can identify with that." His gaze landed back on me. "Really? What are you?"

"Flesh and blood, just like you. As you saw, I can bleed. If Val wasn't around, I probably would have bled out on the floor." I shrugged. "While I can destroy things, she can heal things."

"Like yin and yang?" he asked.

"Pretty much. But she..." I searched for the right word. "...inherited her gift from me."

He shifted in the chair with skepticism written on his scowl.

"I guess maybe we were meant to be," I shrugged. "When I met her, the powers shifted to what they are today. Split kind of like yin and yang."

"You never answered why they are after you," he said staring me down.

"Why do you think?" I asked and leaned back, crossing my arms.

After a moment, his cocky expression turned serious. His mind putting together the pieces with the limited knowledge he held. "They want to control you?"

I nodded. "The same way governments and crazy terrorist organizations would want to control me if they knew what I could do. That's why they went after my wife. They know without her, I'd be more likely to bend to their will."

"Shit," he whispered. "I don't envy you."

I laughed and sighed. "There're only a handful of people who know what we can do." I pointed between the bathroom door and myself and let the statement hang on the air. Threatening someone to remain silent wasn't in my makeup. If he chose to go announce what he saw to the world, I wouldn't stop him, but I didn't get that vibe from him, especially after the litany of things his grandfather recounted. All of which he had originally discounted, but now he wondered how much of it was real.

Akamu glanced at the knife, studying it for a moment before picking it up again. "You might need this," he said, offering the talisman to me.

"Give it to my wife," I said as the shower silenced. "She is the one who needs protection."

"But..."

"Besides the freaky power, I've also got a black belt, so I'm better prepared to fend off an attack. She doesn't have that advantage."

Akamu bit his lower lip.

"She's been hurt more than once," I said, soft enough so my words wouldn't reach her ears. "If that thing works…"

"It does," he interrupted, assuring me of its mythical nature with an emphatic nod.

"Okay." My gaze moved to the bathroom door as it opened and Valerie stepped out in jeans and a halter-top, her hair in a single braid and her lips shining with a gloss that set the heat level switch inside me to the on position.

"Has anything?" Trailing off, she twirled her finger, and I shook my head.

"No, nothing else has happened," I said. "Akamu and I have just been shooting the breeze."

The twitch of her lips was her attempt at a smile.

"Akamu has something for you," I said.

Our chauffer stood, crossing to her. "I present you with my grandfather's talisman. It will now serve to protect you." He held the knife out in his hands as he bowed his head. The presentation of the weapon seemed overly formal to me, but it was necessary for the blade to know who it needed to protect from darkness.

It almost drew a laugh from me. I hadn't realized I had walked into a bad horror movie until just this moment, and I turned away, choosing to look at the beauty of the Hawaiian landscape to ground myself in some level of reality.

"I trust this entire ordeal will remain between us?" I said without turning.

"Yes, sir," Akamu said. "What time should I pick you up tomorrow?"

I glanced over my shoulder, relieved he wasn't going to bolt in the opposite direction as soon as he was out of here. "If you can be here by eight, that would be appreciated. We have a Safari Catamaran tour in Haleiwa setting sail at nine."

"Will do, sir." He gave me a slight bow, and I dropped the shield I had put around the cottages. As soon as he pulled out, I moved my gaze to Valerie.

"This is beautiful," she said, studying the knife before sheathing it and clasping the sheath on the inside of the cowboy boots she unpacked.

"It's supposed to kill anything inhuman," I said, even though I knew she had been privy to Akamu's side of the conversation.

"Maybe it'll kill Lucifer," she said, and a wicked gleam danced in her eyes. One I had never seen in her before. I knew she hated him, but that gleam promised payback in ways I didn't even want to consider.

"You're not wearing that on the ride, are you?" She waved at my shorts.

"You don't think this would work?" I asked, opting for humor instead of where the conversation had veered.

A more genuine smile appeared, and she rolled her eyes, crossing until she stood in front of me. The light caress of her fingertips sent a thrill through me, along with a shudder of goose flesh.

"The lack of a shirt is okay, but I think you'll get saddle sores if you wear the shorts."

"You can fix them." I smiled.

"Go change," she said and swatted my ass.

I leaned down and kissed her gently. The taste of berries came with the kiss, and I licked my lips as I pulled away, enjoying the sweet taste of her gloss. A quick glance at the clock told me I didn't have time to explore that taste and I turned, bending to her sensibility.

Chapter 8

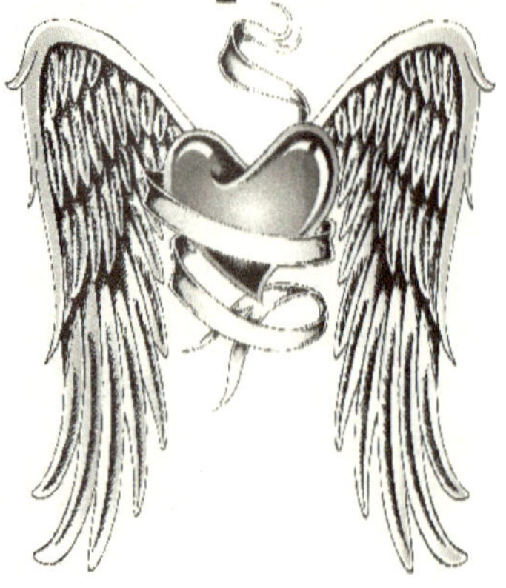

THE IDEA OF BEING on a secluded trail was not as comforting as I thought it would be when I booked the excursion. Both Valerie and I had a healthy dose of apprehension accosting us. I didn't realize the level of our unease until the moment we strolled into the stables and every last horse whinnied. Basically, we spooked a barn full of horses and their wild-eyed reaction took the stable hands by surprise. Even the three horses in the center, being prepped with saddles, pranced around in an agitated fashion.

I traded a glance with Valerie and took a deep breath, forcing my raw nerves into a lockbox at the pit of my stomach for the benefit of the now skittish animals. Valerie did the same, and our conscious effort to quiet our internal turmoil seemed to work its magic. The horses calmed, and I inspected the ones being groomed for the ride.

A gray speckled appaloosa and two chestnut quarter horses had saddles already placed and the stable hands were making sure everything was in order. Valerie and I approached the three horses, and a petite Hawaiian woman stepped out from behind the brood.

"Mr. and Mrs. Ryan?" she asked.

"Yes, ma'am," I said, giving her a nod.

"We have Koa," she said, patting the appaloosa, "and Mahina and Lanikai," she finished waving toward the two quarter horses. "You may take your pick," she added with a smile.

"You first," I said to Valerie, and her gaze moved from one horse to the other before she stepped closer. It wasn't so much she picking the horse, but the other way around when one of the quarter horses stepped forward and nuzzled her.

"Lanikai likes you," the little woman said, and she turned her gaze in my direction.

I stepped forward, focused on Koa. She threw her head back in defiance and met my blatant stare. The horse moved with grace and placed her head on my shoulder. It was the damnedest thing, and I could tell from the woman's expression that she hadn't seen anything like it either.

"I guess I get Koa." I smiled and got a nuzzle in response that knocked me back a step. I scratched the white patch between her dark eyes. After the horse settled down, I focused on the little woman and the other stable boys who fit the last horse with a saddle that came equipped with a large picnic basket. "What's your name?" I asked her.

"Jenna," she said and gave us a nod. "Once we get to our destination, dinner will be served and when you are done, we can head back."

"Or we can send you back with the basket and return when we're ready?" I asked, raising a hopeful eyebrow.

She laughed politely. "I'm sorry, but that is not our policy."

I glanced at Valerie and ran my hand down Koa's neck, waiting for our guide to instruct us to mount. Something about animals always calmed me. It had been years since my father's guide dog died; Sam hadn't crossed my mind in the last few years. He was the best damn dog in the world and I couldn't believe it had been so long since I thought of him.

"Have you ever ridden before?" Jenna asked, stepping in front of the two of us and our chosen rides.

"Yes," we both said at the same moment.

"But it's been years," I added after we exchanged grins.

"Would you categorize your skills as closer to a novice or to an expert?"

"Expert," Valerie replied. "In middle school, I used to ride on the equestrian team."

"Novice," I said when Jenna looked my way. "I'm not nearly as experienced as my wife," I added. Her history was the reason I booked this excursion.

Jenna gave a nod to Valerie, indicating she could mount. The grace with which she climbed onto the horse made my breath stick in my chest. Some of the simplest things she did could leave me breathless, and this was no exception. I smiled when my brain-stall kicked back in gear, pulling air back into my lungs.

"Do you remember how to get up into the saddle?" Jenna asked me.

I refrained from rolling my eyes. "Yes, ma'am," I answered and reached for the horn on the saddle. When my fingers brushed the horse's mane, I glanced where I thought the thing was supposed to be. There was no horn.

Jenna suppressed a grin. "It's an English saddle."

Heat filled my cheeks. That was one thing I had requested because Valerie competed with an English saddle. I just never considered what style I should choose. "I know," I muttered. Before I made a complete fool of myself, I slid my left foot into the stirrup and gripped the lip of the saddle where the horn would have been had this been western style. I swung my leg over and took the reins after I got situated in both stirrups. I was much less graceful than Valerie, and I caught her smirk when I finally looked up.

"You sure you don't want a western saddle?" Valerie asked, as Jenna mounted her horse.

Jenna's horse was the only one of the three with a western saddle. I could have easily switched with her, but now my ego was a bit bruised, and my pride wouldn't let me back down, no matter how unsteady I felt.

"I'm good," I said.

Jenna made that familiar clicking noise and her horse took the lead. Koa and Lanikai followed. Riding in an English saddle took some getting used to, and thank god Koa and I seemed to be on the same wavelength. All I needed to do was adjust the tension on one side of the reins or the other and she went the way I wanted her to.

"Do you want horses?" I asked when we trotted onto a private stretch of beach. The flash of interest in Valerie's eyes came and went like a firefly in the dead of night.

"Horses are a lot of work. I'm not sure I'd have the time."

"I'm not doing much," I shrugged. The idea of having such a majestic creature really piqued my interest.

"We're traveling enough to make having any sort of pet difficult."

She had a point, but I had unlimited resources. "I could hire a caretaker," I said.

Jenna had stopped a few feet away, meeting our gaze, and I got the silent message even before she spoke. "I believe you wanted to gallop?" She waved her hand at the open stretch before us.

Valerie nearly salivated at the thought.

"Beach or surf?" I asked, and she grinned at me, taking control of her horse.

"Yahh!" she yelled and headed straight for the water. Her form was impeccable, and I traded a shrug with Jenna before I followed suit.

Koa reacted, taking off like a bolt. I nearly fell out of the saddle before I regained my balance and figured out the natural rhythm. Water splashed under her hooves, and I caught up to Valerie easily. Koa was faster than her horse, and I held both reins and a handful of her mane to help with the balancing act.

This was as close to the feeling of pure freedom as surfing was for me, and I grinned like a drunken fool as we galloped side by side in the shallow surf. Valerie's laugh filled the small beach, and I couldn't tell you how much sheer joy pulsed through me in that moment.

It nearly wiped out the darkness that hung on at the back of my mind. The sunset shimmered on the ocean, and as we reversed course, the click of the camera caught my attention. Jenna had unpacked her Nikkon and was snapping away per the package specifications. Not only did I contract a three-hour horseback ride, but I had a candlelight dinner and picture package included.

We pulled to a stop at the shoreline, and I leaned toward Valerie to catch a kiss in the trail of the sunset on the water. Jenna snapped a few more pictures before making that clicking noise that called the horses back to the normal trail ride pace.

We climbed out of the thick canopy at the edge of a steep incline. Our dinner destination was the plateau above and the ride up the hill was unnerving for me. I had to focus my concentration on staying in sync with the horse's movement, otherwise I would have ended up on my back on the ground.

Surveying our surroundings every few minutes was also wearing my nerves thin, and I hoped my exhaustion wouldn't interfere with this dinner date. I also prayed we wouldn't be attacked by anymore of Lucifer's henchmen.

Jenna arranged the picnic on the smooth rocks near the bluff and I sat down, looking at the spread of cheese and crackers, roast beef sandwiches, and fresh fruit decorating the disposable paper plates.

It was simple, and the wine bottle sitting in the travel ice bucket made me smile. As simple as the meal was, it was incredibly satisfying to my growling stomach. After we wolfed down the food, I settled on the rocky ledge. Valerie took a seat next to me and intertwined her fingers through mine.

"Are you okay?" she asked softly while Jenna cleaned up what was left of the meal.

I glanced away, ignoring her question now that the silence surrounded us; a twinge started in my gut, like we were being watched by monsters just out of sight. Instead of answering Valerie, I turned, addressing Jenna. "I really would like to stay for a while. However, you can start back if you want," I said.

"Rules..." she started.

"Fuck the rules," I said, and her hesitant gaze hardened.

"It's..."

"A liability," I finished. "What if I granted you a waiver against all liability?"

"I still can't," she said.

"Do the horses know the way back?"

She nodded, but wasn't budging on her stance.

"Leave without us. We'll be fine," I commanded, and she blinked with surprise as her body did what I ordered, despite her emphatic desire not to leave us to our own devices. "I promise we will be okay, and we'll see that the horses are taken care of properly before we leave," I added with an apologetic smile as she mounted her horse and started the trek back without us. Granted, she had no choice in the matter.

"You really didn't have to do that," Valerie scolded me. "And you never answered my question."

"Am I okay?" I said and scanned the darkening horizon. "I honestly don't know." I turned, meeting her gaze. "What that thing said earlier..." I trailed off and looked out at the rainbow of colors painting the islands. "It twisted my insides."

"I'm sorry," she whispered and turned my face towards her. Our lips met and the soft kiss became much more insistent. Where we were was as secluded as you could get, so when I pulled her away from the edge onto the grassy knoll, she didn't stop me.

Just as I was pushing her shirt up to kiss her sexy belly, something spooked the horses. They didn't take off, but they whinnied and pranced closer to where we had stretched out. Their senses were much more in tune with nature than mine, so I paid attention and pulled away from Valerie, scanning the woods beyond their restless nickers.

"I think we should head back and resume this at the cottage," I said, moving my gaze to hers, but her eyes were scanning the dense brush just as quickly as mine had.

Valerie reached down to her ankle and pulled out the knife. "I think that might be a really good idea."

The sigils on the blade let off an eerie glow, and I hopped to my feet, pulling her up with me.

"Do you know how to get back?"

"The horses know the way," I said, and we wasted no more time. We mounted the horses, and I took the lead. I closed my eyes, willing a protective cocoon around us as we descended the hill, praying whatever was stalking us wouldn't spook the horses enough to throw one of us. Once we hit the beach, we took off at a gallop.

A shadow that reminded me of a dog slunk just inside the woods, and I caught the red glow of eyes tracking us.

"Fuck," I whispered, and Koa whinnied like she agreed, yet she pushed faster, leaving the sand behind in favor of the beaten path through the tropical forest. It was almost as if she knew nothing would get to her as long as she had me on her back.

Valerie's horse was on our heels and one glance over my shoulder told me her mare wasn't as sure as mine. The shadow darted forward and the sudden appearance of a hellhound in the path made Koa slam on the brakes. I, on the other hand, kept going.

Thank God for years of break falls in karate class. I tucked, somersaulting as I hit the ground and rolled to my feet, into karate form. The impact knocked the wind out of me, and I think it may have cracked a couple of ribs. Each breath brought forth a wave of pain. However, I didn't have time to noodle on the damage to my body. I was face to face with a snarling demon dog and still had the protection wrapped around the horses and Valerie a few yards back.

I inhaled and yelled, "Get!" waving my arms like a lunatic.

The hound's growl faded, and it cocked its head for enough of a pause to let me catch my breath. The inhuman snarl filled the space, and the thing launched at me. A flash of silver shot by me, and Valerie's blade caught the creature between its eyes, just as its paws hit my chest.

I went down, half expecting its powerful jaws to snap my neck; instead, I was slammed to the ground by dead weight. An audible "Oof" escaped as I hit. I blinked at the night sky and Koa's snout leaning down to inspect whether or not I was all right.

My already damaged ribs were singing a hellish tune at the weight of the dead dog, and I attempted to push it off, but it wouldn't budge. My gaze met Koa's intelligent eyes. "A little help," I hissed from my compressed lungs. I had never seen a horse carry an expression of disgust, but Koa's face displayed just that. Yet she leaned down with her lips pulled back and clasped her teeth on the dog's ragged ear, pulling it to my right as I tried to roll out from underneath.

As soon as I was clear, Valerie was by my side, and she planted her healing kiss before moving on to the dead hellhound. With her foot on its jaw, she clasped the knife and pulled it out. The air sizzled around us and the dog disintegrated into a dust swirl.

"Damn," I whispered and just lay on the ground, staring at the canopy of stars and palms overhead.

Koa nuzzled me and I glanced at her, reaching out to rub her nose before I finally climbed to my feet. "You certainly lived up to your name," I said, taking her reins before turning to Valerie.

My entire body tingled as the last of the healing mojo faded. I debated on walking the rest of the way because I really didn't want to take another turn at flying, but I also didn't want to linger in the tropical forest for longer than we needed to.

Valerie's complexion was waxier than I cared to see, and I pulled her into a hug before we both mounted the horses. Instead of leading, the horses trotted side by side and I got the sense they were just as freaked out by the experience as we were.

I stroked Koa's neck as we rode, trying to loosen the tension I could feel in her taut muscles. "I got you covered," I said and gave her a pat before trading a glance with Valerie.

"I think they understand you," she said with a tremor in her voice.

I smiled and shrugged. "I've always been real good with animals."

"Being good and being on the same wavelength is different," Valerie muttered. "I bet you could let go of the reins and just think the commands and she would follow your directions," she added in that moody way that told me she had a bit of envy flowing through her.

"Are you upset with me?"

Her gaze snapped in my direction. She shook her head, but the way her lips pressed together told me she wasn't pleased about something.

"What's eating you then?"

"It took me years to ride with such ease. You've been on that horse for maybe a total of an hour, and it's like you've been riding all your life."

I laughed. "Babe, you weren't thrown from your horse. I was."

She chewed her lip and then sighed. "Okay, maybe not all your life," she conceded.

The path opened up to the far edge of the hotel grounds and the stable was within view, creating another notch of relaxation in both the horses and us. Once we delivered the mares to the stable hands waiting for us, we headed back to our room.

The quiet walk ate at my nerves. I could see the things that attacked us at the cottage being native to the area, but a hellhound? That meant a portal had to be on the island. I sighed, glancing at Valerie before I pulled my cell out of my pocket. I stared at the cracked screen and irritation flashed.

"That fucker cracked my phone," I muttered. It was always a royal pain in the ass to replace an iPhone. I powered it up and blew out my breath as the display came to life. It still worked, so that was a plus. I took a seat on the knee wall near the edge of the grass in front of our cottage and stared at the display, scrolling through the numbers before I settled on one.

I met Valerie's stare, as she stood a few feet away with her arms crossed and her features tense.

"Hi, Tom," I said to the mechanical voice that answered.

"Are you okay?" he asked.

"Yeah, but I think we might have a problem."

"What kind of problem?"

"I think there might be a portal on the island."

"Excuse me?"

"Today, we've been attacked twice by hell's agents."

Silence filtered through the line. "Shit," his automation program replied.

"Yeah, that was close to my first reaction."

"What do you need from me?"

"I need you and Damian to pinpoint it for me and let me know the coordinates so I can close it."

Valerie's arms dropped, as well as her jaw, and then she spun, stomping back into the cottage, leaving me with the ruined night and Tom telling me he's on it.

After ending the call and pocketing my phone, I stayed in place, unable to face Valerie's aggravation. The thing she didn't understand was now that they had waged war against us, I had no choice in the matter.

"IT'S OUR HONEYMOON!"

"Would you prefer it to be our funeral?" I countered, knowing it was low, but with the history we'd had with Lucifer, it was a distinct possibility.

"Fuck you, Chris," she snarled and turned to stomp off.

I grabbed her arm, pulling her to me. I stared down into her wild eyes; the heat in me wasn't fueled by sexual tension this time. I was bordering on furious.

"They started this. I'm just ending it before we go home," I snapped. "Otherwise, they'll send more and more until they overpower us, and I'm not about to let them tear us apart."

"They already have," she said, her eyes glistening with unshed tears.

"No. They haven't." I softened and inhaled, closing my eyes and doing that silent countdown to calm my nerves. "If there's a portal here, I have to close it." I gave no leeway for argument, and I didn't let her go.

She struggled in my grasp, and finally, she stopped and met my glare.

"By the way, I never thanked you for saving my ass. Your aim was impeccable," I said, changing the subject. Her glare warmed and she let out a nervous laugh.

"I'm not sure I can miss with that thing."

Her statement shed the last traces of irritation, and the colors in her eyes swirled slowly. I glanced up at the open deck, willing the screens closed, followed by the curtain. The concept of only a locked screen and fabric curtains between us and whatever attacked us left me skittish. I unwrapped my arms from around Valerie and crossed to our stowed carryon suitcase. When I pulled out the container of Morton's salt, Valerie let out a chuckle.

"It'll keep out the demons and hellhounds," I said and laid a line across the floor, thankful that the salt blended with the grout as I followed the groove from one side to the other. I did the same with the front door and put the container back in our bag. "And maybe I'll get a little sleep," I said, turning towards her.

She yawned, mirroring the sudden layer of exhaustion pummeling my muscles. I walked to her and delivered a sweet kiss. The thought of making love to her crossed my mind, but I was actually too tired to follow through. Instead, I led her to the bed, undressed and crawled under the covers, with her in my arms.

"I love you," I whispered and kissed the side of her throat.

She shivered in my grasp and pulled me tighter around her. "I love you, too."

Chapter 9

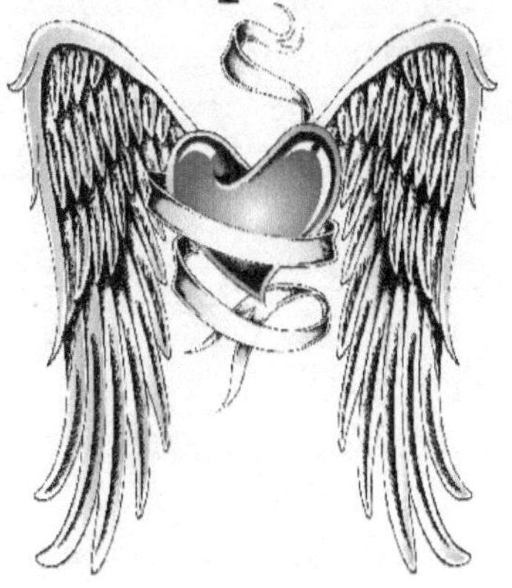

THE BUZZ OF MY phone on the nightstand interrupted my sleep, and I glanced at the display, wondering who the hell was calling in the middle of the night.

Tom's name flashed, and I picked up the phone.

"Hey," I whispered, my voice thick with sleep.

"We didn't wake you, did we?" Raven's amused accent filled the line.

The clock on the table blinked at four-fifteen and I rubbed my eyes, calculating the hour at home. "What do you think?" I muttered and her laugh filled the line.

"We're even then," she said.

"Sorry about that," I whispered. I knew it had been late when I called, but the circumstances warranted it. "Did Tom stay up?"

"Yes," she said, and her tone was less than amicable.

I slid out of bed and slipped out onto the patio, taking a seat in the pre-dawn darkness. "Did he find what I asked him to look for?"

Silence came over the line, and I looked at the phone just to make sure I hadn't lost the call.

"Raven?"

"Right between Laie and Pupukea. If you draw a line between the two, it's right smack in the middle. In the mountain range."

I remained quiet for a moment. "How far south from Turtle Bay?"

She sighed. "Five or six miles due south. It's almost as if you are the median between the two points."

"How the hell am I supposed to get there?" I muttered. I didn't mean to speak out loud, and Raven's sigh didn't help.

"I think you have to hit it from the air."

"That's fucking insane," I said.

"What's insane?" Valerie's voice pulled my attention to the cottage, and I turned, glancing at her rumpled hair and sleepy eyes.

I almost forgot what she asked as I stared at her.

"What's insane?" she said again, and I shook the cobwebs from my head.

"That I have to get to the portal by air."

She blinked at me, and her sleepy features sharpened to irritation. She spun on her heel and disappeared back inside.

"She can't be happy," Raven said on the other end of the line, and I couldn't help the laugh that cropped up.

"She's pissed."

"Can you blame her?"

My laughter subsided. "No. But if I do nothing, they'll keep coming until we leave, and people could get hurt. Hell, I've already had my guts shredded and my ribs broken," I said. "We might not be as lucky next time."

Raven blew into the phone. "Tell her I'm around if she needs to talk."

"Will do. Text the exact location and give everyone back home our best." I didn't wait for a response. I ended the call and ran a hand down my face before going back inside to my bride. Valerie was on her stomach with her face turned away, and I bit down on my aggravation.

"At least they didn't crash the wedding," I said, crossing the dark room.

She turned her head, meeting my gaze as I slid under the sheet next to her.

"By air?"

"I'm as excited about it as you are," I said, staring at the curtains moving in the light pre-dawn breeze. I really should have been sleeping, but I was wracking my brain to figure out a way to get into hell's domain and then out again as soon as I cleansed the area.

"Isn't there another way in?"

I pulled up my phone and clicked on the location they sent and stared at it on the map. "It's a little over five miles due south from here."

"That's shorter than the walk to the lighthouse and back from our house at home."

"True, but there aren't any roads through the area."

"What about ATVs or even the horses?"

I turned to her. "You're not going with me."

"The hell I'm not," she said.

Every muscle in my body tensed at the thought of walking into danger with her at my side. "Val," I started.

"Don't Val, me. I'm not letting you walk into a trap alone."

"It's not a trap, and I'm not putting you in a position to get hurt again."

"Then you're not going." She crossed her arms and pouted, setting me on edge.

"Valerie." I waited until she turned towards me and when she did, the resolve in her eyes pulled a sigh. "I can't do this with your there."

"Didn't you listen to my vows?"

I closed my eyes and covered my face. "I did," I whispered. I listened, and I thought they were perfect, but I didn't translate the stronger together part into going after Lucifer. Any other situation rang true, but not this. "But I'm not stronger with you in the mix. If anything, I'm vulnerable because he knows how much I love you. He knows how to completely fuck me up."

"Chris," she said, and I glared at her. Her mouth popped closed in response.

"He will kill you," I said. "And if he does, you know damned well what that will do to me."

She bit her lip and rolled onto her back, staring at the ceiling. "If he kills you, it will destroy me," she said.

I didn't speak, instead I reached for her hand and threaded my fingers through hers.

"So, we're at a stalemate," she said.

"No. We aren't. You are not going." I stared at the ceiling, and when she tried to pry her hand from mine, I clamped down. "You are going to stay here and wait for me to return." It wasn't a request, it was an order, and the filth that came out of her mouth when I got out of bed could have curled my mother's toes. She continued her angry rant while I pulled my jeans on. I had to give her props on the horse idea, and I knew I could get into the stables and hijack Koa. I glanced at her from the doorway.

"I love you. I promise I will be the one to come back."

"You son of a bitch, let me go!"

I glanced at the clock. "I'll be back before the car gets here to take us to the marina." I stopped and turned back. "You can get ready, but you can't leave the cottage."

"Fuck you!" she screamed.

I knew there was going to be hell to pay when I got back, probably more than at hell's gate. I took off at a jog toward the stables. The gate was locked, but locks don't mean shit to me. A flick of my wrist opened the doors, and I stepped inside the dark barn.

As I walked down the center of the barn, I realized I had never saddled a horse before, never mind put a bit in. I stopped at Koa's stall, and she stood facing her door, like she had been waiting for me. I stared at her a moment and flipped the door lock, freeing her from the stall.

"I really have no clue what I'm doing," I said. Koa nudged me and walked toward the equipment wall. I followed like an inept child. The horse was smarter than I was at the moment, and I nearly laughed when she shook her head at a particular bridle.

"You understand we're going somewhere dangerous," I said as I pulled the bridle off the wall, inspecting it before I turned toward her. Koa dipped her head for me and willingly opened her mouth for the bit. I fit the bridle over her head and then turned toward the array of saddles, quickly zeroing in on the one that had been on her last evening.

I draped the soft blanket over her back and fit the saddle, buckling it as tightly as I dared and tested the stability. It slid a little, and I repositioned, tightening it a couple of notches. "Is that too tight?"

Koa just turned and looked at me. I tested the stability again and it didn't budge.

"Are we good?"

The horse actually nodded, pulling a laugh from me. I gave her a pat on the neck and mounted her. "You ready to run?"

Another nod of her head and I clicked my tongue. Koa trotted out of the barn, and she started in the direction of the path we took last night, but that wasn't where I was taking her. With a new direction, we trotted across the deserted freeway and disappeared into the tropical forest. I checked the direction on my phone as we cantered.

"I'm not sure how bad the terrain is," I said softly and gave her another gentle pat. "I figure we've got a little time, so you don't need to barrel ass across the landscape. Okay?"

Koa slowed to a trot.

Twenty minutes in, we hit our first steep grade, and according to the beeping light on the map in my hand, we had to crest this peak, and then the spot we were looking for was less than a mile down the other side. However, this hill was treacherous for Koa. Every step was a struggle, and the ground shifted under her.

"I might have to do this alone," I whispered as she slid a few feet before pushing on again. The concentration in Koa's stance told me she wasn't giving up and neither should I. What should have taken a few minutes took us a hell of a lot longer than I anticipated, but when we reached the crest, I gave her a gentle pat as I scanned the majestic vista. To the east, the sun had just crested the horizon, and I snapped a few pictures before turning to the south. The vista dipped into another section of dense vegetation and I sighed, glancing at the directions again.

"We need to go down there." I pointed to what looked like a small clearing to the right of where we stood. "When we get close, I'll let you take a rest while I take care of business, okay?"

She turned her head, leveling a look that I could almost read. It matched Valerie's this morning when she insisted on coming with me, and I raised my eyebrow.

"Don't tell me you want to barrel into danger with me.

Koa nodded her head, and I had to laugh. This was by far the weirdest experience I'd ever had and the fact that this horse was given a Hawaiian name that translated to fearless wasn't lost on me.

I scanned the forest below.

"Well, then. Game on, Koa," I said and clicked my tongue. She obeyed, keeping the pace at a light trot. Once the thick canopy swallowed us, I glanced at my phone and slowed Koa to a stop. We were almost on top of the dot, and I sighed.

"I really don't want to put you in a position to get hurt," I said, but she was already sniffing the air and shaking her head in derision. Her small huff and agitated prancing told me more than the dot on my phone, and I slid the electronics back into my pocket.

I took a minute to gather my strength at the same time the wind shifted and the burning smell that had spooked Koa hit us full force. We were in the portal's circumference and my heart thundered at the realization.

I didn't know how big this was, and I hoped like hell there was no one out here right now, because my only goal today was to shut this down. I wasn't up for a confrontation and the shifting of light through the forest, freaked me out as much as Koa.

"Fuck," I stuttered as a pair of red eyes appeared and then another and another until we were surrounded by hell's hounds. Koa didn't like this either, and her wild-eyes caught mine for a minute. Concentrating, I wrapped us in a protective bubble and let go of the reins. I spread my arms wide, sending white light over the landscape and obliterating everything in our path.

The ground rumbled under our feet and Koa pranced. "My angel rain won't hurt you," I whispered and grabbed hold of the reins. "Yah!" I yelled and Koa darted in the direction we came, jumping over the deep crevices that now carved the landscape until we hit solid ground.

I turned in time to see the caverns close and the light fade, leaving a weird round crop circle marking the cleansed land.

"That was entirely too easy," I whispered, and Koa whinnied her agreement.

Shadows pulled at our attention, shifting under the sporadic cloud cover, and I shivered in the morning heat.

"I think I'll just leave the barrier up for a little longer," I whispered, and we continued back towards Turtle Bay. I didn't take a full breath until we were at the crest of the mountain slope. I stopped Koa and stared at the steep grade down, and glanced around us at the bright morning sun now above the horizon. I pulled my phone out and glanced at the time. I had a little over an hour left and I sent a text to Valerie, telling her the portal was closed and we were on our way back.

I swung my leg over Koa's head and slid off the saddle, onto the ground next to her. "It might be wise for us to go down together," I said, taking the reins. "Just don't drag me, okay?" I said, trading a glance with the horse. My first step sent me sliding, and I let go of the reins, falling on my ass for a good thirty yards before my boots dug into the muck. My heart clamored in my chest, and I sat, catching my breath before looking up the hill.

Koa still stood in place, waiting for my command. I still had three quarters of the mountain to scale down and if I slid, I was sure Koa would, as well. With trepidation, I made the clicking sound to call her down, and I didn't wait for her to barrel into me. I got back on my feet and started my descent again. The slide, stop, catch my breath, and slide some more continued. Except at the halfway point, Koa passed by me, her steps more cautious, and her ass nearly in the dirt like mine. She didn't slide nearly as much as I did and God bless the mare; she stopped at the bottom and waited for me.

The last few feet were easier as the base of the hill leveled out. My entire backside was covered in wet mud and greenery, and I crossed to Koa.

"You should have told me I'd be okay on your back," I muttered and climbed back in the saddle, gritting my teeth at the soggy squelch of mud on the fine leather. I wiped my hands on the front of my shirt and pulled out my phone to check the time. My little excursion down the hill took longer than expected and I sighed, pocketing the phone again before I picked up the reins.

"Let's see if we can make it back in twenty minutes," I said, and patted the side of her neck. Before I settled into the seat, it was like a gun went off. Koa launched forward and nearly unseated me. It took me a minute to find my balance, and I put most of my weight on the stirrups, riding like a jockey would. I cleared the path in front of us so she wasn't running through brush and by the time we reached the highway, I had to stop traffic in place as we flew across the four lanes and back into the forest, coming out of the woods onto the grass field that separated the resort from the stables at a gallop and I'm sure my face reflected the sheer joy of speed just as much as Koa's.

When Koa slowed down to a trot, I saw the guide who took us the night before and she did not look happy. Both Koa and I were filthy, and Koa was huffing pretty hard after the workout.

"What the hell do you think you're doing?" Jenna snapped when we came to a stop in front of the barn.

"I took Koa for a ride this morning." I dismounted and ran my hand down Koa's neck. She nudged me like she didn't want me to leave, but I had to go clean up and head out on a sailboat today.

"You can't do that," she said.

"I'm sorry, but I needed to borrow her for a bit. Trust me when I tell you it was important," I said and wiped the sweat off my brow. "I'll pay to have her rest for the remainder of the day. Koa deserves it."

"I can't do that," she said, and I raised an eyebrow.

"Yes, you can. And you will. Koa needs a bath and some TLC today."

"You don't own her. You cannot dictate her schedule."

I glared at Jenna. "Who owns her?" I asked.

Jenna pointed towards a man with a clipboard and I crossed to him.

"I'm CJ Ryan and I'd like to buy Koa," I said, hooking my thumb over my shoulder at the magnificent, mud-covered mare.

"She's not for sale," he said without looking up from his clipboard.

"I'll give you one hundred thousand for her."

His head snapped up and his jaw tightened. "I don't have time for your games, kid," he said.

"It's not a game. I want to buy that horse and I am offering you one hundred grand. Do we have a deal?"

His gaze narrowed. "Do you even have that kind of money?"

I grinned. "Yes. I do. So, is Koa mine?"

He looked beyond me at the mare being rinsed off by the staff and then at me. "Are you for real?" he asked, his face registering more hope than irritation.

"Yes," I said and pulled out my phone dialing. "Hey, Randy, it's CJ, can you assure this man that I have one hundred thousand to spare," I said and when Randy Kincaid said sure, I handed the man the phone.

After a couple of moments, the man rattled off a number and slowly handed the phone back to me.

"Are we all set?" I asked Randy.

"Yes, I'm faxing documentation to him and once he signs and faxes it back, I'll transfer the money."

"Thanks, Randy." I hung up the phone and met the man's stare. "I don't want Koa going out on trail rides today. She needs some rest after our morning ride," I said, and he gave me a nod. "I'll be back later to make arrangements for her."

I walked off, leaving him with his jaw hanging open.

I jogged back to the cottage and collected myself before stepping inside. What greeted me chilled whatever heat I had built on the run. Valerie stood in the center of a pile of bodies, her breath hitching as she brandished the knife at the last of her attackers.

The ease of my mission was explained in that nanosecond. Lucifer had sent his minions after us. He hadn't planned on me taking action so quickly, but he knew I would eventually, and by the looks of things, this was an attack meant to kill, not capture.

Fury overrode my senses, and I roared, pulling both their attention to the door. I let loose; the anger rolled across the room and incinerated the dead bodies and the last Kapua still on the attack.

Valerie's chin quivered as her gaze landed on me. "They told me you were dead," she said, and the gore-covered knife dropped to the floor. "Your text couldn't have come at a better time." She sniffled and stood her ground, glancing at the massacre surrounding her. "I started fighting the moment it blinked on the screen, otherwise..." She trailed off and met my gaze with a shrug.

The way she trailed off sent my heart to the floor, and I crossed, pulling her into my trembling arms. When the shakes subsided, I whispered, "I bought Koa."

She pulled back, meeting my gaze. I shrugged and offered my best conciliatory smile. I knew it wasn't really the right thing to say at this moment, but it was what popped out of my mouth from the shuffle of information going through my head.

"You what?" she asked, and unwrapped her arms, staring at the muck covering them before she turned me around so she could see what I was covered in. Her initial thoughts centered on blood, and I could see her point based on the tacky wetness saturating my clothing.

"I'm fine. It's mud," I said, and she met my gaze.

"You fell off the horse again?"

I let out a shaky laugh. "No, I didn't want to ride her down the hill we climbed, but I really should have. She did fine. As you can see, I didn't fare as well." I leaned forward and planted a kiss, but she stiffened in my arms. "We need to get cleaned up. Akamu will be here any minute."

"I'm still pissed at you for making me stay here," she said and peeled out of my grasp. She headed into the bathroom without another word.

I glanced at the dust-ridden room and willed it clean, rolling the gray cloud out of the sliding screens and onto the lawn where it settled into the damp grass. The grimy knife lay at my feet and I picked it up and headed into the bathroom. The warm water in the sink washed away most of the blood and gore from the blade and when I was done wiping it with a cloth, the shine from the overhead light sent a reflection of my dirty face back at me.

I glanced in the mirror, and my eyebrows rose at the mud streaking my face. I knew my back was covered, but I didn't think my face was as smeared as it really was. No wonder Koa's owner gave me shit. I would have, too, if someone looking like I did offered me one hundred grand for a horse.

Stripping, I tossed the ruined clothing into the garbage pail and opened the frosted shower door. Valerie stiffened, wrapping her arms around her chest in a protective reflex, and the glare she sent over her shoulder almost made me step back out and wait my turn. Unfortunately, we were due to leave in less than five minutes.

"Sorry," I said, and reached for her, but she swatted my hand away. I stared at her, at her complete unease at my close proximity. The tightness in her features made me sigh. I hadn't even thought about her state of mind when I returned.

She was unhinged, and it had nothing to do with killing Kapua. It had to do with her doubts that I was me.

"Complete mind fuck, huh?" I said and her tense features relaxed a fraction, but her lips pressed together and her chin quivered. This time when I reached for her, she came to me.

"You can't ever do that to me again," she said into my chest.

New York came to the forefront of my mind, and I clamped down on the thought before she could get a hint.

"I'm sorry." There wasn't much more I could say. "It was easier than I thought it would be," I added and pulled away, reaching for the soap. It took a scrubbing to get the muck off both of us and I washed her hair twice under the warm spray.

"Where are we going today?" she asked as we wrapped the towels around our bodies and headed to the main room to dress.

"Sailing and snorkeling," I said. "It's a private charter, so they'll wait for us." My phone buzzed, and I picked it up, sending a return text to Akamu telling him we would be out in five minutes.

"The car is here, so..." I said, trailing off as I filtered through the suitcase looking for my backup swim trunks. They weren't in the suitcase, and I looked at Valerie. "We did pack my other swimsuit, right?"

Valerie rolled her eyes and pointed at the beach bag that sat in the corner.

I shuffled the extra beach towels and yanked the swim trunks from under the tanning lotions and sunglasses, pulling it on under the bath towel. By the time I turned, Valerie had her bikini on and was pulling a sheer cover over her head. I never understood the use of a sheer beach cover. It didn't block out the sun the way a t-shirt did, but I have to say, it was incredibly sexy on her. Much more than an oversized t-shirt would have been.

With a few strokes of a brush and an elastic band, her hair was transformed to a tight ponytail, and she tossed me the brush. My hair took less time than hers and we slid on our beach shoes and I grabbed a clean v-neck t-shirt for the ride. With our wallets and phones stowed in the beach bag, we headed out to meet Akamu by the limousine for what I hoped was a relaxing day on the ocean.

Chapter 10

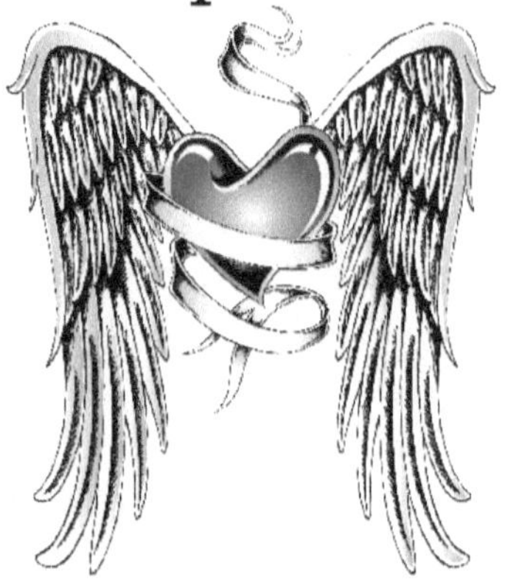

THE CATAMARAN CRUISED ACROSS the water and I sat with my arm draped over Valerie's shoulder. She sipped champagne between snapping pictures. The dolphins jumped in time with our boat, and she put the camera down, giving me the widest grin I had ever seen.

After all that had happened over the past twenty-four hours, I really needed to unwind, and this was the perfect environment. The blow of a whale to our starboard side jarred me out of relaxation, and when the creature jumped out of the water, it sent a splash onto the deck, rocking the catamaran. Valerie had her camera back in hand, and was snapping pictures like a pro.

"Oh, my god, did you see that," she asked, and I chuckled, pulling the wet t-shirt away from my chest.

"I not only saw, but I think I wore most of that splash."

She turned toward me, taking in my waterlogged state and pointed the camera in my direction, snapping off pictures until I wrestled the camera from her. Her laughter rang out over the boat, bringing a genuine smile to both our faces and that of the crew. It was a rare state for us, but the total release of stress, and childish antics, really made my day.

I captured her laughter in at least a dozen snapshots and then looked up at the crew trying not to join in with us.

"It's okay to laugh," I said to the captain. He tipped his hat and grinned.

"We're almost to the reef and you have your choice of lunch then snorkeling or snorkeling first," he said.

Valerie and I traded a glance. "Snorkeling," we said at the same moment.

I grinned and sat back, watching the wonder etched into her features as she caught sight of the vibrant sea life surrounding us. I couldn't imagine giving up forever with her for anything, and my smile faded. What we had was complex and drove us at the cellular level. I would gladly lay down my life for her, and couldn't imagine a future where she didn't exist.

She glanced at me, and her smile faltered a notch.

"You okay?" she whispered in my ear and then planted a kiss on my cheek.

"I'm perfect," I said, meeting her gaze.

"Liar," she said, and sat back.

Heat pooled in my cheeks, and I allowed the smile to form, but I didn't argue with her. I knew at some level I was lying to myself. This perfection we found here would be tested when we got back to Maine. At home, I wouldn't be able to get away from my father's memory or the knowledge that I was the one who sentenced him to eternity in hell. The responsibility of closing the portals was mine, but so was trying to figure out some sort of rescue mission.

If I didn't try, I wouldn't be able to live with myself, and Valerie was going to fight me every step of the way because it meant I'd be putting my life on the line.

The boat slowed to a stop, and the captain dropped anchor. I could see the multiple colors of the coral a few feet away when the first mate approached us.

"The snorkel equipment is aft," he said, pointing towards the back of the ship.

I stripped my t-shirt, dropping it on the seat in the back where we had stowed our bag. Valerie peeled off her sheer cover and turned to the captain. She glanced at his name tag again, and I had to smirk because I couldn't bring myself to refer to him as Captain Jack. Every time his name ran through my head, so did the Billy Joel song.

"Captain, um, you said you had underwater cameras available?" she asked.

Apparently, Valerie couldn't call him Captain Jack, either. She sent a sideways gaze my way, picking up on my benign narration.

"At least his name isn't Jack Sparrow," she whispered to me when he stepped out of sight.

I actually snorted and had to turn away.

"And you need to stop with the song, unless you're going to belt it out," she added.

I glanced over my shoulder with a grin.

"Maybe on the way back, after I've hit the bar," I said, nodding toward the interior cabin and the spread they were just setting up.

Captain Jack stepped back outside, along with his first mate, whose name I couldn't remember. There were three crew members, and you would think I'd be sharp enough to remember all their names, but I couldn't concentrate after the captain introduced himself and the song started looping in my head.

Valerie shot me a smirk. She knew me well enough to know I was embarrassed by my inability to address the first mate by name.

"Thank you, Tom," she said as the first mate handed her the camera.

Now I got her smirk. Of all the names in the universe, I should have been able to remember the name Tom. I shifted and offered a nod of thanks just as the captain handed out the equipment and instructed us on what to do in the event of an emergency.

"What constitutes an emergency?" I asked as I pulled on the flippers.

He leveled a heavy stare in my directions. "There are predators in the water and while we have been lucky, there have been shark attacks in the area." He looked out over the horizon. "But with the whale and dolphin traffic that we've seen today, I highly doubt sharks are nearby," he said, sending an unsettling smile in my direction.

"When was the last attack?" I asked, cursing the nervous lilt in my voice. While I had set a pretty decent barrier around me when I went surfing, I really wasn't sure I could put protection around us without toasting the fish and ruining the entire snorkeling experience for Valerie.

"A week ago, but it was a few miles south of here," he said.

"Okay, I'll keep an eye out," I said, and Valerie rolled her eyes. She wasn't the least bit nervous, but then again, she had the human shield at her side.

"You two have an hour. Enjoy."

"Thanks, Captain Jack," I said and clamped down on the need to break out in song. Valerie bit her lip and jumped into the water without waiting for me. She adjusted her mask and inspected the camera while I eased into the water from the stairs.

"You're on lookout duty," she said, meeting my gaze as she held up the camera. "I'm the appointed photographer." She winked at me and pushed off.

When we were far enough away to not be heard, she surfaced and whispered, "You are so bad."

I grinned and winked, and we continued over and around the reef, diving to inspect the bright sea anemone living on the reef. Bold colored fish swam in small schools around us and in the distance, we saw a large turtle heading in our direction. It was an amazing adventure, and we had close to one hundred snapshots on the digital underwater camera they provided. I couldn't wait to see them.

Valerie aimed the camera in my direction and her eyes widened behind the mask.

I turned in time to see teeth. Water pulsed and all I could do was blink as my heart thundered in my ears and the shark went flying, tumbling away from me along with anything else caught in my sudden burst.

When I turned back, Valerie wasn't there and panic bit at my skin. I shot to the surface, taking a breath. What the hell had I done? The boat rocked on the waves, but it was farther out than when we jumped in. The captain pointed beyond me and I turned back towards the reef, scanning the water until our eyes met.

Panic filled Valerie's eyes, and I swam towards her, aware that the top of the reef wasn't that far under the surface. The boat's engine seemed to get louder, and I chanced a glance back. It was approaching as close as it dared to the reef, and both the captain and the first mate were motioning for us to get back.

As I got closer, the water turned pink in places, and shock skittered through me. My gaze jumped to Valerie, and her strained smile told me more than I wanted to know. The coral had ripped her up, but by the time I got to her, there wasn't a mark and somehow, she had kept hold of the camera.

I helped her swim toward the boat, and I didn't give a damn. I set a protective barrier around us with enough juice to stun anything that hit it, knowing full well the presence of blood would draw the sharks. When we got beyond the reef, I wasn't disappointed. We were met by three agitated tiger sharks, and I could see at least two more coming from the deeper waters.

The boat was twenty feet away, and they were calling us in. We didn't hesitate; we kept swimming. One shark went on the attack, and Valerie's fingernails bit into my arm as we watched it coming. When it just grazed off the bottom of the barrier and started sinking to the ocean floor, she glanced at me. It recovered just as we reached the boat.

I let her go up first and the minute I was out of the water; we backed onto the floor of the boat and both of us let out shaky laughs.

"Holy shit," I breathed, as the captain checked Valerie for damage and came up empty.

His brow creased, and he turned his attention to me. "I thought I saw blood in the water," he said, and sat back on his haunches.

I exchanged a glance with Valerie and sat up, peeling the flippers off before I met his gaze.

He reached forward, grabbing my shoulder and turning my back towards him. "Tom, can you get the first aid kit?"

I blinked and my gaze shot to Valerie before I glanced at the gash in the back of my shoulder and the red spreading on the deck below me. "I guess it got me," I said.

Valerie peeled off her flippers and stepped to my side, inspecting the wound. "This looks more like its tail cut you and not its teeth," she said, and took the first aid kit from the captain.

"I would agree. It seems like that seismic anomaly may have saved your life, son." Captain Jack took off his hat and ran a hand through his hair as he scanned the area. "Damnedest thing I've ever experienced."

"Seismic anomaly?" I asked, as Valerie ran a wipe across the cut. I winced and pulled away from her, meeting her gaze now that the pain made itself known. She paused, raising an eyebrow. I couldn't help the sudden shakes that gripped me as the entire ordeal sank in. I could have killed her, and that realization made me physically ill.

I scrambled to my feet and leaned over the railing, hurling my breakfast all over the pristine water.

"Chris," Valerie said, and I spit before I glanced at her.

"What?"

"You're going to need stitches," she said, pointing to my shoulder.

I looked at Captain Jack. "Do you have what she needs to stitch me up?" When his jaw dropped a fraction, I added, "She's a doctor."

"All we have is that kit," he pointed to the kit on the seat and Valerie sighed.

"Okay," she said, and moved the contents around. "I think I can get him patched up with what you have here. Do you mind if I bring him into the head to do this?"

The captain hesitated.

"I'd rather have her patch me up than either of you," I said, and the captain nodded, pointing us below deck.

As soon as the door closed, Valerie wiped the cut again before placing the healing kiss on my shoulder. I sucked air through my teeth at the gnawing pain of the healing process. She quickly rinsed the blood and attached a large bandage over the spot before it completely healed.

"I could have killed you," I said in only a whisper.

She palmed my cheek. "You didn't."

"But I hurt you," I said, and she met my gaze without responding. The water had washed away all evidence, but I knew better. "I'm sorry. I just... reacted, and you got torn up in the process."

She let out a little laugh and sighed. "If you hadn't reacted, I think you would have lost your arm, or worse," she shivered, thinking about the alternatives.

"A seismic anomaly," I said, and pressed my lips together against the grin that wanted to surface.

"Yeah. How fucked up is that?" She winked at me and patted my bandaged shoulder, dropping the bloody gauze in the garbage before leading me up to the interior deck and the lunch spread that had been put out for us.

"I'll get us underway now that you're all patched up," Captain Jack said.

"I'm fine to finish lunch and the rest of the boat tour," I said, meeting his gaze. "All I need is a stiff drink."

"But, sir," he started, thinking of the liability.

"I'm fine. You warned us about sharks, and we went into the water of our own accord. I believe the waiver we signed absolves you of any liability in this matter."

"But you're injured," he said.

"It's just a flesh wound," I said, adopting an English accent and the line directly out of Monty Python. I pressed my lips together, trying not to laugh at the captain's sudden smirk. "Honestly, I've had worse," I said, after I got control over the need to burst into laughter.

"There was only one small section that was deep enough for a stitch or two, but I was able to close it up with a couple of butterfly bandages. If it opens up again, we'll see the signs through the bandage and can head back, if that happens, okay?" Valerie asked, as she handed the captain the first aid kit.

His gaze traveled between us, and he handed the kit to the man behind the bar.

It disappeared under the counter, and the Jack Daniels appeared on the bar top.

I actually laughed and then sang the chorus to the song stuck in my head. When I finished, all eyes were glued on me, and I shifted. "Sorry, but ever since you told us your name, that song has been stuck in my head."

The captain snapped his fingers. "You're that singer," he said with a grin.

"Ayup," I said, and reached for the jack and coke on the rocks that the bartender had already poured for me. "And I have to apologize. I don't remember your name," I said, when the glass passed hands.

"Howey," he said, and flashed a smile of impeccably white teeth.

I pounded the glass back and let the alcohol warm the chill that remained, and I focused on

having a good time despite the close brush with
death.

Chapter 11

"MMMM," HER PURR SATURATED my bliss, and I turned my head towards the other massage table.

I decided our last day on the island needed to be a complete pamper session for both of us. The last few days of activity had taken its toll. Mentally, we were both trashed, more from the constant tension of wondering what horrors would crop up next, but luckily, the shark fiasco was the last of the attacks.

We expected to fall out of the sky on the helicopter tour, or have the lines snap while parasailing, or the wheels blow on the mountain bikes as we sped down the lush mountain terrain, but nothing happened on any of the other excursions. The rest of the honeymoon left us with a slew of exceptional photographs, satiated by wonderfully romantic settings in private coves along the shoreline, and some outstanding dinners while we did some island hopping.

And now, the massages. A little slice of heaven to end our honeymoon, before we stepped back into reality.

"You enjoying that?" I asked, and she peeked at me with a smile.

"Mhm," she mumbled, and we both settled back onto the table for the remainder of this part of our spa package.

With my body still tingling from the massage, the small rotations in the back of the pedicure chair seemed to enhance my relaxation. I had never experienced a pedicure in my life, so I had no idea what to expect, but the chair left me feeling like a piece of silly putty and the warm water bubbling around my feet felt incredible.

"I can't believe we have to go home tomorrow," she said.

It was my turn to grunt a response and her hand covered mine. I opened my eyes and met her smile with one of my own. "We could always stay," I said.

"You have a show next week," she said. "And I have my patients."

"Yeah, yeah," I muttered, a crust of annoyance grew over me at the unwelcome thoughts of going home. I had gotten used to the pampering and royalty treatment. Back home, I'd have to do things for myself again.

"What time is Ted picking us up?"

"We need to be at the airport at eight."

"In the morning?"

I nodded. "That will get us into Boston around ten tomorrow night and home by midnight."

"Midnight?"

"It's going to be a long day," I said with the same amount of enthusiasm as she displayed. "That's why I had this day planned. At least we'll be relaxed for it."

She let out a musical laugh and squeezed my hand.

"Where you from?" the petite Asian pedicurist at my feet asked.

"Maine," I said.

"Wow, that is far."

I smiled and shrugged. It was the farthest state from Hawaii, but it wasn't like we were halfway across the globe. "The water here is a little warmer than at home," I said and sent a wink in her direction.

The woman blushed and focused on scrubbing the dead skin off my heels.

The rest of our last day was uneventful, and as we sat on the beach watching the sun dip on the horizon, Valerie leaned over and planted a kiss on my cheek.

"I love you," she whispered.

I brought her hand to my lips. "Love you, too."

Quiet settled.

"You're going after the portals when we get back, aren't you?"

It wasn't a question, and it really wasn't a conversation I wanted to have right now when my body was so relaxed. Just the thought of what I had to do created tension in my core, and I met her gaze, keeping my mouth shut.

"Chris," she whispered, her eyes begging for some denial. Anything to appease her.

"You already know the answer."

"You know how I feel." She pulled her hand out of mine and her arms crossed across her chest.

"And you know I have to try to get my dad out." I stared at the darkening ocean.

This time, she didn't argue like she had every other time. "How?" she asked, after I thought the conversation was over, but the way she said it made me glance at her. It wasn't a facetious tone or condescending in any manner. It was a valid question, and it wasn't meant to shut me down.

"I don't know," I said. "I haven't quite figured that out." I would not put myself in the same situation I had with her. There would be no trade, no negotiation. I'd have to steal my father from Lucifer, and I was sorely lacking in the criminal mastermind department.

"I need to be there if you try," she said, and as much as I wanted to argue the point, I just focused on the water and gave her a single nod.

"Then we have to figure out a way to keep you safe, even on his turf."

Her eyebrows rose at the fact I didn't argue.

"I have a feeling I'm going to need all the help I can get," I said, to the visible surprise in her features.

"Wow. I think I need to make sure you get a massage and pedicure every week," she said with a laugh.

It was my turn to raise an eyebrow. "I think you need to bring me here every month." I pointed to the sand and flashed the smile I knew revved her engine.

Our attention diverted to the noise at the far side of the beach. The next sunset horseback ride was just beginning and this time there was a group going on the adventure. I sure hoped like hell they didn't encounter some of the less than friendly wildlife like we had. I was pleased to see the guide riding Koa and not any of the guests. I had an agreement drawn up that stated only guides could ride her and only one excursion a day, not multiple.

I wanted her to have exercise, but I didn't want her ridden into the ground.

"Should we bring Koa back home with us?" I asked, turning back to Valerie.

"On the plane?"

I laughed. "No, we'd have to ship her separately. Or we can buy a cottage around here and come out a couple of times a year. It's up to you."

She chewed her lip, debating. Her mind jumping around at the possibilities and when the idea of kids cropped up, I raised an eyebrow. Granted, I loved my niece and Damian's kids, but I wasn't ready for kids. Hell, I was second guessing bringing a child into this world, especially with a fourth angelic bloodline in the mix.

Valerie's soft features hardened. "You don't want kids?"

"I never said I didn't want kids," I said. "I'm just not quite ready for them right now." I knew it was selfish, but I wanted my time with just her and no distractions, at least for a little longer.

She sucked on her bottom lip as she considered my words. Now that she was done with medical school and residencies, she was feeling more settled into a life in Maine. We had roots now, and she wanted children before she was thirty.

"I eventually want a couple of kids," I said, so she could hear the words from my mouth. "A boy and a girl." I shrugged and glanced at the painted sky. "Preferably not at the same time," I added with a grin. I saw just how ragged Damian was with triplets. Of course, he was twenty-five-hundred years old, but who was counting?

Valerie's lips curved into a smile. "You don't want twins?"

I shook my head. I had a feeling one at a time was going to be enough of a handful. Besides, being a twin had its downside. Sharing everything from birthdays to parent's attention was not always the easiest, no matter how close the twins.

"You regret being a twin?" she asked, surprised by my open train of thought.

I weighed my response, thinking about the benefit of always having Tom around and the pain I felt when he shut me out. It was a double-edged sword, but I guess that was true of any sibling relationship. "No," I said, and glanced at her. "But before I even entertain bringing a kid into the world, I need to close every last gate to hell."

Chapter 12

TED STOOD AS WE entered the private flight waiting area. This time he listened to me and was wearing a Hawaiian print shirt with Bermuda shorts and beach sandals. He looked as comfortable as you can get, and his wife, Heather, stood next to him, looking just as comfortable in a long sundress.

They looked as thoroughly relaxed as we felt, and I shot out a hand to go along with my welcome smile.

"You finally listened," I said, and he let out a laugh.

"We decided to take a bit of a vacation ourselves. We've been in Waikiki for the last week," Ted said. "I hope you don't mind, but Heather's my co-pilot for the trip home."

"I don't mind at all," I said, as he walked us into the adjoining hangar where they were prepping the plane.

"Is that the plane we flew out in?" Valerie asked, as I hauled both our bags across the length of the hangar.

"No," I said, studying the familiar jet. This was the one I had ridden on at least a dozen times over the years and while it was comfortable for long flights, it wasn't the luxury we had been spoiled with on the way out.

"Sorry. I couldn't take our flagship plane off the market for a week," Ted said.

I gave him a nod. "I wouldn't expect you to. Hell, I didn't even expect the accommodations we had on the flight here."

"Well, it was our little wedding gift upgrade," Heather said, and handed Ted her bag before she took the stairs up to the smaller aircraft.

Valerie climbed up after Heather, and Ted let me lead the way onto the plane. Our bags went into the closet between the passenger space and the cockpit, and Ted closed the door after the ground crew pulled the stairs away.

With everything buttoned up, I stepped into the passenger section, where Valerie had already taken a seat in one of the swiveling captain's chairs by the window. A leather couch lined the opposite side of the plane, along with a little kitchenette, and the bathroom lay in the back section beyond the kitchen area. The television screen was in the same general area as it had been in the prior plane, but it wasn't as big.

"This one doesn't have a bedroom, but if you need to rest, the couch pulls out and those chairs also recline, so you have either option." He rubbed his hands together and then pointed to the small hallway in the back. "Bathrooms are back there, along with blankets and pillows, if you need them.

Drinks are in here, as well as a couple of frozen meals Heather cooked for the trip."

"Thanks," I said.

"Feel free to come up front if you want," he added, and then gave us a nod, disappearing into the cockpit to do his last preflight check before we got underway.

"So, no mile high this time?" Valerie whispered to me, and I grinned.

"I don't believe he said that wasn't allowed." I reached for her and pulled her to me, planting a lingering kiss before she pushed me away with an eye roll.

"We had private quarters before," she whispered and took her seat again, pointing for me to take the adjoining chair.

"I can make this private," I grinned.

"You can't make it soundproof," she said.

The girl had a point, and I shrugged. "You know where to find me if you change your mind." I stretched out in the recliner and yawned. Getting up early this morning wasn't really what I'd wanted to do. I would have rather just slept in and forgotten about going home.

We didn't make any decisions last night regarding Koa, kids, or my father and I put up the barrier in my mind that rendered my thoughts unattainable, and Valerie cocked her head at me. I didn't acknowledge it, instead I closed my eyes and focused on trying to come up with a viable plan. New York wouldn't be the venue and I wasn't bringing Valerie anywhere near that landmark. Not with what Lucifer did to her in that space. I'm sure a crop circle in New York would draw a great deal of attention, and she'd probably see it on the news, but it had to be done. That property needed to be sanitized; scrubbed clean of the evil it bred.

I debated on doing it before the concert, but I knew revisiting the location where Lucifer almost destroyed us would fuck me up big time. Especially if the bastard made an appearance. If that happened, the likelihood that I'd be in shape to perform would be iffy, at best. Even if there wasn't any physical damage, my mental state would be challenged. Hell, it would already be challenged, knowing I have to go take care of business as soon as the curtain falls.

"What are you thinking about?" she asked, as the plane started rolling from the hangar.

"How to keep you safe," I said, opening my eyes.

"I might have an idea that could work," she said, and I sat up, interested in what she had to say. "Well, you know how you can project that barrier?"

"Yeah," I said.

"I know you can do it on a large scale, but how targeted can you get it?"

I shrugged. I was always worried about protecting a group of people, so I never really focused on harnessing it into a small scale. "What'd you have in mind?"

She inhaled and blew a stream of air out. "I'd be willing to bet wherever we go, he will have his henchmen surrounding the area."

I thought about the hellhounds in Hawaii and nodded.

"And if I'm with you, even if I'm not within the perimeter, he'll make sure I'm captured and dragged back into the mix," she said, studying her hands before her gaze met mine.

I shook my head. "I'd never let that happen."

She crossed her arms. "You know it's going to happen. Even if he has to kidnap me before you get there. We both know I'm his bargaining chip. He already knows your willingness to trade for me. But this time, he will not let me get away. At least, not alive."

I shivered at the thought, knowing she was right, and I thought I understood where she was going with this. "What if I don't have any power on his turf? I wasn't able to protect myself last time, or you, for that matter." I bit my lip, watching the land speed by as the plane sped up for takeoff. "You didn't have the power in the warehouse, either," I added, thinking of the view I had of everything Lucifer did to her while I watched helplessly on the shores of Heaven.

"Why do you think Damian has his powers on Lucifer's turf?"

I shrugged. I had no fucking clue why Damian could use what I gave him while I was useless in the same position.

"He's infused with angel grace."

Her comment tore my gaze away from the window.

"And now you are, too."

Her statement hung on the air between us while I combed through Damian's history. He didn't beat Lucifer until he was infused with angel grace. It wasn't that he went on the offensive, like I originally thought, and my gaze moved back to Valerie. She was nodding her head in agreement before I even spoke. "So are you," I said and smiled. I had given her a piece of Uriel's grace after I came back from the dead, along with the healing powers and a small strand of what ran through my blood.

Her eyebrows rose at my silent revelation. I guess she hadn't realized the dark nature that lay dormant within her, along with the grace and healing power I infused her with.

"I told you I never wanted you to be vulnerable again," I said.

"Yeah, but I just thought you gave me back the healing mojo along with a piece of angel grace. I didn't know you gave me..." she waved her hand at me.

There really wasn't a specific word for the powers that ran through my blood, and I smiled.

"So, I could hold you down if I wanted to?" she asked, and her voice carried that coy quality that matched the mischievous sparkle in her eye.

"Oh, I don't know about that," I said, toying with her. "I think you might need to practice when we get home."

Her grin was my answer, and she glanced away as clouds filled the window and the plane leveled out. "I'll have to take you up on that," she mumbled, and then refocused from the sexual innuendo. "Anyway..."

"Back to what we were talking about," I finished, and she nodded, her humor drying up at the sobering conversation.

"If you can target your shield, we might have the element of surprise."

"How?"

"Around me."

"That's easy..."

"Let me clarify," she said, holding up her hand. "Around me so they can grab me and maybe even break skin, but nothing more."

"You w...want me to put a bar...rier in...side your skin?" The surprise her statement hit me with brought forth the full force of my stutter.

"Yes."

I leaned back in my seat and ran my hands down my face, looking at her over my fingertips. "I don't know if I can do that," I said through my fingers. The only time I may have come close to her concept was when I tapped the power within me in order to remain standing after Lucifer's henchmen nearly beat me to death. I had never tried putting a protective barrier below the surface of my skin, let alone someone else's.

"Try," she said, like it was simple, and all I could envision was making a mistake.

My mistakes weren't little, either. I shook my head, and she rolled her eyes.

"Just try."

"Not in a plane," I replied. I knew my limitations and if I screwed up, we could be free-falling to the earth in a matter of seconds. "Maybe when we get home," I said, waiting for the argument, but it never came. Instead, she nodded and unhooked her seatbelt, crossing to the refrigerator to see what sort of refreshments we had at our disposal.

"Want anything?" she asked, glancing over her shoulder.

"What are the choices?"

"Soda, orange juice, cranberry juice, water," she rattled off the listing of beverages waiting for me to make a decision.

"I'll take water for now," I said, stopping her from continuing to read off the alcoholic choices. Valerie tossed me a bottle on her way back to the chair.

I drained my water and smiled at her as she sucked down hers. The way her lips wrapped around the neck of the bottle stirred the heat inside me. As soon as she finished, I grabbed her hand and dragged her down to the restroom at the back of the plane. It was larger than your average plane restroom, but nowhere near as big as what we had coming out. Either way, it would do for the things I had in mind.

She protested, and I pushed her against the door, drowning her voice with a kiss. Time stopped and my hands explored her curves through the silky fabric of her sundress. The smoothness of the fabric from her back all the way down to her thighs pulled me away from her lips.

"You're not wearing any underwear," I whispered, my voice husky with the need riding through my bloodstream.

Her devious chuckle was my only answer before her mouth crushed over mine. I pulled at her skirt until my fingers found her skin and I shifted to get a better angle to the wet satin of her pussy. She breathed a soft moan as I started the soft rub that always made her squirm. I smiled, breaking the kiss and pulling far enough away to see the bliss in her eyes.

Her hands slid under my shirt and she ran her palms down my chest until she found the button on my shorts. She navigated the button and zipper quickly and her gentle stroke sent a shiver through me.

"Do you want to fuck me or my mouth?"

It wasn't an easy choice, and it stalled my mind for a minute. "Both," I finally said, and she smiled, lowering to her knees. Thought stopped the moment her lips swallowed me, and I closed my eyes, leaning my hands against the door, enjoying her seductive technique.

When I couldn't hold out anymore, I reached down, pulled her to her feet, and yanked her dress up at the same moment she wrapped her legs around my waist. I forced myself to hold on, to not come until she had. Luckily, I didn't have to wait long. Her pussy contracted, pulling a groan from my lips as I lost control, slamming my hips to hers until the heat exploded from my core.

"Holy shit," she whispered against my neck.

"That's the right way to do the mile high club," I whispered in her ear and then nibbled her earlobe. She squirmed in my grip, letting out a high-pitched squeal. I laughed and continued nibbling while she continued to squirm and giggle.

I pulled away and met her gaze.

"I love you, Mrs. Ryan."

She grinned. "I love you more than I thought I ever could love someone."

I slid out of her and placed her on the floor before tucking my junk back in my pants and zipping myself up. My muscles started that tired throb that always accompanied a good round of sex, and I grabbed a kiss before heading back to the comfortable leather seats. The recliner felt good, and I considered another drink, but my eyelids weren't cooperating, and the last thing I remember was the creak of the bathroom door.

Chapter 13

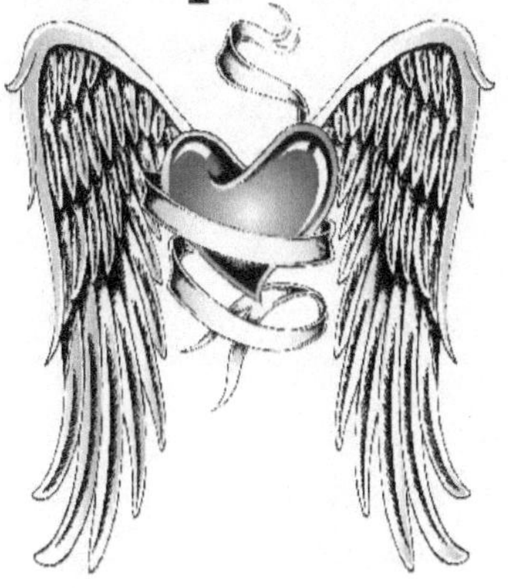

I SHIFTED AND MY eyes blinked open. The chair next to me was empty, and I rubbed my eyes before glancing at the light blanket draped over me.

"Val?" I asked and tried to swallow, but the dryness in my mouth made my tongue feel like sandpaper against the roof of my mouth. There was an unopened water bottle sitting in the cup holder next to me and I took a drink before looking around. My brain was slow to recognize where I was, and it took the purr of the engines to snap it all together. The plane.

I had no idea how long I had been out, and I headed for the bathroom, thinking maybe she was there, but it was empty, and I did my business before heading toward the only other place she could be. The cockpit.

As I got closer, I heard her laugh through the cracked door and I pulled it open. Heather and Valerie looked up at me.

"Sleeping beauty arises," Valerie said with a laugh.

"Where are we?" I asked, glancing out at the green mountains spread out in the distance and the solid land mass under us along with the darkly painted sky.

"Over Indiana."

"Indiana?" I asked with the water bottle halfway to my mouth.

"Yes," Ted said.

"You slept through most of the trip," Heather added, stating the obvious.

"I guess so." My stomach growled and Valerie stood.

"Come on. Let's get some food into you." She linked her elbow in mine and gave Heather and Ted a finger wave as she led me from the cockpit. "They have some very amusing stories about you and Tom growing up," she said, when she deposited me in the seat and crossed to the refrigerator.

"Like what?" I was still foggy-brained, and my focus landed on the sandwich she pulled out. "Bring me one of those Coronas, too, okay?" I asked, before she had stepped away from the serving area.

"You sure?"

I nodded. A cold beer and the roast beef sandwich sounded like a perfect combination and the bag of chips she brought just added to the noise my stomach made. I practically inhaled the food and followed it with cold beer. It wasn't the nice Polynesian food from Hawaii, this was the type of roast beef sandwich you'd get from a deli in New York.

I let out a ripping burp, and Valerie's eyebrows rose. I'm usually not that uncivilized in the presence of a lady, but I was too content to really care. I offered a shrug and got to my feet, depositing the empty bottle in the trash along with the paper.

"You want one?" I asked, holding up another beer.

"Nah," she said and stretched. "I'm good."

"That you are," I said under my breath.

"What was that?"

I brought the bottle to my mouth, choosing to take a sip of beer instead of repeating what I had said. Besides, the smirk on her face told me she heard me perfectly and just wanted the ego boost.

"Assuming I can target my power, what then?" I asked, bringing us back to the original conversation from earlier this morning. "How is that going to help get my father out of hell?"

She bit her lip and shrugged. "It might give us the distraction to be able to snatch your father, but that assumes he's there at the same time."

I let out a huff. "That's one hell of an assumption."

"I never said it was a perfect solution," she muttered.

I reached out and took her hand. "At least you have something close to a plan," I said. "I've drawn a blank beyond knowing I have to do something."

I may be a genius on paper, but in situations where a devious mind was needed, I was clueless. I had snowed the devil once. I doubted he'd be dumb enough to let me do it again. But I also knew Lucifer was a bit of a megalomaniac and he would want to show off just how broken my father was, so, she might just have something that I could work from, even though I wasn't at all comfortable with the risk.

"Maybe Damian and Tom will have some ideas," she said.

"Maybe, and Steve might have some decent advice, too," I said. After all, he's the one with the closest association with criminals. His undercover career was legendary for someone so young, so he might have a few tricks up his sleeve that he could coach me on. "In the meantime, I'd rather just table this for the next hour or so until we get back to the real world."

She smiled her agreement, and we turned towards the television, electing to watch a few sit-coms for the rest of the plane ride.

Chapter 14

HOME.

I dropped our bags on the floor and fell back on our bed. Valerie was downstairs sorting through the mail before we focused on the wedding gifts piled on the kitchen table.

"Chris?" she called up the stairs.

"I'm coming," I mumbled. I shouldn't be as tired as I was, especially since I had slept for a solid four or five hours on the plane. Jetlag whipped my ass, but I forced myself up and trudged down the stairs, putting a halfway interested expression on my face. The couch hugged me as I took a seat, tempting me to close my eyes, but I knew I'd get a swat from Valerie.

She had moved the pile from the kitchen onto the coffee table. With enthusiasm that reminded me of a kid at Christmas, she handed me the basket of cards and started ripping wrapping paper.

I shuffled through the envelopes. All but one was addressed to either Mr. and Mrs. Ryan or CJ and

Valerie. The single envelope had my full name scrawled across the front and I stared at it as a sudden chill hit, making my stomach roll. Valerie gasped, and my gaze bounced to her.

She pulled a beautiful embroidered throw blanket out of a box and held it up. Our names and the date were imprinted, and I gave her a smile before focusing back on the letter in my hand.

Valerie continued with the next box, and I slid my finger under the tab, ripping the top of the envelope.

I pulled the card from the sheath and stared at the front. My smile faded. The perfectly appropriate wedding card was splattered with something rusty. I glanced up as Valerie displayed a silver frame; her smile was still as bright as before. I pressed my lips together in a tight smile and glanced back at the ruined card. Dread I couldn't quantify licked my soul, and I bit my lower lip, opening the card. I swallowed hard at the picture enclosed. The words were even worse.

Paper had stopped being crumpled, and I tore my gaze away from the promises listed in the card, and met Valerie's gaze. She was staring at me, and the paper slipped from my fingers. I sprang to my feet, bolting to the phone.

My heart thundered in my chest as I dialed.

"Connor residence," the familiar voice muttered.

"Dan?" I asked, unsure if it was actually Dan or someone else who answered.

Silence met my question and I glanced at the clock. It was way too late to be calling under normal circumstances, but this was far from normal.

"CJ?"

"Yes."

"You heard?"

Heard. I wish it had been a verbal announcement and not a picture with her blood splattered all over it.

"What happened?" I asked and turned in time to see the horror form in Valerie's features as she stared between the picture and the words scribed in the card.

"They say she slit her own throat," Dan said, his voice just a ghost of what it used to be. The last of his children was dead and buried and I couldn't blame him for the defeat in his tone.

Lucifer waged war by killing someone who had a line to my heart, but not enough strings to devastate. Killing Sandy was a warmup. A kind end to life compared to what he promised to do to those closest to me, and he wouldn't stop until I was dead or agreed to let him take control. He promised I would watch every depraved act. Every drop of blood and every scream of pain would be on my soul.

"Why?" I heard myself say, and the growl that came over the line told me enough.

"Because of you," he said in that accusatory tone that made my knees weak.

He didn't know just how true that statement was, and I hung up the receiver, numbed by the confirmation that the picture was real, and that Sandy was truly dead.

"Holy Jesus," I whispered, and lowered into the chair. I stared at the phone in my hand for a moment and then started dialing. My family was spread out too thin. Steve and Jen were in New York, and Tom and Raven were on the other side of town. They both might as well be on the other side of the globe, and panic started like a bulldozer.

"Steve?" I said, as he picked up the phone.

"Did you just get back?" he asked.

"A little while ago." I glanced at the clock and closed my eyes at the late hour. I never even considered the time when I called the Connors. "Sorry for calling so late, but we got a detailed threat from Lucifer, and it covers everyone."

"Shit," Steve muttered.

"He killed Sandy," I whispered and put my head in my hand.

"What?"

"Yeah. I guess you could say that was his final warning and a warmup to what he has in mind for all of you."

"Are you sure it's not just a trick?" Steve asked.

"Lucifer sent a fucking picture, and I already talked to Dan. He thinks she killed herself. Because of me."

"Jesus," he whispered.

"Her death is on me," I said meeting Valerie's gaze. She was shaking her head, mimicking Steve's sentiments that it wasn't my fault, but it was. I was a walking death magnet and whether I was with those I loved, or halfway across the globe, Lucifer would still use my family to get to me, and he wasn't above killing them. In fact, I think he fancied the idea of slowly driving me insane.

Chapter 15

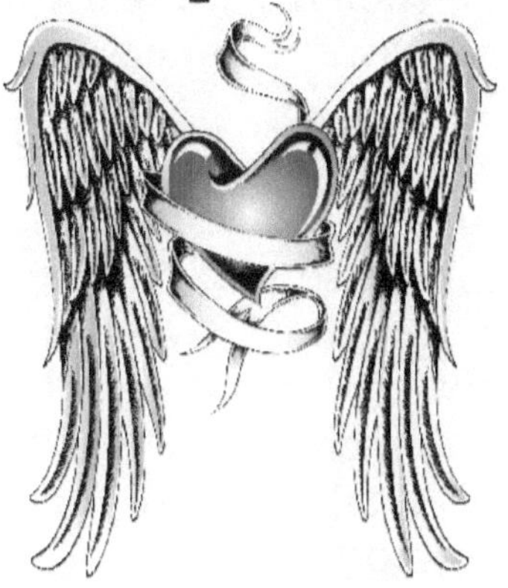

I SAT ON THE couch, staring at the drawer where I had tucked the wedding card from Lucifer. Sandy's picture was no longer in view either, and my entire family argued behind me as to what needed to be done to stop this lunatic.

I hadn't slept.

Neither had Valerie, and I raised my gaze to her on the adjoining couch. She looked as haggard as I felt, and the knife Akamu gave her twirling idly in her hands told me enough about her state of mind without taking a peek myself.

Her eyes rose from the blade to mine, and she offered a shrug.

I needed to take control of the situation before the whole purpose of having my family close derailed. "How many portals have you identified?" I asked, interrupting the chaos.

Damian pressed his lips together, trading a glance with Tom.

"Sixteen," he said, after Tom waved toward me, giving him a glare fueled with annoyance.

"Is that all of them?" I asked, and silence settled over the room.

"It's all we've found on this side of the globe," Tom signed, and his gaze dropped. "We haven't looked on the other side yet."

"I need to know where every one of them is." I stared them down, appalled that they hadn't broadened their search in all this time. "Think you can handle that?" I asked, and Tom's jaw tightened. He gave me a curt nod.

"We know the signature, but we don't have unlimited access to satellites on the other side of the world," Damian said, trying to diffuse the aggravation building between my brother and me.

"You've had two years. What the fuck?"

I was waiting for you to come up with a plan to save Dad. Tom's accusatory tone accosted my brain, and I met his glare.

I checked my frustration. It wasn't aimed at him, anyway, and I stood up facing him.

"You want a shot at me?" I asked, spreading my arms wide, sensing more than just frustration with the situation in my brother.

He pressed his lips, and the muscles in his jaw jumped. The shake of his head didn't come right away, either.

I waved to the backyard, opening the silent invitation. His forms were nearly as perfect as mine and his anger wasn't unwarranted. It had been two years, and I didn't have a plan. He wasn't the only one frustrated by that, and if he kicked my ass, maybe I'd feel a little better.

Tom didn't hesitate. He stormed outside, and I followed. When he turned, throwing the first punch, I didn't block. I let his fist connect with my eye socket. It was hard enough to knock me on my ass. I climbed to my feet as his chest huffed and his hand clenched and unclenched against the sting.

"I don't have the foggiest clue of how to get Dad," I said, shaking the stars from my head. "And I was a little busy trying to put Valerie back together," I added.

His hands curled into fists again, but now a glaze covered his eyes. His fingers uncurled. "We can't leave him there," he signed, and I looked at the ground.

"I know. But the things Lucifer will do to you and Raven..." I trailed off, leaving out Lucifer's horrific detail about their daughter. "I have to close the portals." I met his stare.

"You have to get Dad," he signed, and then his fists clenched. He hadn't read the threats. I only let Damian see what Lucifer had actually written.

I stepped closer. "I don't know how, and if I don't start closing portals, he's going to get loose. When he does, do you want to know what he has in store for Raven?" I couldn't help the growl in my tone, and Tom blinked and stepped back.

"But what about Dad?" he signed, and I shook my head.

"Lucifer said he was going to stuff her so full of blood stones that her intestines would burst and then he'd set her on fire inch by inch until she choked on her own screams."

The description was less eloquent than Lucifer's, but it summed up the gist, and my brother turned the color of waxed paper.

"Is that what you want?" I snarled, stepping so close that I crowded him.

He stood his ground, searching my gaze for any hint of exaggeration, and then he slowly shook his head, taking a step back.

"No," he signed.

"That's the decision I have to make. Dad or everyone else and it fucking sucks," I whispered, with a voice filled with unbearable bitterness. "My death won't save anyone, either. I considered that option."

His eyes widened a fraction and then the pain appeared in his irises.

"If I thought that would work, I would have swallowed a bullet last night. Just like that." I snapped my fingers. "But it would only fuel that bastard's fury and leave you all at his mercy." The admission of the darker thoughts that played through my mind last night brought forth a fresh layer of tears that I blinked away.

I turned away from my brother and crossed to the rock wall, to the spot that seemed to be my go to place when the world dished out too much shit. His shadow followed, and he took a seat, facing the house.

"I have to close the portals," I said. "There isn't any other choice."

His head dipped in a nod, and he studied his hands.

"If we can figure out a way to get Dad out before I close the last one, I'd be willing to try, but it's not something that will stop me if it doesn't work." I dropped my gaze from the ocean view to his. "And I'm scared shitless it's going to kill everything good in me."

I moved my gaze away and took a deep breath, exhaling and steeling my emotions behind the iron curtain in my heart. Until this was all over, I couldn't feel, and I certainly couldn't allow myself to second guess my mission.

If I did, people would die.

It was a sobering thought, and I gave Tom a forced smile and turned, heading back inside to find a map. It took me a while to find a large map of the world in my old closet and I brought it downstairs, where everyone was quietly discussing what to do. I knew what I had to do and now time had run out.

I spread the map out on the table and handed Damian a marker. "Show me where they all are."

My brain was too foggy to follow the number of dots, but when he stopped, I counted sixteen marks. New York wasn't one of them, and my gaze moved from the map to his. He moved his hand toward that last spot, hesitating before I grabbed his wrist.

He and I exchanged a look, and I shook my head. I didn't want Valerie to know that portal was still open, and he nodded, understanding even without words. I scanned the marks and pointed to the one in Hawaii.

"That one's closed." I tapped, and he crossed it off.

"That leaves fifteen," he said, and my gaze moved back to New England.

Beyond the one in New York City, the closest mark was in Canada, just north of Quebec, and the farthest was down in Argentina. I figured anything east of the Rockies in the U.S. and Canada was the biggest threat.

"We need to hit this first." I tapped the one in eastern Canada. "And it will need to wait until after my concert next week," I said, meeting Damian's gaze. "In the meantime, I need you to figure out where the portals are on the other side of the world. Okay?"

"I'll do my best," he said, and scanned the map before exhaling.

"I'm surprised to see the lack of clusters," I said, scanning the map. "New England had three portals within a few hours of each other, but there isn't anything like that in the rest of the states." I met his gaze, and he nodded.

"I had the same impression as well, but I've got no real explanation. The closest cluster is in the southwest." He waved toward four dots between Nevada, Southern California, Arizona and New Mexico. "But even those aren't as close as the ones here were." He sighed and glanced back at me. "Why don't you get some sleep," he added. "And then you and I should have a conversation regarding options."

"Options?"

"Rescue options," he clarified. "After you get sleep. You're exhausted and you and I will need both our minds sharp to figure something out, now that you're closing these things in earnest. The more we close, the more relentless Lucifer will be."

His statement just turned the knife inside me, and I bit my lip to control the reaction. "I'm fine. What did you have in mind?" I really wanted to hear his ideas, especially after the bloom of pain in my core at his comment. Basically, the more portals I closed, the harder Lucifer would be on my father. The fact that Damian had some ideas on how to get my father out of hell shined a little hope into my foggy brain.

He laughed at me. "You and Valerie haven't slept for what... something like thirty hours now?"

"I slept on the plane," I said, but he was right. My mind wasn't working very well, and as much as I wanted to focus, my eyes kept drifting to the map and my thoughts followed. I needed at least a few hours of sleep in order to focus on any one thing. I glanced at the crew gathered in the family room and then back at Damian, suddenly worried about a surprise attack.

"I promise to keep everyone safe. Go sleep." He pointed to the stairs, and this time it wasn't a request.

I sighed and nodded before I crossed to Valerie. Grabbing her hand, I pulled her away from the family with a one-word explanation. "Sleep."

She came without question and neither of us spoke while we undressed, and I moved the suitcases off the bed. We slipped under the sheets, and I just kissed her cheek, pulling her into the spoon position. She wrapped her arms around mine and squeezed, reminding me without words that she loved me, and I squeezed back.

Lucifer's hideous promises kept looping in our heads like a nightmare we couldn't wake from. No matter how hard I tried to push back, the fear of what the future held kept coming, hitting me with the full force of a runaway train.

Chapter 16

THE HEAT OF THE sun woke me, and I squinted at the blue sky outside the window, wondering when the hell sleep finally grabbed hold of me. It took a few minutes to realize it was morning, and I yawned, rolling on my back and stretching without taking my arm out from underneath Valerie.

I rolled back, molding into her, and squeezed her close. "Babe, we need to get up," I whispered in her ear, and she whined, burying her face in the pillow.

If I could hole up in the room all week, I would, but I needed to have a talk with Damian and hear what his grand rescue plans were. I'd also need to start practicing what Valerie had mentioned on the plane because I knew damned well she wouldn't let me go off on my own to destroy the portals.

New York would be my last solo act.

Her eyes blinked open, and she turned towards me. "I thought you were singing with Jen?" she asked, and I strapped down on my thoughts, admonishing myself for not being more careful.

"I'll be in the city without you," I said, quickly enough to cover up my mistake.

Her eyes softened, and she kissed my cheek before rolling out of bed and heading towards the bathroom.

I stared at the ceiling and then rubbed my face, forcing myself out of the warm bed. "I want to go back to Hawaii," I muttered, and started making the bed.

Valerie stuck her head out of the bathroom. "You and me both," she said, and I uttered a soft laugh, meeting her gaze. "I have to go into work in an hour," she added.

I turned and stared at the clock. Crap. It was Monday, and that unsettled nervous energy started in. I'd have to weather eight hours with her out of sight, and that didn't sit well.

"Val," I started, and she glared in my direction.

"I'm not putting my life on hold," she snapped, and disappeared into the bathroom.

I finished making the bed and crossed, ripping the door open and leveling a glare in her direction. "After what he promised?"

Her eyes shifted from her own reflection to mine. "I've been running from Lucifer for ten years. I'm not running anymore," she said around a toothbrush, and then she spit in the sink.

"I can make you..." I started, and she spun on me, the storm brewing in her irises.

"Chris, I swear, I'll rip your heart out myself if you even think about issuing a command for me to stay put." She stomped past me into the bedroom.

I brushed my teeth trying to justify all the reasons to keep her here, but the look in her eyes told me not to fuck with her. Not today. Especially not after what happened in Hawaii, and after I rinsed the paste from my mouth, I leaned on the counter, hanging my head while I tried to figure out the best course of action.

"He's not going to strike today," she said from the doorway, and I turned to face her.

"How do you know?"

She bit her lip and shrugged. "It doesn't feel right. It's not happening. Not today."

I didn't have the same conviction. At least not on the surface, but deep down, I knew she was right. My nerves had to do with my insecurity, not the sense of a pending disaster, and she raised an eyebrow.

"I..." I stopped myself from admitting I was scared. She already knew the turmoil wringing my stomach into knots. Voicing it wouldn't make it go away.

"I know," she said, and sighed before slipping behind the half-open door. Drawers opened and the soft whisper of fabric reached my ears.

I dragged the brush through my hair and grabbed a pair of sweatpants, pulling them on while Valerie pinned her hair up. She chose a turquoise pair of scrubs from the drawer and the color reminded me of the ocean we had left behind.

"We never settled on what to do with Koa," I said and slipped a t-shirt over my head.

She paused at the door. "Koa's used to the warmth of Hawaii. It might be a hell of a shock for her to come here."

She had a good point.

"Then maybe we need to get a couple of dogs," I said.

She smiled. "If that makes you feel better, go for it."

"I'm thinking more for you than me," I said, and her hands dropped from taming the last of the stray hairs.

"Why?"

I shoved my hands into the pockets of my sweats and looked at the ground. My justifications for a guard dog had everything to do with going out on my own to stop Lucifer and not having her along. I knew it was in contrast to what I said in Hawaii, and when I looked up, Valerie's features hardened.

"No." She turned and stomped out of the room.

"But Val," I followed her, catching up to her on the stairs.

"We already had this discussion," she said, glaring up at me. "You need to figure out how to do what we talked about. I'm going to work." She tore out of my grip and, as soon as we turned on the landing, we both stopped.

We stared at the group sitting around the table. I think we just assumed everyone had gone home. If they had, they certainly came back bright and early.

"I have to get to work," Valerie said, and turned to me. "We will talk when I get home," she added, pointing at my chest.

I nodded and gave her a soft kiss. "Have a good day, and if something happens..."

"I'll call," she said and patted my cheek. "I love you."

"I love you, too."

She stepped out of the house, and I watched her until her car turned the corner, disappearing from sight. My stomach tightened with irrational fear, and I closed the door. My back burned from the singular focus of everyone in the room, and I turned to face my family.

"Have you guys been up all night?" I asked.

"Not everyone," Steve said and leaned back in the chair. "Tom, Damian, and I have been tossing ideas around all night, but the girls got some sleep." As if on cue, he yawned. "I'm too old for this shit," he muttered, turning back to the map and the steaming carafe of coffee.

I crossed to the cabinets and pulled out a coffee cup, helping myself to the fresh brew before I slid into the empty seat. "Did you figure out anything that you think is viable?" I asked, searching their features.

"Why don't we bring the kids over to our house," Naomi said, and stood. Raven and Jennifer followed suit, collecting the kids from the family room where they were happily coloring. As soon as they left, everyone turned to me.

Steve ran a hand down his face. "We have a few options, but honestly, they're all wild cards." He met my gaze.

"Valerie isn't going to let me go alone," I said and traded a glance with Damian. *These guys have no clue about New York, do they?*

Damian's slight shake of his head confirmed my thought, and I wanted to keep it that way. I could see Steve insisting on coming, and without power, he'd be just another one of Lucifer's pawns. I couldn't walk him into that, not after all he'd done for us.

"Are you serious?" Tom signed.

"Yeah. She has the crazy idea that I can focus my power and store it under her skin so they'll think she's defenseless." I stared into my coffee and the silence pulled my gaze up.

Steve bit his lip like he was seriously contemplating that option, and then he met my gaze. "That actually could work."

"Excuse me?" My eyebrows rose.

"Look, one scenario we came up with was Damian grabbing your father. We all think the next time you go up against Lucifer, he will flaunt what's left of your dad in order to knock you down a peg or two," he said, and my jaw tightened at the thought.

"But if it's just you and me..." Damian trailed off and inhaled. "If it's just you and me, this could backfire."

"It could backfire anyway," I said, meeting their gaze. "If Valerie is there and I can't protect her, I'm as fucked as they get." I paused, focusing on Damian. "You've been there. You know what kind of sick bastard he is. If he gets a hold of Valerie..." I couldn't finish. Instead, I closed my eyes and bowed my head.

"She could distract him long enough for me to grab your father," Damian said. "I know using her as bait isn't what you want to do, but it may be the only shot we have. We both know Lucifer has her on the top of his hit list. If you can do what she proposed, it could be a more palatable risk."

I stared at him and exhaled. "Would you put Naomi in that position?"

Damian struggled with the answer and finally lowered his gaze and shook his head. I moved my sharp stare toward Tom and Steve.

"Would you gamble with Raven's life?"

Tom shook his head and when I moved along to Steve, he sat back with his arms crossed. I just raised an eyebrow.

"I used Jen as bait on more than one occasion, and every time I put her at risk, something bad happened. She was gang raped because I was a jackass and didn't listen to my gut. I didn't make her leave New York when every instinct I had told me to get her out. She nearly died because of my miscalculations. My daughter died because I underestimated the criminals hunting us. I've never gotten over that. It haunts me every day, but Jennifer is alive, and God bless her, she's still with me." He kept my gaze. "You know the mistakes I've made, and do you know the shit thing of it all?"

I shook my head.

"If I had to do it all over again, I would probably make the same fucking mistakes." He let that sit for a moment while he leaned forward and took a sip of coffee. "I've lived my life on the borderline of reckless and left a hell of a bloody trail behind me because of it, but I did my job and caught the bad guys."

I gave him a nod and studied my coffee for a minute.

"Sometimes, you have to take that risk. The bigger the bad, the bigger the gamble in order to stop them," he added, and I looked back at him. "But there's a world of difference between this situation and everything I've lived through. I'm not you. I'm not standing in your shoes."

"I'm scared," I admitted directly to Steve.

The tension in his features loosened. "I would have you committed if you weren't."

I cracked a smile.

"Look, CJ, you know I love you like my own, and I do not want you walking into a trap," he said and paused, focusing on the table in front of him as he drew a breath. "But we all know every portal you step into is a trap. It's just how we approach it. If it was me, I don't know if I would follow through on the promises you made in heaven. Not when it puts everyone you love at risk, but at least the powers you possess give you an edge here."

"I don't have a choice. If I walk away from my responsibility, everyone is already at risk and my father's sacrifice was wasted. The more portals I close, the more desperate he'll get. Either way, no one is safe, and I'm totally screwed."

"And you don't want to use Val as bait," Steve said.

"No. But she will not let me go alone, so I have to figure out how to make this work. Hell, I already ordered her to stay behind in Hawaii, and she said she'd cut my heart out herself if I ever pulled that shit on her again."

Damian pressed his lips together, trying to shut down the smirk that appeared.

"Yeah, it nearly ruined the honeymoon," I replied, and now all three of them wore the same smirk. They didn't say a word, and I appreciated it. I was sure at some future date they'd use that information to needle me, but today, it wasn't something to screw around with.

"Besides the outstanding questions of whether I can protect Valerie, or whether I even have any of my mojo on Lucifer's turf, I'm not comfortable leaving the rest of you vulnerable while we're off trying to rescue my father. He's already dead. You aren't." I pointed between Tom and Steve. "I don't want to leave you and your families unprotected." My gaze landed on Damian.

"What if we stayed at our cottage?" Steve asked.

"I'd have to bring your father to Paradise Cove in order to get him beyond Lucifer's reach and it's the only way back to Heaven that I know of," Damian said.

I scanned the map, focusing on the dot near Quebec in Canada. "I know it's five hours to Quebec, and it looks like at least a couple of more from there."

"That's if you can drive right to the spot."

I hadn't considered alternate transportation, and I ran my hand over my face. "Do we have access to a helicopter?"

My question surprised everyone, and I focused on Steve, not Damian or Tom. He chewed his lip and nodded.

"I can call in a favor, but it won't get you in the middle of that reserve. Maybe we could get you into here." He tapped a township at the southern tip of the reserve. "And then use snowmobiles for the rest of the trek," he added with a shrug. "I'm not sure if I have the kind of clout that's needed to pull that off, but I certainly can try."

"Does Ted have one?" I asked.

Steve shook his head. "At least I don't think so. I know the FBI does, but I'm sure there will be a thousand and one questions that neither of us is prepared to answer. I know a slew of people who still haven't gotten over what happened in court. There are those with significant reservations about not having me under their thumb, and you are a wild card in their minds. I don't think opening that door is wise."

I huffed a laugh. "You think?"

He grinned. "Yeah. I think."

"So, who owes you a favor?"

He glanced at his hands. "O'Keefe."

"The York Police Department? They don't have a chopper."

"They don't, but O'Keefe's brother does some of the shoreline tours over the summer."

I leaned back in the seat and bit the inside of my lip. "Well, that would cut the trip by at least a couple of hours," I said.

"I've had helicopters land in my yard during the summer, but not the winter, so I'm not sure what options we have. In the meantime, we should figure a backup plan in case this falls through."

"Seems like the snowmobile options are pretty sound for getting in and out of the reservoir," I said and received nods from everyone. I leaned back in the chair. "But what if the bastard doesn't show off the hell he's rained on Dad? What then?"

"You really think he's going to pass up the opportunity to rub your face in the sacrifice you made?" Damian asked with an incredulous laugh. "After twenty-five hundred years of experience with the lunatic, I say he won't pass up on the chance to push your buttons."

I traded a glance with my brother, waiting for him to weigh in. He gave me a nod.

"Okay. We have half a plan," I said, but something didn't sit right. It just seemed too easy, just like Hawaii. "What happens if he sends his army after you?" I asked, looking directly at Steve before moving my gaze to Damian and Tom. "There's no one here to protect you."

Steve slowly leaned back in the chair. "You once loaned your father a slice of your power," he started and I nodded, but it wasn't Steve that my gaze slid to.

"Think you could handle it?" I asked Tom.

He pointed at his chest and his mouth popped open before his gaze bounced to Steve.

"You're the one with angel blood, not Steve," I said, and glanced at Steve. "I know you meant for you, but he's my blood and I know he's got my back along with the same impulse to protect Grace that I have." Steve opened his mouth to argue, but I put up my hand. "I know you were an FBI agent and have that ingrained in your blood, but you are also an expert shot. He isn't." I pointed at Tom. "If I'm going to leave you vulnerable, I need you to be protected on multiple fronts. I figure a tiger, a marksman, a psychic freak, and a Wiccan should do the trick."

"Fee?" Tom articulated.

"Yeah, you're a fucking freak, just like me," I said, and couldn't quite keep a straight face.

He pressed his lips together against the smile, but the small creases at the corner of his eyes told me he found the grain of humor I tried to pass. Tom nodded and signed, "I appreciate the offer, but do you think you can teach me how to use it in the time we've got?"

I shrugged. "I don't know. I also don't know if I can do what Valerie suggested, but it's worth a try. If it doesn't work, Steve can be the fall back, okay?"

Everyone exchanged glances and then nodded.

I stood up and pointed my chin toward the sliders. Tom got up and followed me outside. I took a seat on the cold rock wall, patting the spot next to me.

"You sure I can handle this?" Tom signed, and the worry in his eyes echoed the hesitation I saw in his hands.

"Yes. The only warning I have for you is to watch your temper. That's when it can do damage if it gets away from you. You remember learning to call for Steve and me?"

He nodded.

"That level of concentration is needed to shut off the surrounding noise. We're all pretty good at blocking our thoughts, but regular folks have no clue and if you're in a public place, the noise is hell unless you learn to block it. You ready?"

He scanned the house and then met my gaze with a nod.

"It's going to feel kind of weird, like something wild is filling your skin. It will settle after a few minutes, so just breathe through it." I closed my eyes, concentrating on tearing a piece of my power off. Like ripping fabric, I felt the tug and the shredding from my core until I mentally held a small extract. I opened my eyes and stared at the glow in my palm. Tom was staring at it, at well, and I turned, slamming it into his chest while I held onto him, so he didn't topple off the rock wall into the ocean.

Tom's eyes went wide, and his breath hitched in his chest as the power transferred along with my memories. Every muscle in his body contracted, and I whispered, "Breathe."

It took him a few seconds, and then he sucked in a large wheezing breath, forcing air in and then out again. His wild-eyed gaze locked with mine and I smiled at him as his memories settled in my head along with the rest.

"Kind of a rush, huh?"

He nodded as his breath returned to normal and his shaking hands ran through his hair. "Holy shit," he whispered and then blinked, his gaze shooting to mine while his fingers verified his tongue was still missing. What came out of his mouth wasn't articulate. It was his thought that was loud and clear and overrode his senses.

"You still can't speak clearly," I said.

"But..." he started and stopped, blinking again.

"Welcome to the world of the genuine freaks," I said, and he burst out laughing.

"As if being an ancestor of Lucifer isn't freaky enough," he said, and traded a glance with me. His hands remained still on his thighs, and it was good to hear him clearly over the bastardization of speech.

"I don't stutter in my head," I said and sent a grin his way.

"Yeah, well, it doesn't come out as smoothly as what you hear in your head."

"Ditto."

He smiled and flexed his hands. "So, you're hitting the warehouse in New York without telling anyone," he said, sliding his gaze to me.

"I forgot to lock that shit up," I muttered, and met his gaze.

"And damn, Jenna really turned out to be a fucking freak," he said. The smile that played on his lips made me want to smack him.

"You want me shuffling through your memories?" I asked and stood, turning to face the water before looking down and meeting his gaze. "I haven't yet, but I'd be happy to play this game."

His smile toned down a notch, and he dropped his eyes, staring at the ground for a minute before he shook his head. He glanced at the house, turning serious. "You've got a lot of shit in your head," he said, looking up at me.

"Ayup." I sighed and nodded. "And you have to lock down the information about New York, otherwise Val will skin me alive."

Tom huffed and climbed to his feet. "So, how does this work?"

"Think you can move the picnic table?"

"How?"

"Just focus and envision it moving to a different spot."

His eyes narrowed as he looked at the table and then at a location a few feet away. When the table moved precisely where his gaze landed, his eyes widened, and his head whipped in my direction.

"I felt it go," he said, and his voice filled with awe.

"Now put the table back."

He did, and he slowly lowered to the rock wall. I took a seat next to him again.

"So, anything I wish..." he trailed off and met my gaze.

"You can move things and even destroy things with a thought. Understand there are limitations and things can go wrong," I said, my mind drifting back to my snorkeling adventure with Valerie and I looked at my hands, picking a hangnail before I continued. "Most people you can hear, but true psychopaths actually create static the way we've learned to do. And you can't hear a demon or a vampire. I'm not sure why, but it could be because they're dead and you just can't get a bead on their frequency."

"But I will still be able to see ghosts, right?"

"Yes. Your inherent gifts don't go away.

"I gather you gave me a small amount?"

I nodded. "Relatively speaking," I said and smiled. "But I gave you more than I gave Dad when we were four."

"Really?"

I nodded. "When Damian and I go do this thing, you need to stand watch over everyone at the cottage. I wanted you to have enough mojo to kill whatever comes after you."

"You think he'll send an army?"

I shrugged. "Even if he does, you are now more deadly than an army of demons."

I stood and left him to noodle on the amount of responsibility he had while he shuffled through the memories emblazoned in his mind. As for me, I escaped to my room before anyone intercepted, overwhelmed by exactly what my little brother's memories revealed.

I had seen a couple of Jennifer's visions when Tom was in Georgia, but I didn't have the full scope of what happened until now. The fact he didn't die of shock, and kept a level head, even when that asshole starting cutting him, amazed me. I wondered how in the hell he made it through that without losing his mind, especially when that bastard placed our mother's head on the end of the table he was strapped to.

Nothing I had survived compared to what he'd endured, and his misguided awe of me was humbling. There wasn't much I kept from him, but the battles he had to keep his sanity intact were brutal. I gained a new appreciation for my brother and knew I'd made the right decision. He would operate with the same moral compass that guided my mother and me, and probably do it with a lot more grace than I could ever muster.

Chapter 17

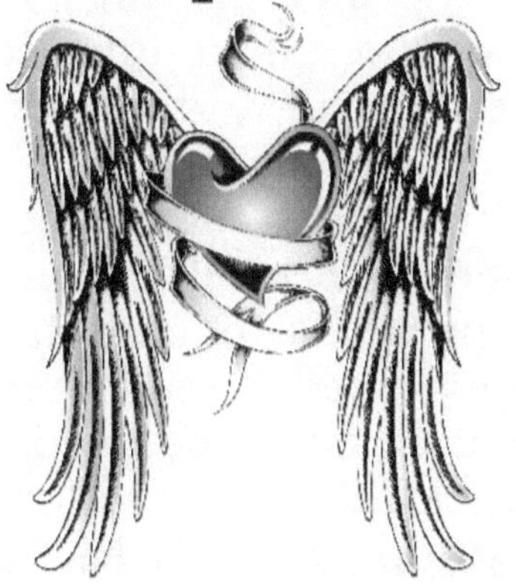

"TRY AGAIN." VALERIE SAID through clenched teeth as the wound on her side healed.

I dropped the bloody knife on the table and walked away. "I can't do this," I muttered and headed for the six-pack in the refrigerator. Over a dozen tries, and each time the knife went too deep before hitting the barrier. If I had been aiming for her heart, she would have died.

I popped the top off using the edge of the counter and drained the bottle in one long chug. I never thought I'd ever plant a knife in my wife's form, so doing it over a dozen times in the last hour was wearing thin.

"Chris," she snapped, and I turned with a second beer in my hand.

"I can't." This time, the words came out with the same force as my hand squeezing the bottle. The glass shattered, sending a spray of beer over the kitchen floor and I snapped my hand, dislodging a few of the bigger glass shards. "Fuck!"

"Jesus, let me look at your hand." Valerie marched over and peeled my fingers back to inspect the array of cuts. She pulled out a couple of smaller shards before leaning in and delivering the healing kiss, bringing with it the sting.

"I can't do this, Val," I said softly, and I looked down at the bloody tatters of her shirt. "I can't keep cutting you." She had no clue how much these practice sessions killed me. Either my protective barrier was too shallow or too deep. I couldn't seem to find the balance and if she didn't have access to her healing mojo on Lucifer's turf and the barrier was too deep, she would die. I had to operate on the worst-case scenario. If I didn't, it would bite me in the ass.

"Then I'll do the knife," she said and walked away.

I grabbed her arm. "No. Give it a rest. I need to prep for the concert tomorrow, anyway."

"Chris, you need to have this down cold," she said.

"I know." She didn't need to remind me. I hadn't put a concrete plan in place for heading north, and I knew on some level I was stalling. I needed to get through the concert and closing off the portal in New York before I thought about the one in Canada. Steve called in that favor and was waiting to hear whether or not it was a go. The timing depended on the weather, and I was all set to focus on that adventure the moment I got back home from my concert.

"Have you figured out when we are going?" she asked, pulling me back to the present.

I grabbed the paper towels and cleaned up the beer and glass from the floor. "No. Not yet. We need to wait for a decent stretch of weather." I glanced outside at the icy winter rain. "We can't fly in this,"

I waved towards the window as I stood and dumped the wet rag into the garbage. With a glance, whatever shards were left, levitated, and landed in the pail at my direction.

"I know, I'm just worried," she said, her quiet voice pulling my attention back to her.

"Well, at least we've gotten to the point I can put the barrier inside you," I said, giving her a shrug. The first few tries sent her flying across the room and into the wall when the power connected. I had to set it to a low-level stun to accomplish it, and pulling it out of her was easy, even to a ten-foot radius around her. We got that part down and it was kind of fun setting up a circle of blocks and water bottles to knock over. However, moving things was a far cry from toasting demons, and we both knew it.

"How's Tom doing?" she asked, giving me a blessed break from this insanity.

"He's still getting used to everything, but at least he can vaporize on demand." I started laughing and got a cross glare from Valerie. "Come on, you don't think this entire conversation is bizarre?"

She pressed her lips together against the smile. "I need to change, since we're done for the day," she said and left me laughing in the kitchen. However normal this was for me, it still had such a strange ring to it when I said everything out loud.

As soon as my laughter eased, I moved to the piano in the living room and started tinkering. It had been a while since I sat down and played and I closed my eyes, letting the notes flow. The tune was familiar now and came as easily as breathing.

When the last note faded, I opened my eyes. Valerie stood leaning on the door frame with that hungry look, and my eyebrows rose. She grinned and blushed, her gaze dropping to the ground and back to me in that coy manner that lit the fire in my core.

I stood and crossed until I was within arm's length of her and stopped, cocking my head. I licked my lips and delivered my famous grin. "You like what you hear?"

She rolled her eyes at me and turned to leave the room. My arm snaked out, encircling her waist and drawing her to me.

"You dare roll your eyes at me?" I whispered and bit her earlobe gently but firmly enough for her to gasp. She squirmed in my grasp, and I pushed her forward, holding her against the wall while my hands wandered.

"Chris!" Her voice carried both humor and now a hint of panic as my lips ran down the side of her neck.

"Yeah, baby," I whispered against her skin. My hands were split, one on her breasts and the other between her legs. Something about her tone almost made me dial back, but she had started this with that hungry tiger look. I was just taking her up on the silent thoughts running through her head while I sang.

"Stop," she whispered.

"Do you really want me to?" I continued to caress her and nibble on her neck.

She hesitated for a minute and then she pushed against the wall. The claustrophobia of being pinned finally winning out over my advances. Without her uttering the word yes, I stepped away with my hands in the air.

"Sorry," I said, but there was no sincerity in my apology, and she turned toward me with reddened cheeks.

"You know I can't..." Her fists clenched, and she stared at the floor, gaining control of the fear that had flashed over.

"I thought we got past this?" Anger now burned just below the surface.

She looked around at everything but me, and her head shook.

"What the fuck?"

Her gaze jumped to mine at the anger in my tone. "I... I don't know," she stumbled over the words. She attempted to wave toward the kitchen, and without words, her eyes expressed her confusion.

"Are you telling me our practicing fucked you back up?" My voice rose, carrying the incredulous tone of the shock skittering through me. "If I had known this would happen..." I stepped back, turning and crossing to the piano. I no longer wanted to screw around, and when I took a seat, my fingers flew over the keys, plucking the chorus of the Bon Jovi tune 'Blaze of Glory' and the words came out in such an angry growl that she backed out of the room in tears.

I slammed my hands on the keys and bellowed in frustration. My anger got the best of me, and I closed my eyes, grinding my teeth as I tried to count myself into a calmer zone. It wasn't until I got to thirty that the shakes gripping me loosened. I blinked my eyes open and forced my breathing into slow, long inhales and exhales until I had complete control.

When I finally stood, the remorse had settled in, and I went searching for her. I found her in our bedroom, face down on the bed.

I crossed and took a seat next to her, but I didn't reach for her or touch her in any manner. "I'm sorry," I whispered. This time I meant it.

She sniffled and turned her head towards me. Her bloodshot eyes met mine and I offered a hint of a shrug.

"I guess I got a little carried away."

She shook her head. "I'm sorry, too. I really thought between our wedding night and the honeymoon we had broken his hold on me."

I moved my hand to her and slowly scratched her back in silence.

"I want to tear him apart limb from limb," she said after a while.

"You're not alone," I said and met her gaze. "Just the fact I had to hurt you once, never mind over a dozen times today, upped the ante for me. I want to feel bones crush under my fist until he can't fucking move."

The venom flowing through my blood was just as potent as the powers lacing my muscles, and I inhaled, moving to leave her alone until she was ready.

Her hand caught mine and the spark lit in her eyes.

I shook my head. "I can't cope with being tied up today," I said, and her hand dropped.

"Why would you assume that?"

"You're going to tell me that wasn't crossing your mind?"

She opened her mouth and then popped it closed. Valerie shook her head and then buried it back in the pillow, looking away from me. I knew I probably should have let her. We had been home for almost a week and hadn't screwed around. We hadn't broken our home in.

I glanced around and grabbed her hand. "Come with me," I said, and pulled her through the house, out the door and onto the front stoop.

"What are you doing?" she asked.

I scooped her up in my arms. "I never carried you over the threshold."

She smiled. "You're such a sap."

"Yeah, but it's tradition for the groom to carry the bride over the threshold. It's a symbol of the start of a new life."

Her hand covered her mouth and her eyes welled up with tears. As soon as we were inside, she pulled my lips to hers. The kiss was soft and sweet. I carried her upstairs and closed the bedroom door with a sweep of my foot.

When I laid her on the bed, she kept her arms around my neck, pulling me on top of her. I pulled away from her lips and met her gaze. "You sure about this?" I asked, before I got too far down the road. I didn't want to be shot down when my libido was in overdrive.

"Yes," she whispered, and I went all in.

I took my time making love to Valerie. My slow progression drove her crazy, and she writhed under my hands, under my mouth, begging me like she hadn't in years. I wanted her to keep repeating my name in that breathless quality she had right before she came. I wanted her wet and ready for me. Hell, I wanted her crying to the gods.

I wanted this bliss to last because I had a feeling I would need all the sweet memories I could pile up before I faced the shit storm waiting for me in New York.

Chapter 18

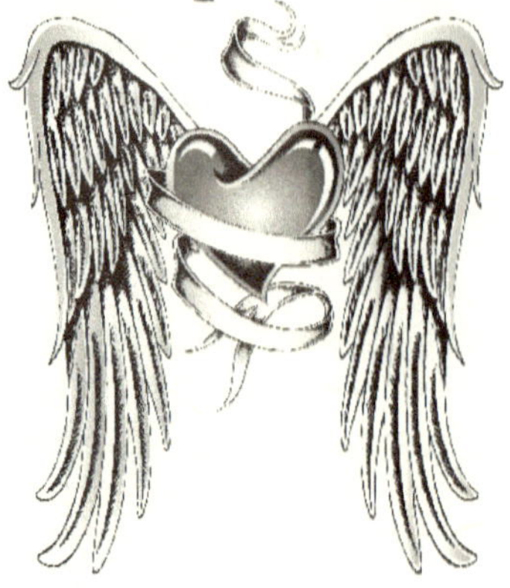

DAMIAN ANSWERED THE DOOR, and I sent a strained smile at him. Beyond him, the noise reached new levels. Grace came running by, laughing as her brothers chased her and Hannah around the first floor.

I let out a small laugh and turned to Valerie, giving her a quick kiss. "I'll call you when I get there," I said. "Enjoy the family," I added, and she chuckled at the chaos.

Tom stepped into view. "Did you want me to come down to New York with you?" he signed, but the words were clear in my head.

"Nah, I'll be okay." I appreciated the offer and gave him a nod of thanks. "How are you doing with everything?"

"He's doing great," Damian interjected. "I think he actually got it faster than I did."

Tom's cheeks transitioned to that rosy color of embarrassment, and he shrugged. "I'm adjusting," he signed, and his words echoed. "It's a pretty heady experience," he added.

"I know." I'd had a small period with nothing, and even though it coincided with Lucifer inhabiting my body, it still was weird not to wield the power of the angels, so I could only imagine what the other way around felt like.

"If you need anything..." He trailed off and looked over his shoulder at the house before focusing back on me. "Let me know."

"I will. Let me know if something happens here, okay?"

"I know how to yell for you," Tom said and tapped his temple.

That maneuver he had down to a science. He could reach me half-way around the world at this point, so I wasn't worried. With both Damian and Tom watching the brood, I was sure nothing would get to them, and if something slipped through, they always had Valerie. She was in good hands tonight. I just hoped like hell I didn't miscalculate the danger on the home front, and I prayed Steve and Jennifer wouldn't be the vulnerable ones. With a nod, I turned and climbed into my car, driving away without a glance back.

It had been a while since I had been in New York and the drive down wasn't bad for a Friday afternoon. I had expected to get to the apartment building with enough time to spare for dinner before we had to leave for Carnegie Hall, but I pulled in a little after three, a good hour and a half before I had planned.

I rolled the window down when the attendant strolled up to the car.

"I haven't seen this corvette in years," the attendant said, appraising it with envy.

"Jason, right?" I asked and my gaze dropped to his name tag.

He smiled and nodded. "You're Chris Ryan's son, right?"

"You remember my dad?" I asked, a little surprised. It had been close to twenty years since my father died, and this was the first time I had driven down on my own. Usually, I was crammed in the back of the truck with Tom and Raven.

"Sure do. He was one of the nicest residents here." Jason sighed as his gaze moved towards the ramp and his memories circled around one of his most horrifying experiences with my father.

"I guess," I mumbled, uncomfortable with the attendant's train of thought.

"He ended up paying for my college education," Jason said, and pulled his attention back to me.

His admission surprised me. I did not know my father did stuff like that. "Really?"

Jason smiled. "Yes. He took good care of a lot of people here," he said, nodding toward the building.

"I never knew that," I whispered, and sighed.

"Your father was a good man," he said. "I'm sorry he's gone," he added, and cleared his throat, adopting more of a professional manner. "Mr. Williams told me you were coming. Did you want me to park the car for you, or do you remember where the penthouse entrance is?"

"I remember," I said and reached for my wallet.

"Mr. Williams already took care of that, sir," he said, and I hesitated, glancing at the older gentleman.

"Can I ask you a personal question?" I asked and fished out my wallet anyway.

"Sure," he said.

"Didn't you get your masters in finance?"

He nodded.

"So, why are you moonlighting here?"

He offered a smile and a shrug. "Times are tough," he said.

I got a glimpse of the hardships he'd been handed and felt the first jab of guilt for having all the money I had when hard-working people like Jason got the raw end of the stick.

I pulled out a few bills and handed them to him. He stared at the cash and shook his head.

"I told you, Mr. Williams covered it."

"I know, but you told me some...thing I never knew about my dad. And frank...ly, it's something I needed to hear. So, this is my way of saying thank you." I stuttered through the awkward moment and pushed the cash into his hand before driving away.

Jennifer and Steve were lounging on the living room couch when I opened the door.

"Did you know my dad paid for Jason's college bills?" I asked when the door closed behind me.

Steve nodded. "He also put the doorman's kids through college."

"No shit?"

"Your dad had more money than he knew what to do with, and I guess those folks that showed genuine interest and kindness benefitted." He shrugged. "Why?"

"I just never knew about stuff like that." I took a seat on the chair facing the balcony. "So, you ready for tonight?" I asked Jennifer, changing the subject before it crawled under my skin.

"Absolutely." She beamed.

I tried to tap into that enthusiasm, but the information Jason gave me weighed heavy on my heart. I put on a fake smile and glanced outside.

Steve put down the paper and stared at me, pulling my attention from the skyline to him.

"What's eating you?"

My smile faded, and I shrugged, opting to keep quiet instead of bringing everyone else down with me. "Nothing," I said.

"Bullshit." He crossed his arms, waiting.

I closed my eyes and dropped my chin to my chest, allowing the turmoil inside to surface for the briefest of instances, and then I inhaled and met Steve's gaze. "My father." That's really all I had to say. Jennifer moved closer and covered my hand with hers.

"He loves you, CJ, and he made the sacrifice because he loves you. That was his choice, honey, not yours. Someday you'll understand."

"I know, but it still doesn't make me feel better."

Silence settled, and she gave my hand a small pat before standing and starting toward the kitchen. She paused at the door. "So, are you changing anything up tonight?" she asked.

"I hadn't really thought about it much," I said and she gave me a nod, disappearing into the kitchen and I glanced at Steve. "Been too busy trying to figure out how to embed my protective wall under Valerie's skin." The moment the words came out, I started laughing. I couldn't help it. We somehow walked into this god forsaken nightmare, and none of us could break the spell. I leaned forward and put my head in my hands. "In your worst nightmares, did you ever think we'd be chasing the devil?"

Steve burst out laughing, too. "Fuck no," he said, and I glanced up at him. "It's kind of a sick joke. Isn't it?"

"Yeah," I said, still huffing. Steve rarely swore around us, so hearing the expletive tickled the laughter out of me.

"Jesus, if I had only known..." Steve trailed off and his laughter faded.

My laughter faded as well. "No kidding, you would have run like hell the moment they introduced you to Eric," I said.

Steve's smile slowly disappeared, and he leaned forward. "The only thing I would have changed, in all this time, was bringing you to Georgia. That's my biggest regret where your family is concerned," he said. "Everything else just enriched our lives."

I looked around the penthouse and back at him.

His eyes narrowed. "That's not what I meant," he said, crossing his arms.

I smiled. "I know. I just wanted to get a rise out of you."

"Jennifer wanted to cook tonight," he said, glancing towards the kitchen.

"Really?" I didn't mean for the disappointment to bleed into my voice, but his smirk and raised eyebrows told me I failed.

"Yeah, really. But I have Chinese delivery scheduled to arrive about a half hour before we have to leave."

My lips spread into a grin, which I suppressed the moment Jennifer poked her head out the door.

"Can I get you something to drink?"

"You have a coke or something?" I asked, turning her way. I could use something a little harder, but I never drank before a performance. She nodded, and I focused on Steve after the door closed. "Does she know you ordered food?" I whispered.

He just smirked and picked up the paper.

"That would be a no," I mumbled, and he lifted his eyes for a second. Just enough to confirm my statement.

Jennifer stepped back in the living room with a tray of drinks and some chips.

"Thank you," I said when she handed me the coke, and I waited for her to take a seat before I asked,. "Did you want to change things up?"

"I kind of like having the last song with you. It gives me the opportunity to be onstage for the encore."

"Okay, then I won't change the order."

She smiled. "We never really had a chance to ask, how was the honeymoon?"

The darkness hanging over me lifted a fraction. "Did you know Ted has a new plane?"

Steve nodded. "Sweet, isn't it?"

"Holy cow, it's beyond sweet. It was nicer than our wedding suite," I said and the heat rose in my cheeks. "It was a great way to start the honeymoon." I grinned. "I bought a horse," I added.

"Really?" both of them said in unison.

"Yes. Koa. She's as bright as they get, and she's the one I rode to the portal."

"Where is she now?"

"Still in Hawaii. I figured it gives us a reason to get over there a couple of times a year."

"Ah, ulterior motives," Jennifer said and leaned back in the seat.

I chuckled. "Not really. It was more of a spur-of-the-moment thing. I didn't want them riding her into the ground, especially after the morning we'd had. I just had a contract drawn up that said the guides could ride her, but only one trip per day." I opened the soda and took a sip. "I need to look into buying some horses, though. Valerie grew up riding."

"Did you do anything else on the island or were you locked up in the bedroom the rest of the time?"

I laughed. Steve and Jennifer had no clue just what had gone on in our bedroom for the last few years, and I wasn't about to divulge that to them. "I had a lot of stuff already planned. I knew how much Valerie wanted to see the islands, so we did a helicopter tour and a couple of island-hopping day trips, as well as an all-day snorkel-sailing cruise. I also treated us to a couple of spa days, too."

"Wow," Jennifer said and sent a glare in Steve's direction. "We didn't do anything nearly as spectacular for our honeymoon."

"Weren't you still in a wheelchair?" I asked.

"Yeah, but a spa day would have been heaven. It certainly would have dulled the pain of physical therapy."

"By the time you were better, I was already undercover. I couldn't exactly take off on a honeymoon when my target didn't even know I was married." Steve reached for a chip and gave Jennifer that annoyed look we both were familiar with. "If you want a spa day, go for it," he said, and she rolled her eyes. "What?"

"I'd like a spa day with you."

"I don't want anyone touching me," he said, looking at her like she was just shy of a deck.

"Seriously, it's worth it," I piped in, and his eyebrows arched. "I wasn't too keen on the idea either, but after the experience in Hawaii, my entire viewpoint changed. I just need to find a decent place around us and go with Valerie at least once a month."

"You're kidding?"

I laughed and shook my head. "No, and if you go, get the deep tissue massage. You can always have them adjust to a lighter touch if you want, but you feel like a slab of putty when you leave and that lasts for a few days. Blew my mind completely."

He traded a glance with Jennifer, but his features still held his skepticism. "I think I'll pass," he mumbled. "On a different note, how is Tom doing?"

"He's doing pretty well," I said. "I'm not as much of a basket case as I thought I'd be, so that's a plus." I grabbed a handful of chips and sat back in the chair. "Is there anything on television?" I pointed to the dark screen. I wanted to keep the conversation as far from closing portals as I could, and I just wanted some down time to gather my wits.

Steve tossed me the remote. "Be my guest," he said. He knew a little of my ritual of unwinding before a show. I wasn't one of those who obsessed about my voice, or planned each step of what I was going to say, but I did do the order of songs in my head. It was my only prep, and since *The Story* was the last one that I did whenever Jennifer was available, I had an idea for the first song that varied from all of my other concerts.

I cruised through the channels, stopping on some mindless HGTV show, rolling my eyes at the false drama. "I'm opening with *New York State of Mind*," I said and glanced at Jennifer.

"That is a perfect way to open a show here," she grinned.

"I thought so, too."

"How many songs did they ask you to do?"

"Just three this time, but I'm the last one on the bill, so I'm not counting any encore in that number." I winked and smiled.

"So, *New York State of Mind*, *Hallelujah*, and *The Story*?"

"No. *New York State of Mind*, *I Don't Want to Miss a Thing* and then *The Story*. Our encore will be *Hallelujah*."

"You got permission to use the songs this time?" Steve asked.

"Yes." We had been slammed for not getting permission the last time. As soon as I knew my song choices, I had my agent get permission to sing them. I had permission for most of Billy Joel's songs as well as Bon Jovi, Aerosmith, and now we had the written permission for both *The Story* and *Hallelujah,* as well. "We tried to get Billy Joel to join me, but he's actually out of town this weekend."

"Have you ever thought about writing your own stuff?" Jennifer asked.

"No, not really. Singing covers for charity keeps me in the shadows, you know?"

Jennifer laughed at me. "CJ, you are kidding yourself."

"I don't see paparazzi chasing me down, do you?"

"No, but you have to admit, the more you perform, the more visible you become. They even did that segment on E about you."

I couldn't help but laugh. The fluff piece they did certainly would have gotten me the sympathy vote had I been running for office, but it just annoyed the shit out of me. They hadn't interviewed any of us, but they had enough surface facts and photos to chronicle the major horrors rained on my family. "You know how I feel about that," I said, sliding my gaze away from her, back to the television.

"They somehow got photos of your wedding."

I blinked at the revelation and bit the inside of my lip. "I got married in a public space. Anyone around the harbor could have easily snapped off pictures, or even up by the road."

"True, but they got on Entertainment Tonight."

"Maybe that's why some folks in Hawaii recognized me," I muttered and sighed. I wasn't interested in any more publicity.

"There was a time I'd kill for the kind of coverage the media is giving you," Jennifer said. Her tone was offhanded, but the underlying disappointment pulled my attention to her. She gave me a smile and glanced at the clock. "I need to start dinner." Without any other conversation, she left for the kitchen.

Steve chuckled the moment she was out of hearing range.

"The media attention bothers her?" I whispered, hooking my thumb toward the kitchen.

Steve's smirk confirmed my question. "She's been working all her life to get the kind of attention you got like that." He snapped his fingers. "And she found out earlier today that she didn't get that lead on Broadway she auditioned for, so she's a little sensitive."

"She really wanted that, didn't she?" Now, I felt like shit. Here I was, blowing off all the attention I was getting like it was a nuisance, when she would have loved every second of the spotlight. "Damn, I'm sorry," I added, meeting Steve's gaze.

He shrugged. "Don't sweat it. She'll get over it the minute she walks on stage with you."

Both of us got quiet and turned our attention to the whiny couple on television looking for the perfect home. I closed my eyes and leaned back in the chair, letting my mind drift to the music. Melodies filled my head and my fingers silently tapped the notes I'd be playing later that night.

Burning bread tickled my nose and I opened my eyes, bringing my gaze to Steve. "Are you really going to let her ruin the kitchen here?" I asked.

Steve chuckled. "I guess not," he said and headed into the kitchen to salvage whatever Jennifer was burning before the fire alarms started. I started flipping through the channels again. The news was on a majority of the broadcast channels and everything coming out was depressing. There was so much darkness in the world already, and with each news story, the hope in my heart fell a notch. I watched politicians lie, intolerance, prejudice, and the complete disregard for human life. I finally turned off the television, throwing the remote on the table in disgust.

I stepped out on the balcony, scanning the city below, my heart heavy with all the evil mankind exhibited. The door behind me opened and Steve stepped to my side.

"What are we fighting for?" I finally asked, meeting his gaze.

"You watched the news, didn't you?"

I nodded and leaned on the rail. "The devil's winning," I said, and sighed.

"That's not true. You know the news focuses on things that boost ratings. Horror and scandal glue people to the television. It's a sick fascination, but that doesn't mean everyone out there condones what is going on."

What he said made sense, but in my current state of mind, it was nice to be reminded why going up against the devil mattered. The fundraisers I did usually lifted my spirits and faith in people, and I hoped tonight would do the same.

"So, did you salvage dinner?" I asked, changing the subject.

"Eh." He shrugged. "The delivery might be the best choice," he whispered, and glanced over his shoulder.

"Gotcha," I said, and we headed inside.

Jennifer stood by the door with the take-out bag in her hand and her hand on her hip. "You did this?" She pointed at Steve.

"I figured edible food was probably necessary," he said, and shuffled his feet, looking at the floor before he gave her a sideways glance.

It was like watching a puppy that had destroyed a pair of your favorite shoes being scolded. Jennifer tried to look annoyed, but Steve's endearing mannerism made it difficult. And when he gave her that half smile, half smirk, and a muttered apology, I covered my smile and turned my back on the two of them. But I couldn't quite stifle my snort of a laugh.

"Really?"

I caught Jennifer's gaze in the window reflection and turned back.

"Was it necessary?" I asked, trying to quell my laugh, but I failed miserably. She pursed her lips, but the dimples in her cheeks deepened.

"Well, I guess I should be thankful you had a backup plan," she said, and lost the battle against her smile.

"I love you, honey," Steve said, and crossed, taking the bag from her.

"Yeah, yeah," she muttered and accepted a quick kiss before he nodded toward the kitchen.

"Dinner's on," he said, holding up the bag, and we followed him into the kitchen.

THE ELECTRICITY IN THE air backstage at Carnegie Hall buzzed in my ears as I waited for my introduction. The pre-performance jitters still gripped me, and I sent a nervous smile at Jennifer. She shined as she waited. If she had any last-minute nerves, I never saw them; it was like the spotlight energized her.

"Go get 'em, tiger," she said when they announced my name.

With a quick inhale, I stepped out on the stage, flashing my brightest smile and letting the applause do its magic. The elation of being on stage grabbed hold, and I crossed to the MC, shaking his hand before the microphone was handed to me.

"Hello, New York!" I said without a hint of a stutter, which made me grin even wider. "You ready for something special?" I asked, as they rolled my piano out and the crowd went nuts. "Before I start, I wanted to thank you all for digging deep to help fight cancer! Rock on!" I sat on the bench and took a deep breath. Closing my eyes, the music took hold.

After the first three notes, the crowd went fucking nuts, and I smiled, sliding my gaze toward the camera with the most playful look I could muster. By the time I got through the opening of *New York State of Mind*, the screaming audience nearly took the roof off.

When my voice was added to the mix, they got even louder. After the first portion, a saxophone joined the arrangement, and I glanced behind me and gave the musician a nod of thanks, letting him have the solo while I continued the soft tune on the keyboard. I started the next stanza, and I wasn't alone. I'm sure my face showed the extent of my surprise when Billy Joel walked out with a microphone and leaned on the other side of the piano.

"Ladies and gentleman, the one and only, Billy Joel," I announced, and we finished the song together, our voices blending in perfectly paired octaves.

The last note faded, and I could almost feel the light dancing in my eyes as I grinned. I stood, taking his hand in mine, and pulled him close enough to whisper. "Shocked the shit out of me."

He pat my back and grinned. "You didn't miss a beat."

"Thanks, man," I said, and pulled away, waving my hand as he took another bow before walking off. I caught Jennifer's grin behind the spotlights, and she pointed her finger at me. Her silent 'Gotcha' made me smile.

"I totally didn't expect that," I said to the audience. "You have no idea how much that made my night," I added and took a seat at the piano again. "I hope it gave you folks as much of a thrill as it gave me." My answer came in the loud clapping response.

"You think Steven Tyler is backstage, too?" I asked, and the noise increased as I started playing the next song on my playlist. Unfortunately, he wasn't in the house, but that didn't seem to matter to the audience. By the time I was done with *I Don't Want to Miss A Thing*, they were in that frenzied state.

"I do happen to have Jennifer Williams in the house for this next song," I said and waved toward her as she crossed the stage. Her dress glittered, and I glanced at the VIP section where Steve stood. His entire body reacted to seeing her in the sequined gown, and I couldn't help but smile. The man loved his wife, and it showed.

I really enjoyed singing with Jennifer. She has always been a quiet strength, the support beam that held the family together, and to share the spotlight with her just felt right. The last note filtered to the rafters, and we stood, taking a bow.

Together, we soaked up the applause, and I grinned at Jennifer. "Do you think we have time for one more?" I asked, and the noise level rose. I sent a raised an eyebrow toward the MC and he gave me a nod.

Instead of sitting down on the piano bench, I took the microphone in my hand and led Jennifer to the edge of the stage, where I took a seat. It was completely unscripted, and we were less than an arm's reach from the audience.

"So, what do you want to hear?" I asked the closest patron, and pointed the microphone in her direction. It was a given, since I was now known as the new face of *Hallelujah* and her voice echoed the same song the rest of the audience cried out. I traded a glance with Jennifer and gave her a shrug. "Do you mind singing along with me?"

"Not at all."

We'd never rehearsed this one together. Hell, I had never sung without instruments of some sort, but I wanted this to be memorable and personal, not me and the piano like usual. I glanced at the audience and took a breath.

The audience stilled when the first words rolled over them, and from my new vantage point on the stage, I could see their faces as they swayed and sang along with me. Jennifer waited until the second verse to join in. I had never seen rapture etched on so many faces before, and I finally understood the power of my voice.

Raven had once said I had the voice of the angels. I think she might have been right. Coupled with Jennifer, we rivaled the heavenly host, and when the last note drifted off, silence filled the auditorium as people's eyes blinked open and fell on me.

"Thank you," I said, and the first sets of hands to clap were Steve's. The rest followed, and we got a standing ovation.

I climbed to my feet and helped Jennifer up before we took a quick bow and headed off stage.

"That was..." Jennifer trailed off, sliding her awed gaze in my direction.

"Fucking awesome," I finished. It was the boost of confidence I needed to tackle the darkness of Lucifer's portal. Now, I just needed an excuse to slip away for a while.

"Mr. Ryan," one of the stagehands approached me. "Some of the other performers and crew are going down to P.J. Carneys for drinks. Do you want to join us?"

"Sounds great," I said and glanced at Jennifer.

"You're invited, too, Mrs. Williams," he said, and I silently wished for her to decline.

"Thank you, but I think my husband and I will head home, instead," she said and glanced at me with a wink.

I immediately got the gist. She wanted some alone time with Steve, and I couldn't blame her. Something about performing made me want to take advantage of Valerie when we got home, and I imagined she was the same with Steve. The rise of blush in her cheeks when he walked in the room confirmed my thoughts and I leaned in.

"I'll take my time," I said, and straightened up in time for Steve to give me a pat on the back.

"That was the best yet. You sure you don't want to record your own stuff?" he asked, and I laughed, rolling my eyes.

"That's all I need," I said, and Jennifer led him away, leaving me to follow the crowd down to the bar. I took a seat at the bar and the group congregated around me. I raised my hand for the bartender, and he stepped over as I pulled out my money clip. I peeled off fifteen hundred dollars and put it on the bar.

"Make sure this group gets anything they need." I said, as we took over the area around the bar. "If that runs out, then someone will have to start a tab, otherwise whatever's left is yours," I said, and the bartender blinked at the amount for a moment and then pocketed the money with a nod. I turned back to the group. "First round is on me," I said with a smile, and everyone started shouting their drink orders. I offered my seat to one of the girls and made my way to the door.

"Kind of chaotic, isn't it?"

I looked up into the dark eyes of Billy Joel and laughed. "Yeah, just a little."

"That was nice of you." He pointed his drink toward the crew.

"It was nothing," I said, and took another step towards the door.

"Bailing so soon?" he asked, and I stopped, meeting his gaze.

"I have something I need to do, and if things go well, I'll be back." I glanced at the people talking and laughing and clinking their glasses to another successful event. "If not, it was a pleasure singing with you." I extended my hand.

He shook it and smiled. "Pleasure was mine. You've got one hell of a voice."

"Thanks, Mr. Joel, I appreciate it."

Before anyone else could intervene, I slipped out of the bar into the chilly October evening. I found the nearest subway terminal and took the 7th Avenue Express to Brooklyn. I made my way down to the river by foot and found the area I was looking for. The euphoria of the show had long vanished, and I crossed to the string of deserted and crumbling warehouses. I walked to the last lot, expecting it to be clear, but I found the remnants of walls still standing with only one wall gone, like someone had taken a rusty hacksaw to the structure. Damian hadn't cleared the footprint at all. He only blew the roof off its rafters.

The stench of evil permeated the small road, and I gathered my wits, focusing my power. I nearly unleashed the cleansing angel fire when an echo of sobs reached my ears. The place wasn't empty, and my gaze bounced to the other buildings. Shadows moved in the abandoned shells, and I realized this was a place the homeless congregated.

"Shit," I whispered, less than thrilled that there would be witnesses to my destruction and I suddenly wished I was wearing my baseball cap and a less high-end coat. The city lights in the distance cast long shadows on the pavement, upping the creepy factor, and I wondered if this was a trick.

Regardless, I couldn't just level the place. I had to make sure innocents were clear. Which meant I had to get a closer look. This certainly wasn't what I had planned. My get in, destroy, and get out scenario like we did in Hawaii wasn't going to happen, and I made my feet move forward against every nerve begging for me to run.

My heart hammered in my chest, making my skin pulse as I stalked closer to the opening. The blubbering got louder as I approached, and I backed against the wall, listening to the plea of whoever was inside.

The rattle of chains caught my attention and pulled me forward until I stood in the opening, looking into the belly of the decayed warehouse. The sight before me nearly took me out at the knees, and I had to blink a few times before I understood just what I was seeing.

Chains, meant to destroy, pulled my father in multiple directions. Bloody welts covered his body, and the image of my mother in the death chair from that movie turned my stomach. Except, instead of Frank Aris slicing her skin, it was my image.

I knew this display was meant for me to see, and the words flowing from my doppelgänger's mouth crushed my father's spirit to nothing. I had never seen my father blubber or beg, and hearing the pain in his voice as Lucifer sliced another piece of my mother was unbearable.

I stepped farther into the warehouse, and Lucifer's insane smile knotted my stomach just as the knife sliced through the throat of my mother's image. My father's wail set my fury switch on high, pulling the angel fire from deep within me, but before it covered the perimeter of the portal, Lucifer's gaze met mine, and then the image of both him and my father were gone.

I roared in anger, letting the fire burn and the ground crumble around me. I hesitated, almost following the debris into hell just to stop my father's torment, but I knew if I did that, I might be stuck under Lucifer's thumb forever.

I jumped back onto solid ground just in time, and the slamming of Earth's plates filled the purified circle. I stumbled away, numbed by the images presented. Halfway down the alley, I leaned over and hurled. The acid burned me back to life, and I gagged and spit, wishing I hadn't come, and hadn't seen the diabolical way Lucifer stripped my father's sanity.

Lucifer was using my image.

My fucking image was doing the damage.

Chapter 19

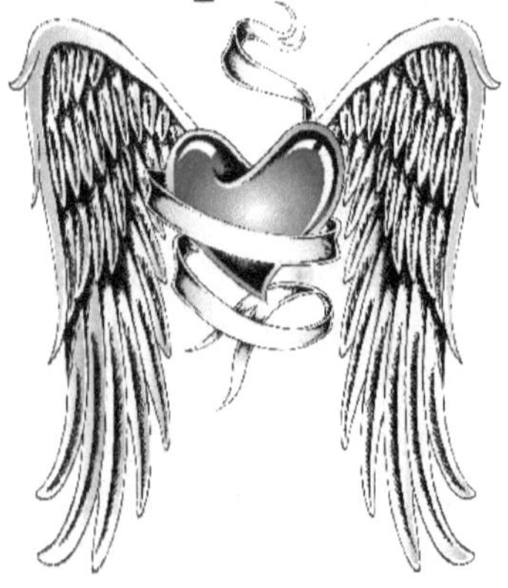

THE MINUTE I STEPPED into the quiet house, I headed for the bar by the sliders and pulled out whatever my hand landed on first. I unscrewed the cap and guzzled, hoping the alcohol would wipe away the images and the pain crushing my chest.

Even when my throat constricted against more, I forced the burning liquid down until the bottle was empty.

"Chris?"

I stiffened, but didn't turn around. I hadn't realized Valerie was in the house. I thought she was with Damian and Naomi tonight.

"Steve called when you didn't show up," she said, her voice closer. "Why didn't you pick up your phone?"

Instead of acknowledging her, I put the empty bottle of whiskey on the countertop and reached for another bottle. Grey Goose spilled into my mouth next, but this was harder to swallow past each hitching breath gripping me.

Valerie grabbed the bottle from my hand, pulling it away, saturating my shirt with vodka before she got the bottle upright. I still didn't turn and meet her gaze. I was too busy pressing my lips together against the turmoil in my stomach.

It only took a moment for the burn to explode and then I sprinted, making it to the kitchen sink as the entire lot poured out, splattering the stainless steel in a fiery storm of acid and alcohol. My knees gave, and I sank to the floor, pressing my forehead against the cabinets.

"Chris, what happened?" her soft voice caressed my ear. The arm she slung over my shoulders warmed the chill in my bones, but it didn't wipe out the images playing against my closed eyelids.

I had wandered around the city, stunned, until I finally hailed a cab to the apartment. I couldn't bring myself to go upstairs and face Steve and Jen, not with so much shit pelting me from all sides. Lucifer had promised blood and pain from this moment on. It was only a matter of time before he slaughtered everyone I cared about, and this little personal viewing was just the beginning of my hell on earth.

"I drove home." Even my voice sounded harsh and raw, and the effort to say those three words rattled my frame.

Valerie tried to pull me so I would look at her, and all I could do was shake my head. There was no chance of a verbal explanation, not with the anguish squeezing my chest. I knew on some level she would be pissed that I didn't have her with me when I closed the portal, but I knew she wouldn't be able to handle seeing the place that nearly tore her to pieces.

"Chris," she said a little more forcefully, and I ground my teeth together against the need to lash out.

"I can't. Not right now," I finally said.

The squeak of the front door followed by footsteps turned every muscle in my body into a tight coil.

"Damian, take her to your house please," Tom's voice echoed in my head, and his inarticulate speech filled my ears.

"I want to stay," Valerie said, and I turned, meeting her gaze.

"Go," I whispered.

"Chris?" she asked, and her lips pressed together.

"Not now, just... later." Talking was difficult, especially since my throat kept squeezing against turbulent acid eruptions in my stomach and the hurt in her eyes was like a knife to my heart. "Please," I forced out, and she stood, walking away. A part of me wanted to wrap my arms around her and never let go, but I couldn't right now. My need for drowning all thought still overrode everything else, and after the door closed, a chair scraped on the kitchen floor.

I looked over my shoulder at Tom.

He didn't speak, but he had a bottle and two shot glasses on the table.

I pushed to my feet and took the seat across from him, staring at the alcohol. Without a word, he poured two shots. I reached for one and he took the other, clicking my glass before downing the drink.

I followed suit and the burn nearly sent another plume of vomit out of my mouth, but I swallowed and closed my eyes, forcing the liquid to stay down.

"Are you going to show me, or what?" Tom asked, his voice soft in my head.

I opened my eyes and my vision blurred through a layer of tears. I just stared at him.

He cocked his head. "Or would you prefer to talk about your wife's bedroom fetishes?" This time he signed instead of speaking in my head and his lips pressed together against a smirk.

I didn't know whether to laugh or punch him, and my hands curled into fists. "Fuck you," I whispered, and reached for the bottle. It moved beyond my reach, and I shot my glare back at Tom.

"Seriously, talk to me," he said, and this time he meant it. He wasn't just poking the bear for fun. He knew that comment would slap me back into control and, damn him, it worked.

"He's using my image to destroy Dad," I said, as the anger overshadowed everything and I opened my mind, giving Tom exactly what he asked for. I watched as his face turned the color of waxed paper. He reached for the bottle, poured two shots with a shaking hand, and downed his before I even got mine to my mouth.

"We have to get him out of there," he said, and I couldn't agree more.

"I'm fucking ruined," I said, folded my arms and laid my head in the crook of my elbow. Hot tears burned my eyes; a few leaked onto my forearm before Tom's hand reached out and gave my arm a squeeze.

"Come on, man. You're stronger than that," he said.

I lifted my head. "No, I'm really not. Getting Valerie to the point she trusted me again was a hellish ride, and she was only under Lucifer's thumb for what, a day or two? Dad's been tortured for over two years. He's going to want to roast me alive on sight," I said. "And I wouldn't blame him one bit. You saw. You know the bullshit Lucifer is feeding him. Jesus, he's not going to believe either of us exists when Lucifer is done with him."

Tom was quiet for a minute, and he studied his still hands before looking up at me. "Doesn't matter." He shrugged. "We still gotta walk that line."

Chapter 20

I BRUSHED THE BITTER taste out of my mouth and stepped into the bedroom. My gaze snapped to the door, and Valerie standing with her arms crossed.

"Are you ready to talk?"

"Did you call Steve and let him know I'm home?" I asked.

"Yes. I didn't know what to tell him, so I said you weren't feeling well and decided to come home instead of stay in the city." She stepped inside the room and closed the door. "You want to tell me what happened?"

"No." I huffed and took a seat on the bed with my back to her. "The warehouse portal wasn't closed," I said after a moment of silence wedged between us. I glanced over my shoulder. "It is now."

Her arms slowly lowered and the sudden mistrust in her eyes stung just as bad as everything else I saw tonight.

"It was a colossal mind fuck," I said, and blinked the burn of tears away; however, I didn't open the memory to her like I had my brother. Some things are better left unsaid.

She crossed to me and cupped my face in her hands. "Why did you go without me?"

I kept her gaze without speaking. I didn't need to say the words. Not this time, and her chin dipped in a slow nod of understanding.

"What did he do?" she asked, and her mind swirled over her hellish time in that facility.

I let a sarcastic smile surface. "He didn't give me a look at what he did to you," I started, and her exhale clued me in as to the extent of her relief. "He showed me what he's doing to my father."

She blinked and bit her lip. She couldn't comprehend what I was shown that would lead me to the near psychotic state she found me in, and I sighed. Articulating what I saw wasn't easy, and I chose my words as carefully as I dared.

"He's using my image," I said, knowing the effect that would have on her, and I was right. She recoiled. When her hands pulled away from my skin, a chill was left behind and I shivered. "And he's replaying the final scene from Survival Games, except I'm the one killing my mom while he watches, just before the chains pull him apart." My fists clenched. "At this point, my father associates my image with death."

I met Valerie's horrified stare.

"So, you can understand just how fucking off the wall I was earlier."

"Oh, baby," she whispered, and tears formed in her eyes.

She wrapped her arms around me and my arms found their way around her waist. I pressed my forehead to her chest, clenching my teeth against the tears that threatened. I hated that I couldn't push the devastation away and replace it with the raw anger that shared the same space. Her hands threaded into my hair and she pushed me away from her chest, forcing me to meet her gaze.

When her lips crushed mine, I couldn't help it. I pulled her down on the bed with me and rolled so I was on top. I needed to feel a sense of control right now. I think Valerie understood exactly what I needed. She let me exercise some aggression with her, and our love-making session was fraught with ripping fabric and kisses that plundered as hard as my hip thrusts.

She met every move with her own growling satisfaction until we lay spent, side by side.

"This is the last time you'll go it alone, right?" she asked, turning her flushed features in my direction.

I rolled onto my side and pushed a few sweat laced strands of hair out of her face. "Yeah," I agreed. "But I have to have what we practiced down to a science."

She pressed her lips together. "Um, about that," she said and shifted, sucking her lip in between her teeth before she exhaled. "We have to be really careful where we put the knife." Her eyes jumped around my face before settling on mine.

"Okay," I drew out the word because my sixth sense tickled, telling me there was more.

"It just wouldn't be a good idea to cut my lower belly," she said and her hand slid down her stomach, stopping below her belly button.

I stared at the placement, and then my gaze bounced to hers. "You're shitting me," I gasped. Her lips twitched to a nervous smile, and I looked back at where her hand was. Without thought, my hand covered hers and I stared, speechless, as a

whirlwind of emotions slammed me from all sides—
wonder, hesitation, joy, but the most prevalent
emotion dried the saliva in my mouth.

Fear.

Fear of taking the next step.

Fear of whether or not I would be a good father.

Fear that Lucifer would kill my child.

Soul crushing fear.

"How far along are you?" I asked.

"Maybe a month at best, but I think this child
was conceived on our honeymoon." Her sigh filled
the space. "I'm as regular as clockwork and when I
missed my period last week, I knew something was
up." She shrugged. "I had Raven pick up a
pregnancy test, and it turned out positive."

"And you still let me..." I dragged my hand away.
Our last training session crossed my mind. I would
have never stuck her with a blade if I had known.

"I had you attack me from the side on purpose."

I pushed into a sitting position and pulled on
what was left of my underwear. A new irritation
scratched my skin, and I glared over my shoulder
at her. "I could have killed our kid," I snapped, and
she rolled out of bed, pulling on her nightgown
before she approached me.

"I wasn't sure," she started.

"Bullshit!"

"I had an idea, but I thought maybe the jet lag
screwed up my cycle."

I bit down on the budding anger and crossed my
legs Indian style, letting the information truly sink
in. She climbed back into the bed next to me,
adopting the same pose while her hand gently
scratched my back.

"You should have told me you suspected you
might be pregnant before we started practicing," I
said softly and slid my gaze to her.

"You should have told me you were closing a portal tonight."

I nodded. "I should have," I said, and stretched out again, running my hands down my face. "Would you have come?" I asked, as she shifted onto her side.

She didn't answer right away, chewing her bottom lip while she debated her answer. She finally sighed and shook her head. "I had afternoon patients, and even if they weren't scheduled, I wouldn't have gone near that warehouse," she said. "But I would have gone to the show," she added.

I rolled towards her and covered her hand. "I thought as much," I said. "That's why I didn't mention it. No sense in you being a basket case all day." Her lips thinned for a minute and she closed her eyes. When they opened again, the storm colors in her irises were slowly rolling.

"How was the show?"

I smiled, due more to the subtle change in subject rather than the actual question. "It went well. I sang *New York State of Mind* with Billy Joel."

Her eyebrows arched. "No shit?"

"Yeah, I'll have to call Jo tomorrow and see if she arranged that one or not. Either way, I was shocked as hell and a little humbled." I let out a small laugh. "It was pretty cool."

Her palm caressed my cheek. "Never take on Lucifer without telling me, okay?"

I didn't agree at first. Instead, I traced her bottom lip with my fingers before moving my gaze back to hers. "You know this changes things, right?"

Her features hardened and lightning flashed in her eyes. "It doesn't change a goddamned thing," she snapped and went to roll away.

I clamped her wrist, holding her in place. "You're not going with me to Canada."

She yanked her wrist out of my grip and rolled away from me, giving me her back. Her back moved with each huff of breath and I waited for the backlash. I didn't have to wait long. She rolled back with a glare.

"I'm going." She turned away again, as if giving me her back ended the argument.

"Not when you're carrying my child," I said, and she slowly turned towards me.

"It's my child, too."

"I'm not having this argument, Val. It's not just your life on the line."

"And I don't want to raise this child alone," she threw the words back at me. This time, she rolled away from me and punched her pillow before snuggling into it. "Stupid ass," she whispered under her breath. Aggravation came off her in waves that her mutter just punctuated.

The ball of tension in my chest expanded. "I will not do this." The growl was back in my voice. "I will not let that monster come between us," I said, through clenched teeth and the muscles in her shoulder tensed.

She sighed and rolled onto her back, staring at the ceiling before she finally looked at me. "Can we meet in the middle on this?"

My gut was saying no, but my head and heart just wanted us on the same page. "How?"

She chewed on her lip and looked back at the ceiling. "What if I just went to the area with you and waited outside the portal for you?"

"He'll have demons or other things around the portal. I don't want you in danger."

Her brow scrunched. "Well, if I'm not near the portal, don't you think he'd send his goons after me, anyway? Especially since you've already started the campaign to close the portals?"

The detailed descriptions of Lucifer's horrific promises drifted to the forefront of my mind, and I rolled onto my back. He promised to finish what Tom and Damian interrupted at the warehouse, whether I agreed to give him what he wanted or not. Valerie was at risk no matter what happened and while I trusted my brother with my life, I wasn't sure if I trusted him with Valerie's if Lucifer truly waged war.

Her vows echoed in my ears, and I closed my eyes, covering them with my arm.

"Chris?"

I lifted my arm and looked at her. "It might be better if you're somewhere that I can get to quickly," I said. "But only if I can work out the kinks. You know damned well even if you're hiding beyond the portal, they'll grab you so he can use you as a bargaining chip." The original idea had been hers, so she was aware of how that would play out.

"If I find I'm powerless on his turf, I will have Damian take you out of there. Understand?"

"But..."

"The entire mission will be aborted." I interrupted. "Because the guilt of knowing what's happening to my dad is nothing compared to what will happen if I lose you."

"And if he gets hold of you? What am I supposed to do then?"

"As soon as you're clear, I'll let the angel fire rip, like I did in Hawaii."

"And what are you planning on doing if you have your powers on his turf?"

I met her gaze and allowed the fury buried inside me to growl out the answer. "I'm going to beat him to a fucking pulp before I send him back to hell."

Chapter 21

VALERIE PLANTED HER TALISMAN into the center of the kitchen table. The anger radiated off her like I had never seen, combined with her pale cheeks and the dark circles under her eyes. I knew she was just as exhausted as I was. The only difference between us was that her hormones were playing hell with her, just as much as continuously having to put the healing power into practice.

It was almost Thanksgiving, and we were no closer to getting this down.

I crossed to her, towering over her with the same ferocity coming off her tense form. Instead of doing this the same way we had countless times, I yanked her into my arms and kissed her. With our bodies touching and our tongues dancing in frenetic circles, I willed the barrier under the surface of her skin far enough for me not to feel the repelling power against my hands firmly planted on her back.

Both our chests heaved as I stepped away and I stretched my hand out for the knife. I didn't take my gaze from hers; instead, I willed the blade into my palm and then grit my teeth as I slice into her side. Her flesh gave, and she cried out in pain. This was always the part that crushed a piece of my soul every time we did this. The pain in her eyes gouged through me as much as the knife sliced through her. I kept going by sheer force of will and a little farther in; I hit the barrier. It was like hitting a live electrical current and my hand jerked away; the knife went tumbling from my grip and I was thrown across the room.

I landed on my ass a few feet away and my gaze dropped to the cut. It was deep enough to draw blood, but not deep enough to do any actual damage.

Valerie inspected the wound, wincing, but then her gaze moved from the gash to mine, and I yanked the power outwards. The furniture within a few feet of her went sliding, banging into the wall, and the recliner toppled over.

I blinked and so did she. Her jaw tightened, and the cut healed, leaving another smear of blood on her skin. She was getting faster at patching herself up. All the practice we were doing was honing her skills as much as mine. She cracked a tired smile.

"Well, shit. If I had known kissing was the fucking key, practice for the last couple of months would have been a hell of a lot more fun," I said from my vantage point on the floor.

She started giggling, to the point her hands covered her mouth, leaving bloody fingerprints on her cheeks. She was a mess, and when I stood, I got a good look at myself, as well. We both looked like rejects from a horror movie, and I started laughing too. I could have easily passed for a scientist gone mad.

I met her giggling gaze and crossed the distance on shaky legs. Running my fingers over the tacky blood covering her side, I sighed and met her gaze.

"We must be completely insane," I whispered and took her face in my hands, planting another kiss before she could answer. "I'm ready for a shower and a nap," I said.

"One more time just to make sure that wasn't a fluke," she said.

"After we get some rest. You look like you're going to drop."

She started giggling again and instead of waiting for her to stop; I scooped her up in my arms and crossed to the stars. I tapped into my inner reserves and climbed to our bedroom and the bathroom beyond. Without putting her down, I willed the shower on and stepped inside with both of us fully clothed. Only then did I set her on her feet.

Tenderly, I peeled off her clothing and tossed it over the top rail before cleaning the blood away. Once her skin was clean, I dropped to my knees and kissed the spot I'd sliced over and over, until I thought I'd scream. Knowing it was a necessary evil didn't alleviate the nightmares I'd had since we started this madness. In them, I slip, and the blade kills our child. I have woken screaming more times than I can count, and so has Valerie.

My lips moved from that area over to the front of her stomach. We hadn't told anyone the results of the test; not with all this other shit going on, and I kissed the almost imperceptible bump, looking up at Valerie.

She ran her hands through my hair and I stood, peeling my clothing off. She ran the soap over my body as we stared at each other.

"What if this doesn't work?" I asked, and the progression of soap on my skin stopped.

"Then you might as well burn both of us up in the angel fire."

Her words silenced me, and I held her face, touching her lips with mine. "We already know we'd die for each other," I whispered against her. "But can you promise me something?" I pulled away.

She put the soap back in the holder and her hands found my chest. "What?"

"That no matter what happens, you will live? Not for me, but for our child?"

She blinked and pressed her lips together. Her tears mixed with the mist from the water, and she gave me a nod.

"Thank you," I said and turned the water off.

I barely remember pulling the covers over us.

Chapter 22

A SLIVER OF LIGHT stabbed my eyes and I rolled away, pulling my arm out from under Valerie. I hugged my pillow, turned my head toward the wall, and drifted off again. My leg jerked from that annoying half-dream misstep, and I opened my eyes, glancing at the clock.

The numbers blinked nine and my brain was still somewhere in sleep land. My lids drifted closed before the fog had the chance to clear. When I blinked my eyes back open, another twenty minutes had sailed by and the bright patterns on the wall caught my attention. My eyes widened and darted back to the clock.

Shit!

"Val, you're late for work." I rolled towards her. I shook her shoulder. "Val!"

She mirrored my initial reaction to the sunshine and rolled into her pillow, whining her discontent.

"It's after nine. In the morning." I shook her again.

Her eyes cracked open, meeting mine, and then they dropped beyond me to the clock. A few quick blinks and then her gaze came back to mine, widening. "Shit! We slept close to twenty hours?"

I nodded, and the covers sailed off her.

"Shit, I'm so late!" She nearly bounced off the bed.

Her mad dash through her bureau drawers would have produced a laugh had I been fully awake, but I was still in that foggy 'holy shit, we slept that long' phase. Valerie was in the bathroom before my feet reached the floor and by the time I entered, she was already dressed and whipping a brush through her hair, collecting it into a ponytail before she wound it into a messy bun.

I stepped to the sink and brushed the cotton from my mouth. Before I finished, Val was already heading back into the bedroom.

"When's your next day off?" I asked, and she glanced at me, the crease between her eyes conveying her disdain at my ill-timed question. Her eyes jumped from mine to my bare chest and back before her brain caught up with the question. "Friday. And I have the weekend off, as well," she said and started for the hallway. "Why?"

"We'll close the portal in Canada on Friday."

My words stopped her dead in the doorway, and she glanced back at me. "We have to make sure last night wasn't a fluke before you set that in stone." Worry lines appeared around her eyes when I shook my head.

"I'm closing it Friday. If it was a fluke—we'll have to figure out a new plan of attack."

She gave me a tight nod and headed out of the room. I pulled on my sweats and followed her down the stairs. When she sat on the bench near the garage door, I crossed to the kitchen, swiping her pocketbook off the counter. I made a stop at the refrigerator and grabbed a juice for her. When I handed both items to her, she sighed and nodded toward the kitchen.

"Do you mind grabbing my vitamins?" she asked and started digging in her purse for the keys.

I retraced my steps and collected the prenatal vitamins for her, along with a granola bar. If she didn't eat when she took these things, her stomach would give her trouble. She dumped them in her pocketbook, offering me a grateful smile as she climbed to her feet.

"Thank you, sweetheart," she said, and stood on her tiptoes for a kiss. It certainly wasn't our normal lingering good morning kiss, but it was still sweet.

"Call if you need anything," I said as she shot out the garage door. I stepped into the opening, crossing my arms over my bare chest to ward off the November chill. When she drove out the gate, I pressed the button to close the garage and stepped back into the warm house.

My stomach protested its empty state and sent a rumbling growl through my abdomen. "Yeah, yeah," I mumbled, but instead of heading to the kitchen to feed the beast, I went upstairs to straighten the bedroom and get dressed.

With a clean pair of jeans and a sweater on, and my hair in some semblance of order, I headed down to the kitchen in search of food. As I passed the phone, it rang, intercepting my trek for sustenance. I considered letting it roll to voicemail, but Tom's name blinked on the display, and I picked up the receiver.

"Good morning, Ryan residence," I said out of habit.

"You're finally awake?" Tom's automated voice asked.

I glanced at the call counter, but this was the first call of the day.

"Yeah, why?"

"We need to talk. Can you come up?"

I paused and the absence of noise in the background prickled my senses. I almost always could hear Hannah in the background whenever I talked to Tom. It was like she was programmed to pitch a fit whenever her parents were on the phone. "Sure, is Raven there with you?"

"No. She's on her way to Damian's. Hannah and Grace have a play date today."

"Let me grab something to eat and I'll head up after."

"I'll cook you something here."

Even though I was listening to an automated voice based on Tom's typed response, I got the feeling there was some emotion behind the request. His offer to cook me breakfast threw me.

"Are you okay?"

"Yes. We'll talk when you get here."

"Okay. I'm on my way now."

I hung up the receiver and slid on my sneakers before grabbing my coat and keys for the short drive. The sunlight dance on the water, giving the illusion of a warm fall day, but I knew better. Winter was only a stone's throw away, and the air this morning had the old man's bite to it.

Tom opened the door the minute I pulled into the driveway, and his haggard appearance sent a shockwave through me. He looked worse than both Valerie and I had yesterday. I stepped out of the car and crossed the distance. Tom just stepped aside, opening the door all the way to let me pass.

"What the hell happened to you?" I asked, as he passed me and took a seat on the couch.

His head dropped into his hands, and he let out an audible sigh. "I had the unpleasant experience of being two places at once last night." His bastardized words were overlayed in my head by his perfect enunciation, and he looked up at me. "Twice," he added, and a chill skittered up my spine.

"Who?" I said and my voice cracked.

"Steve and Jen were attacked last night. He was able to hold them off, but you were... un-fucking-reachable, so he called me."

His glare said more than I wanted to hear, and I slowly lowered onto the couch across from him, dreading whatever he was going to say next. "Are they..." I trailed off when he shook his head.

"They're fine. I vaporized those motherfuckers."

His gaze still held anger, and I didn't understand why, but the relief in knowing they were okay drew an exhale, releasing the tension in my body a fraction.

"If I had been any longer, I would have been a widower," he said. "Or a fucking soul without a body. Either way, that little jump left me open to attack. Raven was able to hold them off, but it scared the living shit out of her."

"I'll bet," I said, raking my hand through my hair.

"Right before I turned them into dust, they told me they already got to you." His mind didn't echo the bastardized words, but his momentary expression of crushed hope and his slow signing hands got the message through. "I panicked and bam..." He snapped his fingers. "...I was standing in your fucking bedroom while both you and Valerie snored up a storm."

My eyebrows rose.

"You didn't hear a thing. Did you even notice the new salt lines blocking your bedroom door and the windowsills?"

I shook my head.

"You have never slept that soundly. What the hell?"

I blinked and shrugged. "Valerie and I were... practicing, and I guess that wiped us out." To the tune of twenty hours, I thought, still stunned by that basic fact.

"Practicing? What the fuck were you practicing?"

I opened my mouth to explain, but sometimes it's better to just show. My mind opened, and Tom's eyes slowly widened in horror. Slash, bleed, heal, rinse, repeat. The insanity that we'd engaged in over the past month rolled in his head, and Tom's disgust carved a grimace in his face.

"Yesterday was the worst. It was fucking grueling, and I was mentally shot by the time we figured it out." Silence fell between us, and Tom rubbed his face. "I don't remember ever being that tired, and Val must have been ten times worse than I was."

His jaw tightened. "If I didn't have a piece of your mojo, we would all be dead," Tom said and stood, heading into the kitchen. I followed. "I thought you were," he muttered and started slamming pans around.

"You want me to cook?" I asked, and guilt gnawed at my stomach along with my hunger pangs.

"No, I got it."

He cooked in silence, his aggravation building, and I couldn't blame him. I hadn't heard Steve's call and I wouldn't have heard my brother's either. I pulled my shoulders back, cracking my spine and shook off the shiver that wanted to take hold.

Tom set an omelet before me and took the seat on the opposite side of the table. I wolfed down my meal in a matter of seconds, and my stomach growled its contentment.

"That was good," I said, and Tom met my gaze.

"I don't think I want it anymore," his thought echoed in my head.

"If you're not going to have it, I'll eat the rest," I said, eyeing his half-eaten omelet.

His eyes narrowed and his lips thinned. "I was talking about the power." He shoved his plate in my direction.

I took the offering and scarfed it down while I formulated a response. Last night was exactly the reason I gave him a touch of my power. I didn't want him vulnerable in the war I was waging.

"You don't have a choice," I said, after I swallowed the last bite. I cleared the plates and tucked them into Tom's dishwasher before I continued. "You're stuck with it until the powers that be decide to transfer it to someone else."

"Can't you take it back?"

I suppose I could have if I wanted to, but that would leave him and his family at Lucifer's mercy.

"No," I said, and his teeth clenched, making the muscles in his jaws tighten. He knew damned well I was lying.

His fists clenched, and he closed the distance, throwing a punch. Instead of parrying, I stopped his hand less than an inch from my face, without the use of my hands. His face scrunched with the fury filling him, and he pushed with more than just his fist, trying to breach my hold.

"You really don't want to tango with me like this, Tom," I said softly, and attempted to convey a silent warning with my eyes. "I get why you're angry. I fucked up, but you were there to save the day, so chill," I added. "That's exactly why I chose you."

He stopped trying to force my hand, and his fist loosened just before his arm dropped to his side. Tom stepped back, putting distance between us. Aggravation carved his features into a tight muscled relief map. "Why now?" his voice barreled into my head, making me wince. "You had twenty-six years to share. Why the fuck did you choose to do it now?"

This wasn't about my sleeping like the dead last night. I looked closer, taking a step toward him. "What the hell is eating you?"

His glare nearly sent me back a step, and he ripped a note card out of his shirt pocket. "This was on my door this morning." He flung the paper at me.

I caught it out of the air, but I didn't need to read the fine script signature to know who it was from. The same looping cursive on the inside of his note was written on the wedding card Lucifer sent to us and the words on this one were just as harsh as on mine.

"I'm on his acquisition list," Tom spat out.

"Well, that's better than being gutted," I said, thinking about Lucifer's threats outlined in my note. Lucifer outlined a pretty sweet deal for Tom. In the event I refused the devil, Lucifer offered to spare Tom's family if he said yes. If Tom stood with me, he outlined in detail his plans for Raven and Hannah.

"Did you see what he wrote about Hannah?" Tom waved at the note and I nodded.

"These... plans, for lack of a better word... are identical to what he wrote in our card." I held up the note before tossing it on the table.

"What the fuck am I supposed to do?" Tom asked, running his hands through his hair. The dark circles under his eyes seemed to grow by the second. The lack of sleep, along with the physical backlash of exercising the power, was draining his strength.

"I'm closing the portal in Canada on Friday," I snarled, feeling the first hint of anger, and his gaze snapped to mine. "And if you say yes to him…" I couldn't contemplate that option. If Tom said yes, then I'd have to destroy him. I wasn't sure that was something I was capable of following through with.

"Don't worry. I'm not thinking about saying yes," Tom said, but the sarcasm in his voice laced my anger even more. "Besides, the bastard is a lying shit. He'll still kill Raven and Hannah, even if I say yes."

We stared at each other as silence filtered through the anger, diffusing it, and I finally looked at the ground. "I doubt it," I said, and brought my gaze back to his. "If you said yes, he might be inclined to keep his word, especially if you give him a super powered vessel."

Tom blinked at me and then turned, storming into the living room, his fury too big to be contained in the small kitchen without striking out at me.

I didn't follow him right away. I let him siphon through the memories of Lucifer. The one thing I found when I examined the memories of our ancestor was that while Lucifer was vile, controlling, devious, and downright cruel, technically, he never lied.

Neither had I, but I played his own game of deception, deceiving him into thinking he was getting something he wasn't.

That's why he took it out on Valerie. If I had given him the vessel he coveted, my family, Valerie included, would have been spared. However, the rest of the world would have burned.

I sighed and entered Tom's living room, meeting his gaze.

"So, my soul for my family?" he asked, and I nodded.

"Your soul for a temporary stay of execution," I clarified. "I'd still have to destroy Lucifer, regardless of whether you were still hanging in there with him or not. So, the promises he made me would still be in play, creating the loophole in your deal."

Tom covered his eyes. "Basically, I'm screwed either way," he said and dropped his hand. "Unless you take this shit back."

I laughed. I didn't mean to. It just came out at the idiotic conclusion. "You're even more screwed without that power." I slid into the seat next to him and patted him on the back. "Welcome to my world."

"Fuck you," he replied, sliding his gaze to mine, but it had less of a bite of anger than before. "You just didn't want to deal with this alone anymore."

He had a point, and I shrugged. "Damian's been living it for twenty-five hundred years."

"What a pisser," he said and for the first time today, he actually cracked a smile.

"No shit," I sighed. "I'm sorry, man. But I couldn't leave you vulnerable. Not after the threats he left me."

"What about Steve?"

I glanced out the window, swallowing the lump that had formed in my throat. I loved the man almost as much as my father and the thought of him dying, whether by Lucifer's hand or not, left an empty spot in my heart. I turned back to Tom.

"He's not my blood," I finally said, admitting the truth to myself as much as to Tom. "I'm not sure how much I can spare before I become…" I paused, searching for the right word. "…in…e…ffective on Lucifer's turf." The stutter interrupted the flow of words, and I pressed my lips together for a moment before continuing. "I made a choice," I said softly. "One I pray doesn't backfire."

Chapter 23

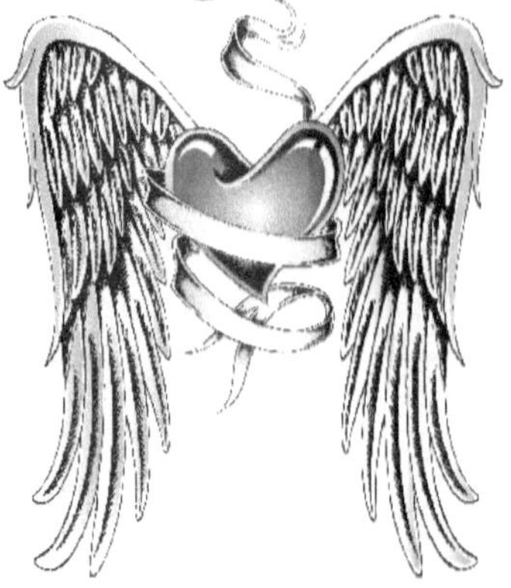

I HUNG OUT AT Tom's while he took a much-needed nap, and I headed home in time to finish dinner before Valerie arrived. When Valerie came in from work, I put a salad on the table and met her gaze.

"Hey," she said and hung her coat before taking a seat on the bench by the garage door, stripping off her shoes.

"Hi," I said, doing my best to send a smile in her direction, despite the conversation I'd had with Tom today.

She paused with the shoe still in her hand. "Are you okay?"

"They struck last night," I said, and her eyebrows arched.

"Where?"

"New York."

The shoe tumbled from her fingers and her hand covered her mouth as the same shock I first experienced.

"Tom took care of it," I said, and she closed her eyes, leaning against the wall. Relief swept over her features. When she opened her eyes, she still had a layer of tears making her stormy eyes shine.

"We need to stop this madness," she said, and walked to the table.

"We do." I reached out and pulled the bobby pins from her hair. I liked it down, and today I really needed to understand why we were fighting such a losing battle. I knew deep down Tom wouldn't take the deal, but I had to give Lucifer props. He pulled all the right strings.

"We have to make sure last night wasn't a fluke," she said, and I closed the distance between us.

"Later," I whispered, and leaned down, planting a kiss on her lips. I stripped the hair tie and dropped the bundle on the table along with the bobby pins. The kiss deepened when I ran my hands into her hair. Every movement of her tongue with mine sent tingles through my form, and I willed the barrier into her without her knowledge. As I ran my hands down her back, I tested the depth until the tingle in my fingertips dulled to nothing more than the heat from her skin.

When I pulled away, I met her gaze.

"I needed that." I said and stepped away, waving to the dinner table and locking my mind. If I'd miscalculated, she'd be able to heal quickly enough, but I had a feeling I'd end up in the backyard from the charge I set. It still wasn't the max load, but enough to do damage to a normal person.

I pulled out the chair for her and lifted the plate warmer. The waft of aroma from the steak smelled wonderful, and even though I was hungry, my stomach knotted with the tension now filling me. I had positioned her so her back was facing the sliders, and I reached for the steak knife and whispered in her ear.

"I love you, babe," I said and stuck the blade in her side. The blast lifted me off my feet and I snapped a protective bubble around me, at least one strong enough so my neck wouldn't snap on impact. As I flew through the air, I closed my eyes and yanked outwards and then I hit the pavers along with enough debris to make my heart slam in my chest.

A buzzing sound filled my world, and I stared up at the star filled night, blinking until she stepped into my view.

"Chris, what the fuck was that?" she snapped, holding the bloody knife in her hand.

"A test," I whispered, coughing at the pain in my back. I glanced at the knife and closed my eyes with satisfaction. An inch. The bloodline on the blade only covered an inch.

"You fucking demolished the kitchen." She pointed toward the house. Her anger was warranted, but I had to make sure I could do it before I made the call to Steve to set things up for Friday.

"Are you okay?" I asked from my vantage point.

"I'm fine," she said, and looked at the steak knife a little closer.

Silence fell with only the sound of buzzing electricity, and I propped up on my elbows, scanning the damage.

"Holy shit," I whispered. "Well, let's see if I can at least fix the wall," I said. Closing my eyes, I willed the house back to its original state. The creak of glass and metal and wood filled the backyard and the power flare in my chest grew until I didn't think I could contain it anymore.

When my eyes opened, the solid face of the back of the house was intact, and Valerie was on her knees next to me with her mouth hanging open in awe. My head dropped to the pavers as exhaustion played havoc with my muscles.

"Shit," I whispered, and before I could say anything else, her lips were on mine. I groaned, wincing at the pain filtering through me like an electrical fire. "Damn," I finally hissed, and the colors swirled in her eyes as she grinned at me.

"I don't know if I put it all back together," I said as the healing tingle faded. "And I'm not sure the steak survived."

She let out a nearly hysterical laugh as I slowly sat up next to her. "Don't ever do that to me again," she said and swatted my chest with the back of her hand.

"The next time I do that, it will annihilate a horde of demons." My gaze shifted from the house to the pathway leading to Naomi and Damian's house.

Damian stood staring at us with wide, wild eyes. "I heard an explosion."

"Yeah. I got it covered," I said and climbed to my feet, helping Valerie up, as well. We were both a little unsteady, and I wrapped my arm around her waist, guiding her toward the house.

"What happened?" he asked, as we got closer.

"I tried to cook," I said, unwilling to share our practice sessions with Damian like I had with Tom. If Damian knew, I'd get a beating from here to hell and back.

"Bullshit," he snapped, and both of us turned to him.

"We're heading to Canada on Friday."

His features tightened.

"So, we had to make sure everything we have planned would work."

His eyes traveled between us.

"I'm okay. He's okay. It's fine," Valerie said, but his gaze had already dropped to the knife in her hand.

"You can't be doing this type of shit right now, CJ," he said. "Not with the stuff that went down last night."

"Okay. We'll stop blowing things up," I said. Damian gave me a nod, and we entered the house, stopping as the slider closed behind us.

Valerie scanned the demolished kitchen table and dusty surroundings. The wall, counter, and sink were all pieced together again by my sheer will, but the table was in ruins, along with our dinner. I'd have to run out and pick up something, but I needed to make a phone call first.

"You're one fucking amazing man," she said, and I cleared off a chair for her.

"We can go out to eat tonight," I said, scanning the destruction. "After I call Steve." The wall phone wasn't an option anymore, so I pulled my cell out of my pocket and dialed the familiar number.

"Hi, Steve," I said, with my back to Valerie. "It's time to call in that favor."

"Are you okay?" he asked, ignoring my statement.

"I'm fine. I was exhausted yesterday. I'm sorry I didn't..." I trailed off, running my hand through my hair. Shards of glass made tinkling sounds as they hit the floor around me, and I stared at the dust that littered my hand. "Are you and Jennifer okay?"

"We're fine. A little shaken that they so easily got into the building, but we're fine now that we're in New Hampshire."

"I'm glad you're okay," I said. I really would never forgive myself if anything happened to either of them, but I took a gamble with Tom that I believed would pay off. I sat on the couch. The leg gave way and the side I was on dropped a foot. Valerie let out a giggle.

"About that favor?" I said again, pressing my lips together against the smirk when Valerie and I traded a glance.

"When?"

"Friday."

Silence filled the line.

"This Friday?" he asked

"Yes."

More silence, and I glanced at Valerie with a shrug.

"You realize what day that is, right?"

I blinked and tried to figure out the significance of the date and when I didn't answer him within a few beats, he filled me in.

"It's black Friday. The day after Thanksgiving."

My head whipped to Valerie, and I mouthed 'Oh Shit!' before glancing at the nearly unusable kitchen. Both of us had completely forgotten about the holiday. We hadn't gotten a goddamned thing to prepare for the feast we were supposed to host in a couple of days.

"What?" she whispered.

"Thanksgiving," I said, and her eyes did the same frantic bounce as mine.

"You are still hosting, right?" Steve asked on the other end.

"Um, about that..."

"We could have it here at the lake if that's easier."

Valerie nodded.

"That probably makes more sense. Valerie has to work that morning, but we could be there by two," I said. "Just as long as you don't let Jennifer cook."

The hearty laugh came over the line. "You forgot, didn't you?"

"Yes. Totally." I gave Valerie a shrug, and she nodded her silent thank you for deferring the holiday dinner somewhere else. "Do you think we'll be able to get a chopper out on Friday morning, with the holiday weekend?"

"I'll check when we are off this call. And CJ?"

"Yeah?"

"The next time I call you, you better wake the fuck up," he said.

"Yes, sir." I hung my head in shame.

"I'll let you know what I find out, and look forward to seeing everyone on Thursday."

"Thanks."

"I love you, kiddo," he said.

"Love you, too," I replied, and hung up the phone, meeting Valerie's gaze.

"I forgot this week was Thanksgiving," she said.

"You're not alone." I stared at the mess I made. "I'm officially an idiot," I added, and she started chuckling. "Come on, let's go clean up and I'll take you to dinner."

As we climbed the stairs, I couldn't help but be thankful. If I was going up against the devil, a family gathering the day before sounded like the perfect thing to remind both Tom and me what we were fighting for.

Chapter 24

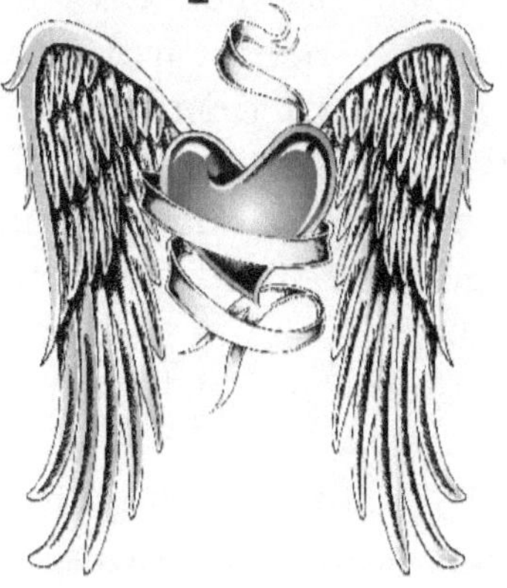

I SWIRLED MY WINE, staring at the way it clung to the glass. My mind was a thousand miles away from the cheerful banter of my family. Instead, my thoughts focused on the things I might encounter in the confines of Lucifer's portal.

I played every conceivable scenario I could think of, borrowing from past experiences where Lucifer aimed to rattle his foe. I kept jumping to the first time he faced off with my father, and how he capitalized on bringing my uncle into the mix.

What would I do if my father was the one being torn to pieces by a hellhound?

Valerie elbowed me, and I glanced at her, raising an eyebrow. She leaned towards me. "Let it go for a little while," she said, in a scolding tone that pulled me out of my reverie.

I blinked, remembering where I was. "Sorry," I said, and refocused on the conversation.

Tom's gaze pulled to mine, and we both sighed. Since I had supercharged him, every time we were together in a crowd, it was like the connection we'd had when we were younger was back online. The connection that had been broken the minute the psycho in Georgia grabbed him.

We spoke without words or thoughts in this case. We had an underlying communication that hummed between us. An understanding. A kinship I was thankful for.

I raised my glass to him, and he followed in kind.

"Thank you," I said aloud, pulling everyone's attention to me and silencing conversations. I shifted under the sudden quiet and cleared my throat, praying my stutter wouldn't tie my tongue. "I wanted to say thank you for a superb dinner." I raised my glass in Steve's direction. "Especially for not letting Jennifer into the kitchen," I added and everyone but Jennifer chuckled. "Sorry, but you and I both know, had he let you in there, this feast would have ended up a charcoal fest."

Jennifer pressed her lips against the smile.

"Thank you for the best singing partner I could ever ask for."

"You're welcome," she said. "Thank you..."

"I'm not done saying my peace," I said, interrupting her. "And I want to say what I need to before I have any more wine," I clarified. I had already downed three bottles myself. "And before my stutter slices up my speech."

Everyone gave a slow nod, exchanging wary glances.

"Thanks for giving us a loving home, a great meal and the sense to know what path to take when given choices." I turned my attention to Damian and Naomi. "I know you feel responsible for all the shi..." I closed my eyes for a second and restarted with a PG version, cognizant of the kids at the table. "Stuff that has happened to all of us, but I wouldn't have met Valerie if you hadn't shown up in York. Despite our rocky start, you two ended up becoming pretty decent friends, even if it's only a ruse, so you can be close enough to protect Valerie." I sent them a wink and moved my gaze to Tom and Raven.

There really were no words to describe how thankful I was Tom was alive. He'd cheated death a few times, and I'm not sure I'd be who I am if he wasn't around. "You have no idea how thankful I am that you're my brother..." I pressed my lips against the sudden swell of emotion and his eyebrows rose.

"Someone take the wine away from him before he gets all sappy and shit," he signed, and Raven smacked him.

"And that he met you," I said to Raven.

"Oh, no. We're too late," she chided, and her dimples made an appearance. "Maybe the wine does have to go," she said. Her Irish lilt made it sound so much more formal than she's ever been and the group laughed at my expense.

I slid my gaze to Valerie, and with a smirk, she reached for my wineglass.

"I love you, but you cannot have my wine." I lifted the glass so she couldn't reach it.

"Tom's right, you're getting sappy," she laughed.

"Yeah, well, I'm facing Lucifer tomorrow and we all know what happened the last couple of times I decided to battle the devil."

Her smile faded, and she sat back in the seat. Silence settled like a wet blanket.

"I'm just saying my peace," I said, scanning the now melancholy crowd. "I love every one of you," I shrugged, and toasted from my little soap box. I downed the rest of the glass and reached for the bottle.

Steve looked at Valerie. "He's cut off."

His statement made me pause with my hand half-way to the bottle. The silence hung on the air until Tom snorted laughter.

"You're toasted, aren't you?" he signed, and the words echoed in my head.

A smile played on my lips, and I reached the rest of the distance, grabbing the bottle and emptying the contents into my glass. "Maybe a little," I allowed.

"Don't get shitfaced," Steve said, despite the young ones gathered around the table. "Save that for tomorrow night, okay?" This request was serious, and I hesitated with the glass in hand.

With a nod, I set the glass on the table and slid it back, trading the alcohol for a glass of water.

"Thank you," he said.

"I may be a little, um, off, but I meant what I said."

"We know, and we love you, too," Jennifer said. "Now, who wants dessert?"

"Who made it?" I asked when no one's hand shot up. She sent a glare in my direction and hooked her thumb in Steve's direction.

"He did."

Everyone's hand shot up.

"You all suck," she said, standing and grabbing the dishes.

Steve stood, and I shook my head. "You cooked," I said, and stood, collecting my empty plate along with Valerie's. Tom and Damian followed suit, leaving the women and kids at the table with Steve while we cleared.

I stepped into the kitchen and Jennifer had three pies sitting on the island.

"You know I'm just yanking your chain, right?" I said, as I passed her and started rinsing the dishes.

"Yes," she said and waited until Tom and Damian had left to get the rest of the dishes. "Want to know a secret," she said, and I met her gaze. "I probably wouldn't eat it if I had baked it," she admitted with a smile.

"Want to know one of my secrets?" I chuckled.

Jennifer nodded, glancing towards the other room before bringing her gaze back to mine.

"Sam wouldn't eat your cooking, either," I whispered.

"Get out. Sam ate everything that fell on the floor."

I laughed as Tom stepped into the room and placed another pile of dishes next to me. "Anything you didn't cook, he scarfed up. But your cooking? Sam just pushed that around with his nose until he found a suitable hiding place. You had to know it wasn't either of us who hid food in the couch," I said, glancing at her. She had started that giggling that would overflow to hysterics any moment, and I traded a glance with Tom. "I even remember one time when I tried to pass something to Sam under the table when you and Steve weren't looking. He covered his nose with his paw and whined. It was the damnedest thing I've ever seen."

She went into the land of the guffaw until tears leaked from her eyes. "You're kidding?"

"No, I'm not," I said, grinning while I finished loading the dishwasher. I glanced behind me at Tom. "Right?"

He nodded. "You always blamed one of us for the hidden food," he signed. "But it was the dog."

"No way," she gasped, through the laughter.

"Yes, way," I laughed. "Your culinary skills are pretty damned sad."

"And you get way too honest when you've had too much to drink." She grinned at me as her laughter wound down.

"Yeah, he becomes one of those bad beer commercials when he drinks too much," Damian said, placing another pile of dishes on the side of the sink.

"Come on, I'm not that bad," I said, tucking the last plate in the washer and closing it. I grabbed a dishcloth and wiped my hands. "Someone else can get the pots. I want pie."

We each grabbed one of the professional-looking apple, pumpkin, and chocolate cream pies and carried them into the dining room. Jennifer followed with the dessert dishes and silverware.

By the time we were done, there were only scraps left and, collectively, we leaned back in the chairs. I glanced at my watch. "The Dallas game is probably still on," I said and chairs scrapped as we all got up, clearing the table on our way to the large family room overlooking the lake. I took a spot on the window seat, leaving the couches for the rest of the family. Valerie sat between my legs, and I split my attention between the sunset painting the sky and Dallas schooling the Eagles.

At seven, both Damian and Naomi, and Tom and Raven took their kids upstairs to the guest rooms to get them settled down. My hands caressed Valerie's stomach, and she glanced back at me with a ghost of a smile.

That was one thing I was thankful for that I kept to myself. Tom knew, and I suspected Raven did, as well, but we hadn't announced it to anyone yet, and Valerie asked me to wait until after tomorrow before sharing our news.

Jennifer crossed to us and took a seat at the window.

"When are you due?" she asked, her voice just a whisper under the sounds of the television.

We both just stared at her. I bit my lower lip and scrunched my eyebrows, pretending not to know what she was talking about.

"Due?" Valerie asked, pushing off the inevitable.

"You didn't have any wine with dinner and you're a little pale," she said. "Either you're coming down with something, or you're pregnant."

"I'm not feeling very well," Valerie said, and that probably was the truth. The morning sickness didn't seem to be confined to mornings.

Jennifer's brow drew together, and her gaze moved from Valerie's to mine, searching. I just shrugged and a bite of guilt bloomed inside me. I hated lying, but neither of us was ready to share.

Damian came down a few minutes later. "What's the plan for tomorrow?" he asked, taking a seat on the couch.

"I couldn't get a helicopter," Steve said. "But Ted is sending one of his smaller, faster planes. You need to be at the airstrip in Wolfeboro at seven in the morning, and make sure you have your passports." He looked at the three of us. "He's taking you to a smaller airport northwest of Quebec and I told Ted that if you aren't back by ten tomorrow night, to leave without you." He paused and took a sip of a beer he had cracked open after the kids went upstairs.

"I rented a truck with a couple of snowmobiles and it will be waiting at the airport."

"How far do we have to drive?"

Steve crossed to a desk in the corner and picked up a piece of paper. "It looks like the drive is a couple of hours to a public park. The snowmobile trails nearest the spot Damian marked look like another hour from where you're parked. And from there, it's about a mile. I'm not sure if you'll be able to get through with the snowmobiles, so I also have a couple of pairs of snowshoes waiting for you as well."

"What time are we landing?" I asked when he handed me the paper.

"Nine. So, you have thirteen hours to get in, close the portal and get back, otherwise you're driving home. If you don't fuck around, it should only take you six hours at the most."

Damian and I nodded, and then his gaze pierced Valerie. "Are you sure you want to come with us?" he asked, but his tone carried a warning.

"Yes," she said, stiffening in my arms, preparing for a battle of words, but Damian just blew out a stream of air and gave her a curt nod.

Tom came downstairs and glanced at us gathered by the window.

"Go over the plan again," he signed, and I met his gaze as the words echoed in my head.

"The plan for you is to stay put and protect this house until I tell you it's okay."

He nodded.

"Not Damian. Just me. When I either show up or..." I trailed off as Valerie stiffened in my arms. "Or you see my ghost," I finished, and his gaze moved beyond me to the lake, but he gave me the nod I was looking for.

"Chris," Valerie started.

"We know it's a possibility," I said. "And if things go south and I'm without power on his turf, you'd better get her the hell out of there," I said to Damian.

"And if I already have your father?" Damian asked, and it was a good question.

My arms tightened around Valerie and I met Tom's gaze. "You have to let him go and get Valerie out of there." I put my forehead to the back of Valerie's head. "And if things don't go as planned, Val, you have to run. Understand?"

She didn't move or speak, and I caught her reflection in the window. Instead of arguing with her in front of the family, I lifted my gaze to Damian.

Can you hear me? I sent the thought out wrapped in a bubble and he nodded, but neither Tom nor Valerie gave any indication of hearing my targeted thought.

"I'll keep my mind open. You'll know if there is any problem, okay?"

"If your mind is open, won't Lucifer be able to glimpse your thoughts, too?"

"I'm pretty sure I can target it." I glanced at Tom. "I'm going to try something and I need you and Valerie to tell me if you can get whatever I'm transmitting to Damian. Damian, make sure you block your thoughts." I concentrated on putting a barrier around my thought while leaving an open channel to Damian. "You ready?"

Everyone nodded.

I stared out the window. *Do not react beyond a nod, but Valerie is pregnant.* I glanced at his wider than normal eyes and got a small nod. *She doesn't want to make the announcement until after... you know... so keep it under wraps. Okay?*

I got another nod. If Valerie had heard the message, she would have sent her elbow into my stomach along with shooting me a nasty glare.

I think we can safely say this channeling thing works.

"But can you do it while keeping the barrier inside Valerie intact and juggling whatever Lucifer is throwing at you?" Damian asked.

I shrugged. "We'll see."

"I heard nothing," Valerie said, and her gaze bounced between Damian and me.

"Neither did I," Tom signed.

"Good." I shifted Valerie so I could stand, and I disappeared into the kitchen, finding a soda in the refrigerator. What I really wanted was a beer, but Steve had a point earlier. If I got drunk and ended up with a hangover, I'd be in trouble tomorrow.

"You okay, babe?"

"What if he shows me the same shit he did in New York?" I asked, turning to Valerie and voicing one of the many things eating away the lining of my stomach.

"Then you'll deal with it. If he's chained, you'll have to break them for Damian to carry him out, though."

I hadn't thought about the condition or placement of my father, and I met Valerie's gaze. The tiny details beyond just having Damian grab him needed to be fleshed out, and I wondered if I'd get any sleep tonight.

"I think we should probably call it a night."

Valerie's gaze shot to the clock beyond me and her brow creased. "It's still early," she said, returning her stormy eyes to mine.

"I know," I muttered and walked past her. Not only did I need to think these things through, I wanted some alone time with my wife.

She grabbed my arm as I went to pass. "What are you doing?"

I sighed and glanced at the family now gathered around the television, watching the evening game. When I brought my gaze back to her, I smiled and gave her a lingering kiss. "Hoping for the best, but preparing for the worst."

Chapter 25

FIVE-THIRTY ROLLED AROUND MUCH too fast, and I banged the alarm with my palm, shutting off the annoying buzz. Yawning, I stretched; amazed I got any shut eye at all. I shook Valerie, and she lifted her head, meeting my gaze and letting off a soft groan of discontent.

"I know." I kissed her forehead. "But you can choose to stay in bed."

"No. I can't." She rolled off the side, heading into the guest bathroom ahead of me. I closed the door behind her while she rummaged through our overnight bag.

When she pulled out an antacid, I raised a brow. "Are you sure?"

For a moment, doubt passed her features, but after popping a Tums, she met my gaze and nodded. "I didn't think I'd ever get to sleep," she said, reaching for the toothbrush next to mine on the counter.

"Neither did I."

She let out a light laugh. "You were snoring before I got settled back in bed," she said after she spit.

"I don't think so."

"Ya-huh," she said. "I thought having to keep quiet wore me out, but apparently it sucked the energy right out of you instead."

I smiled. Making love to her last night was far from the wild romp we usually got into at home. It was subdued and slow, and I loved every second of seeing her struggle with keeping quiet. It was the perfect ending to the perfect night, and just what I needed to fortify my inner strength.

"I hope you packed the long johns," I said, and she pulled them out of the bag like a magician.

We dressed in layers. Light thermal underwear underneath jeans with a fleece lining. I opted for my work boots instead of the bulky snow boots. I could stuff foot warmers in if I needed to, but the steel toe gave me a little more protection in case it came down to another fist fight. My leather jacket fit snugly over the sweater, and this time, I remembered my ski hat and a scarf. It wasn't frigid, but it was below freezing, according to the weather maps, and I didn't want to be frozen solid by the time we got there.

Valerie had the same idea of layers, but instead of a leather bomber jacket like mine, she wore her down coat that almost reached to her knees. The last thing she pulled out of our bag was the knife from Hawaii. I stared at it and then traded a glance with her. She gave me a nervous smile and strapped the sheath to her belt. It couldn't hurt having something like that, and maybe it could destroy an angel. We would certainly find out.

I tapped lightly on Damian's door, letting him know we were ready to go.

Downstairs, I grabbed a juice out of the refrigerator and tossed it to Valerie just as Damian climbed down the stairs. He was equally bundled up as we were.

"Passports?" he asked, holding up his.

"Yes. In my wallet." I tapped my jacket to make sure I had my wallet and phone in place. "Good to go?" I asked, glancing at the two of them. The creak on the stairs pulled my attention.

Tom rubbed his eye with one hand. "Be careful," he said. I wasn't the only one who heard the words perfectly in my head.

I crossed. "You, too," I said and gave him a quick hug. With no more words, I turned and stepped outside with Valerie and Damian, heading towards our car. The morning was bright, but the pending stand-off weighed heavily on me as I drove the short distance to the airstrip in Wolfeboro.

Ted was already standing at the counter as we walked in. I gave him a strained smile and shook his hand.

"I didn't think you were going to be our pilot today," I said.

He gave me a shrug, but didn't say anything until we were safely tucked in the plane. "I got the distinct impression this wasn't a joy ride," he said, meeting my gaze.

I didn't want to drag Ted into this. He was not, in any way, equipped to deal with monsters, but he had a right to know. "No. It's not. And if none of us are back by ten tonight, it's wheels up for you, okay?"

His lips pressed tight, and his gaze traveled over the three of us.

"You aren't doing anything illegal, are you?"

The three of us let out a laugh. "No. We aren't," I said. "All you need to know is we're going after the bad guy and when I pour a line of salt across the entry before I leave, know I'm not insane, and as crazy as it sounds, that line will protect you from what we're hunting."

His rapid blink put me on edge and then he turned, closing the hatchway.

"Steve once dragged me on one of his vigilante quests, and I always had a grain of regret about asking so many questions, especially when he gave me answers," he looked between all of us again. "And I know I'm going to regret this, too, but what the hell are you hunting?"

Damian reached into his pocket and pulled out another blood stone necklace. "Raven asked me to bring this for the pilot," he said and held it out towards Ted.

I took it from his hand and crossed to Ted. "You really don't want to know," I said and handed him the necklace. "But this will also offer you some protection."

He stared at the necklace and then met my gaze. "Are you packing?"

I shook my head. "A gun wouldn't do any good."

He swallowed and took the necklace, slipping it over his head. "Then why isn't Steve here with you?" he asked. He had seen enough of the things Steve was capable of over the years, but I wasn't sure he knew about me.

"I'm better suited for this trip than he is," I said, and Ted's gaze narrowed.

"You sure about that, son?"

I smiled. "Yes." *I'm the one who supercharged Steve.* I sent the thought into Ted's mind and his eyebrows rose. "Well, technically, it was my father, but I was the one who originally gave him the juice," I said aloud.

Ted uttered a laugh. "Steve never let on about you," he said and gave my shoulder a soft pat.

"Can you blame him?"

"No, can't say that I can. And I've gladly kept his secret all these years. Yours is safe with me, as well," he added before turning and marching into the cockpit.

The fact he didn't press for more answers was a relief, because if I had to burst Ted's bubble with what really existed out there in the world, it would have put a target on his back.

I bit the inside of my cheek as the realization set in. Ted was already a target, at least as much of a target as Sandy had been. His longstanding friendship with Steve made him vulnerable, and I wondered just how thin I could spread myself today.

I took a seat next to Valerie, and she covered my hand.

"You can't protect the plane."

Damian's statement pulled my gaze to his. "Why not?"

"Because you're right, that would spread you too thin," he said, throwing my train of thought back at me. "You need everything you have, and you're already splitting it, so don't even think about safeguarding the plane while we're gone."

I glared at him, but he was right. I needed everything I had. Instead of dwelling on what was coming, I pulled up the table between the four seats and opened the compartment near the window, pulling out a deck of cards.

"Five-card stud?" I asked, and both Valerie and Damian's eyebrows rose. "It will pass the time," I added as I shuffled the deck.

"What are we playing for?" Damian asked, leaning forward.

I bit my lip and glanced at Valerie. "Babysitting hours," I said, and Damian grinned.

"You're on," he said.

Valerie leaned forward, her gaze jumping between us. "You told him?"

I nodded, dealing the first five cards. "Can you grab the pen and pad in there and keep track? I have a feeling this might be a very valuable game." I winked at her, knowing she was irritated with me, but something else danced in her eyes.

I think this is the first time I have looked beyond today, and it filled both of us with hope.

By the time we landed, the damage was done; whatever hope we had in the future included owing Damian forty-five hours of babysitting. He just grinned while I muttered under my breath, sliding the cards into the box and stowing them away.

My luck was equally tested when we arrived at the car rental place to find the truck we rented. It was old enough to make me doubt it would make the trip, and the single snowmobile in the back added to the frustration. At least the thing was long enough for the three of us, so that was a plus.

Damian pulled me aside once we got the snowmobile down from the truck bed. "You need to get into the right frame of mind before we get there," he said, and I crossed my arms. "I know you're irritated with how the cards fell on the plane, the condition of the truck, and even the single snowmobile, but you ever think that maybe your luck was reserved for a reason?"

I blinked and my arms dropped, the shock stilling me for a moment, and then I let out a little laugh. "God, I hope to hell you're right," I said. "I was thinking we should just turn around and do this another day."

Damian let out a chuckle. "I hear you, but that's three things that haven't gone as planned." He pulled up his coat sleeve, showing me his watch. "But if you hadn't noticed, we're ahead of schedule," he said.

I hadn't noticed, and I offered him a nod of thanks.

Valerie stood by the snowmobile waiting for us, and I caught a quick kiss before we piled on the contraption. I took comfort in the thought that Valerie would benefit from our warmth as we squished together on the seat. I took a moment to pull out my phone and turned the snowmobile toward the blinking dot. I tucked the phone away and took off in a straight line toward whatever waited for us in the deep Canadian woods.

The snowmobile may have been big, but it certainly hauled ass.

Chapter 26

THE THREE OF US stood outside the perimeter of Hell's portal. Evil spilled over like a nasty oil slick sliding over the water, destroying everything in its path. You could almost smell the foulness.

I glanced at Damian. "When my dad appears, you know what to do," I said, ignoring the plumes of white our breath created in the frigid Canadian air.

Damian gave me a nod. "Get him the hell out of dodge."

My lips curved at the cliché. I'm sure my dimple made a brief appearance, too. "Yeah, but wait until I give you the signal."

"Got it. Be careful. I will not be here to bail you out this time."

"I will. I think I'll be good, and if not, we'll have to table the rescue mission." I glanced at Valerie. "If my powers are blocked, you'd better run like the place is on fire. Understand?"

She hesitated and traded a glance with Damian before bringing her gaze to mine. I pulled her close.

"We talked about this," I said, and she nodded, but the set of her jaw and the tight line of her lips told me she wasn't leaving no matter what. "If this goes to shit, promise me you'll get out of here," I said, unwilling to move forward with the plan without her concession. My hand drifted lower to her belly and the reason for my hesitation. We had more to lose than just our lives.

Her gaze dropped to my hand. I knew she didn't want to raise our child alone, but she also knew if Lucifer got hold of her, I wouldn't be able to say no. Not with my child's life in the mix. When her gaze came back to mine, she nodded.

"Okay. I promise," she said.

"I love you," I whispered, and planted a kiss, taking a moment to let our tongues intertwine. The heavy winter attire made the transfer a little more difficult, so I dropped my gloves and unzipped her coat, wrapping my arms around her waist until the tingle dulled in my fingertips. I pulled away from her lips and pressed my forehead on hers, closing my eyes and willing the full force of my power into the barrier I layered inside her.

Damian cleared his throat, and I glanced at him, slipping my hands out from under Valerie's coat, and zipping it up before I stepped away. I gathered my wits and focused my energies on the pending battle. "Stay out of sight," I said to Damian, just before he transformed and took flight. The human-to-hawk thing still startled me, and I watched his graceful ascent until he ducked out of view, hoping like hell Lucifer didn't catch sight of him.

"You, too," I said to Valerie, and she slid farther back into the woods, using the big pines like shields.

Nerves bit at my stomach, and I closed my eyes, steadying my breathing and centering my power. I didn't know how much Lucifer knew, now that he had my father under his domain. All I could do was hope Heaven's secrets were still under wraps.

"Game on," I whispered, adopting my dad's favorite battle line and moved forward, breeching the portal boundaries. Brimstone hung on the air, and I rubbed my nose, suppressing the tickle that wanted to turn into a sneeze. I still had one hundred yards of dodging trees and thick shrubs before I got to the epicenter. The place where Lucifer would be waiting for me.

I found it odd that no demons approached, and tension filled my muscles, turning me into a coil waiting for the surprise attack. I had the benefit of Uriel's grace, in addition to my self-defense skills I hadn't had with my last encounter with Lucifer, and I was confident that the little extra juice I received in heaven would push the advantage to my side of the chessboard this time around.

I cleared the woods line, stepping into the confines of the small glen, and stopped.

The form leaning against the rock at the opposite side of the clearing set my heart banging on my ribcage. I swear my shirt vibrated in time with the beat.

The familiar face smiled, but it wasn't the warm smile I would have expected from my father. Instead, it held the promise of pain.

I took a tentative step forward, unsure of myself.

"You like the new digs?" He spread his arms out, and I recoiled.

Lucifer's curve ball hit with the level of devastation he probably expected. My chest ached like I had been sucker punched, and I steadied myself, focusing on the power swirling in my abdomen.

"Where's my father?" I asked, when I was sure my voice wouldn't shake. Everything about this was wrong.

Lucifer snapped his fingers and the meanest, ugliest hellhound I had ever seen appeared by his side. The beast snarled, pulling at the restraints holding him in place. He wasn't the only rabid dog in the vicinity, either. Shapes dotted the woods line, blocking my exit from the clearing. There must have been one hundred hellhounds all gunning for their chance to tear my flesh from the bone.

It wasn't until I took a closer look at the dog next to Lucifer that understanding overtook me. The hellhound's vibrant blue eyes followed me, and despite the violence reflected in his irises, I would have recognized those eyes anywhere.

"You turned my dad into a hellhound?" I asked. Both anger and anxiety filled my voice, and I met Lucifer's gaze.

His lips spread into an evil grin.

"And you figured I wouldn't have the heart to kill the likeness of my father?" I added, taking a step forward.

"I like this look." Lucifer waved at the fine physique. His smug smile set my fury level to almost unbearable. "And whatever was left of your father when I was through with him has turned into the most viscous hound I've ever had."

Lucifer unclasped the chain holding the hound in place and, like an obedient dog, he stayed next to Lucifer's side, waiting for the command to attack. I dropped my gaze to the ground, praying the abort information was relayed, because if Damian swooped in and grabbed the image of my father, he'd be carrying the devil out of danger.

I took a deep breath, exhaled, looked back at the bastard, and straightened my back in defiance. "You played this kind of sick mind game with Val, and it fucked her up. But I'm a different beast all together." I said, and my fists clenched as I imagined a protective shield surrounding me. "I don't give a shit what form you take. I am going to end you."

His smile faltered just before he gave the attack command. My gaze dropped to the blue eyes of the lead hound as he bounded toward me. His snarl carried on the air like a rifle report, and all I could do was prepare for the impact.

When the hound launched, my muscles clenched.

The beat of wings sent a whirlwind around us, and the yelp of a dog punctuated it. Before my brain could process any sort of response to Damian snatching the hellhound out of the air, he cleared the trees, heading south, and disappearing from sight with the hound still in his talons. I had time to blink before the rest of the hellhounds attacked.

None of them reached me, and the stench of burned fur mingled with brimstone. If Damian hadn't snatched my father from the air, he would have had the same fate as the rest of Lucifer's canine army.

I smiled, relieved that I had my mojo on the devil's turf. If not, I was certain I'd be near death right now. His smug grin faded and his eyes narrowed.

"You little shit," he said.

"Me?" I pointed to my chest. "You're the one who turned your kin into a fucking dog."

He chuckled. "I ripped my brother's head off. What'd you expect? That I'd treat Uriel's blood line any differently?"

"I didn't expect that, but I would think you might feel a little differently about your own bloodline." I dropped the bomb and from the rapid blink and loose jaw, he had no fucking clue. I crossed my arms and squared my feet. "And you know what that makes me, right?"

His jaw tightened. "With your little slut, that gives you the possibility of siring a dark trinity." His eyes danced at the prospect, and I leveled a smile.

"My mother has two angel bloodlines, as well," I said, springing these additional facts on him with a bit of glee.

His smile disappeared. "You're a... trinity?"

"Ayup," I said and tilted my head. "Funny that you never picked up on that. But I guess it was masked by the double dose of your blood."

He actually stepped backwards.

"That, along with a little infusion of angel grace, and I'm your worst fucking nightmare," I said, dropping my hands to my side where they balled into fists. "This time, I'm ready to tango, gramps." I allowed the sarcastic overtone to bleed through.

He seemed to recover much quicker than I imagined, and he squared off, crossing his arms as a little smile spread on his lips.

The bushes to my right rattled and in stepped a group of demons, all holding weapons from guns to knives, and in the center of the group stood Valerie with her arms bound behind her back.

She met my gaze and lifted one of her shoulders. The minute she had stepped in the confines of the portal, her powers were useless. I guess the trinity piece was the important one and not the angel grace. My heart pounded as I made a small calculation, wondering if what we practiced would work.

"You won't be able to save her," Lucifer said, reading my intentions, and I moved my glare to him.

What he didn't know is I had already done it before I left her in the woods. I knew an ambush was possible, and so did she. She even accurately guessed the pricks would puncture her skin just to make a point. I just hoped they didn't go too deeply because then the element of surprise would be ruined, and I prayed she still had the knife.

When she gave me a slight nod, I exhaled. She still had the knife, and that gave us more of an edge. We both wanted to reduce Lucifer to a trembling mass of flesh before I closed off this portal.

"You really are an asshole," I said, and mentally yanked outwards. The power crackled in the air, annihilating everything in its path. Guns, knives, demons. They all fell to the sharp blast before the creatures used their weapons.

"My, my, aren't you just full of surprises today," Lucifer said, and despite the jovial tone, the hesitation in his eyes gave me some level of satisfaction.

"Looks like your bag of tricks is nearly empty," I said, trying not to gloat at the small win. I needed to remember not to get cocky. Even with the advantages I had, I knew he was just as dangerous.

Valerie went to move, and an invisible hand clamped around her throat. She clawed at her neck, her panicked gaze locking with mine.

"I never got to finish what I started in the warehouse," he said, and the slow, salacious smile appeared. The buttons on her jeans undid and a pitiful whine escaped her lips.

"No fucking way," I growled and sent a mental shove.

Lucifer stumbled back, landing on his ass. The initial shock that I had enough power to derail him on his own turf gave me the window I needed to get Valerie behind me and away from his direct control.

She stumbled in my direction as her breath wheezed. I didn't move, but I made damned sure she was insulated behind me before I cocked my head at Lucifer.

"That's the last mistake you'll ever make," I snarled, letting a bomb launch from my chest. My power expanded and rolled forward, killing whatever monsters there may have been lurking in the woods. I toppled trees and turned the mighty oaks into fire tinder in one fell swoop. The portal lay barren, with only Lucifer and us standing.

"Go," I said to Valerie, and this time, she didn't hesitate. She ran in a straight line, using me to block Lucifer's access. The moment she stepped beyond the portal, she sent me the all clear.

"No display of white light or heavenly fire?" he asked.

"Not yet," I said and took a step closer. "That will come, but first I'm going to kick your ass."

He took the same form I was familiar with and then he snarled, "Game on."

It was enough to make me hesitate. I stared at the likeness of my father, knowing damned well it wasn't him inhabiting his form, but it still played with my head, whether or not I wanted to admit it.

Instead of acknowledging the bloom of fear that formed in my throat, I waved him in.

"Let's see what you can do when we are on a level playing field."

He charged, taking me by surprise, but it was sloppy enough for me to parry and send him tumbling to the ground. He glared at me and scrambled to his feet. I inhaled, finding my center and waiting for him to try something as inept.

"You would kill your own blood?" he asked, as he wiped off the dust.

I considered the question. "What do you think?"

"I think you don't have the stomach for it," he said. "You aren't like your father."

I smiled. In that respect, he was absolutely right, and that was the one thing that differentiated us. The one thing that made me forsake the dark side of my heritage. "No, I'm not."

He took a step closer, and his right hand formed the deadly claw I was familiar with, but I didn't move. I kept my hands loose and my ready stance intact.

He launched again and this time I spun away from his claw, and he roared in anger when my elbow caught his jaw, knocking him to the ground a few feet away.

"I'm not like my father. I've never killed for sport." I refrained from adding 'until now' because this really wasn't for sport. It was filled with liquid revenge.

"You're playing with me just like your father did at first, but I broke him, just like I'll break you, boy."

I laughed. "I've got trinity wrath in my blood. Bring it on," I said, and took my form again. This time, when he came in for the kill, I landed a punch, crushing his nose with a little extra juice behind my fist. Lucifer was tossed like a rag doll and hit the ground hard. His head bounced, and I couldn't help the smile that plastered on my face. My hand didn't even hurt from the effort.

Kill him. Valerie's voice invaded my mind, but I ignored her. I was enjoying the game.

He shook his head and glanced up at me.

"CJ?" the bastard asked, like he was just waking from a long nightmare. I knew damned well it was a ruse. My father was headed to Paradise Cove, regardless of his less than desirable form.

"I'm not buying it," I said, and sent a mental punch right into the bastard's balls. He made an 'oof' sound and curled into a fetal position. "That was for Valerie."

His bloody nostrils flared with anger, and he rolled onto his hands and knees. I took advantage of the situation and stepped in, setting up for a kick. Unfortunately, my foot never connected. Lucifer rolled and swept my leg out from under me. I landed on my back, and he was on me before the daze cleared.

His snarling growl caught me off guard, and his fingers pierced the skin over my heart.

"If I can't control you, I'm going to kill you and eat your fucking heart," he said, pushing farther into my skin.

I bellowed at the burning pain and threw a punch right at the bastard's throat. It knocked him back far enough that his hand was dislodged, and I threw him off me. I rolled clear and hopped to my feet, now leery.

Warm blood dripped down my chest, and the welts stung. The fact his fingers punctured through my leather coat and my thick flannel shirt sent a shiver up my back. As much as I wanted to pummel him, I started to doubt that strategy, but I knew if I sent him back under with no damage, he'd be back much sooner than if I decimated him.

"Is that all you got?" I said, egging him on.

His gaze shifted, and a flash of silver caught my eye. Lucifer caught the blade in his hand, hissing in pain as he threw it toward me. It dropped at my feet, slicing into the ground. Blood dripped from his hand and the smell of fried flesh hit me. It took me a second to understand what had just happened, and then I looked at the knife at my feet.

Valerie's talisman.

Valerie's knife had the power to damage angels.

Valerie. Shit.

The thought produced the metallic taste of fear, and my heart plummeted when Lucifer let out a growl of anger. I forgot my cardinal rule and glanced over my shoulder.

Valerie was within the perimeter, but she wasn't on the ground. Horror filled every fiber of my body, freezing me in place. She was elevated above the earth with her head bent so far back I didn't know how her neck hadn't snapped. The arch of her spine was equally alarming, as some unearthly force tried to break her in two. The scream that finally escaped from her tore at my soul.

"Say yes," Lucifer said, his voice close enough to pull my attention back to him.

The snap and sudden silence that filled the space broke through me like nothing I've ever experienced. I completely lost control.

"No!" my voice barreled out along with the lion's share of power, sweeping Lucifer into a ball of fire. I swept the knife off the ground and turned, running toward Valerie, willing whatever the hell was holding her in place to disintegrate as the ground rumbled around me.

Panic layered over me and shot out in waves. She tumbled from the sky and I caught her limp form in my arms. Without slowing down, I sprinted for the safety line, dodging the breaks in the ground as Hell's gate crumbled from my building wrath. I dove the last few feet, rolling with her in my arms.

When I glanced back, white fire rained on the portal, sending everything down into the canyon I had created. The flurry quieted as the earth fused and the righteous light faded. It wasn't until the dust settled that I glanced down at Valerie.

Her gaze looked through me like I wasn't even there, and I leaned down, putting my ear to her chest. Her heart wasn't beating.

"No!" This time my cry echoed to the heaven's. I refused to let her die, and I focused, forcing her heart to beat while I administered CPR. "You can't die. You hear me!" I bellowed, willing her body to keep functioning. "Breathe, goddamn it!"

When nothing happened, I split my focus, concentrating on keeping her heart beating and her lungs filling with oxygen while I forced Uriel's grace out of my body and into the tight, brilliant ball in my hand. I opened my eyes to prisms dancing around us and without hesitation; I plunged it into Valerie, praying angel grace held the miracle that the fraction of healing power I held couldn't.

Light filled her and healing sparks danced over her form. Valerie's breath sucked in, and then her scream filled the silent forest. Her back arched and the crunch of bones realigning made me grit my teeth, but whatever magic the grace held seemed to work. I knew better than anyone what kind of hell the healing mojo created, but it was temporary and her scream softened to a shaking whine before it stopped all together.

Her chest moved up and down as her breathing steadied into the normal cadence of life. When she opened her eyes and met my gaze, I bit my lower lip, willing the tears to remain locked away.

Valerie blinked at me with wide eyes, and then her head turned toward the clearing. "Mind fuck," she whispered and looked back at me.

Our little secret phrase brought a relieved smile to my lips, and I pulled her into my arms.

"I thought..." I couldn't finish and buried my face in her hair.

"Me, too." Her hand ran over her belly. "I don't know if the baby survived," she said, and I glanced down at her stomach.

My hand covered hers and we sat in silence, holding on to the dream that was our child just a little longer.

Chapter 27

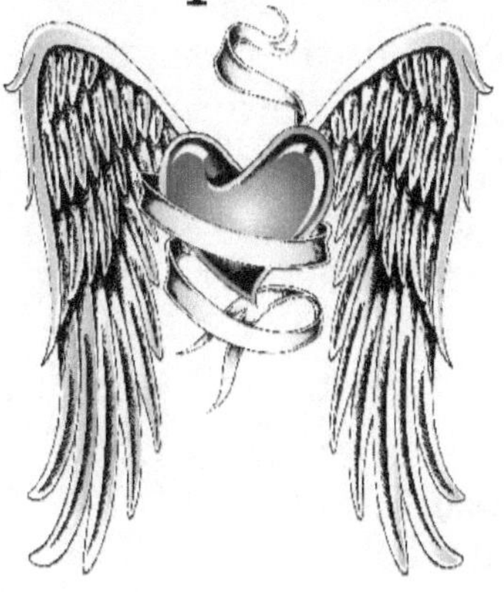

AFTER THE LONG TRIP down to Brooksfield, New Hampshire, I left Valerie in the care of Jennifer and Steve at the cabin and trudged to Paradise Cove. Damian sat on a rock watching the mad hellhound trying to get out of the salt barrier he was placed in. The beast snarled at the sight of me.

"Chill," I said, and put my hand up.

"What the hell are we going to do with him?" Damian asked, standing.

"I don't know, but it was worth a try," I said, meeting his gaze. "I'm just glad you got the message."

"This is royally fucked up." He ran a hand through his hair, and I couldn't agree more.

"Sit," I commanded, and despite the divisive snarl, the beast sat on his haunches.

I went to step inside the salt ring, and Damian grabbed my arm.

"I'm his son. He won't hurt me," I said, meeting Damian's gaze.

"That isn't your father anymore." He held fast, his gaze hard and unyielding. "And after what you told me Lucifer was doing to break him, I doubt he knows who you are."

"I gotta try, man," I whispered, and his hand dropped.

"If he attacks, he's toast," Damian promised, and I sighed.

Footsteps pulled our attention to the path and Tom stepped onto the moss.

"Holy fuck," he said, and I laughed as his eyes widened at the rabid beast.

"Yeah, Lucifer is more of an asshole than I gave him credit for." I crossed to my brother. "He turned Dad into that." I pointed, and the thing growled, its eyes bouncing between the two of us as saliva dripped from its sharp teeth.

I glanced at the sky and sighed. "I was going to step in the ring, but I have a feeling he's too far gone and would try to kill me," I said, and Tom nodded in agreement. "But there is one person he wouldn't attack." I met Tom's wide eyes.

"Mom," we both said at the same time.

Mist rose off the frozen water and the shift in air pulled our attention to the cove. My mother stood a few paces away from the wild dog. Her gaze locked on the beast and his snarling subsided. It was as if no amount of torture could erase her power over him.

His snout rose in the air, and he sniffed, and then a pitiful whine escaped, and he stretched on the ground, crawling forward until his paws stopped at the salt barrier. He laid his head on his paws. For the first time since I saw him, I got a good look at his pelt. The damage to his form was substantial. Evidence of torture laid waste in the scarring crisscrossed over his exposed flesh.

My mother saw it too, and her eyes welled with tears. "Jesus, Ty," she whispered and kneeled on the other side of the salt barrier. His head lifted parallel to hers and he whined.

Her hands moved, breaching the barrier, and cupped his massive jaws.

Damian laid a salt ring around my mother to protect us and she glanced at me before she wiped away the barrier keeping the hound from her. He crawled forward and laid his muzzle in her lap.

A lump formed in my throat, and tears burned. I had annihilated his human form, and all that was left was a beaten and butt ugly hellhound. My chin dropped to my chest, and Tom put his hand on my shoulder.

Wonder filled his eyes. "Look," he whispered.

My mother's tears fell on my father and the light that filled each prism wiped out the blackened form, replacing it with human skin, until it was actually my father's beaten and scarred form lying on the ground with his head in my mother's lap. Tattered clothing covered his body, and he lifted his head, pushing himself to his hands and knees and just stared at her.

His hand rose to her cheek, but his eyes didn't believe she was actually there.

"Baby, I'm here," my mother whispered.

His forehead dropped to her knees, and he crawled closer, wrapping his arms around her waist. His form shook.

"If this is another game, just kill me," he whispered, his voice hoarse and filled with agony.

"It's not, Dad," I said, and his body stiffened like he expected more horrors. His head turned and the glare he sent in my direction turned my blood to ice. The scene I witnessed in New York crawled back into my mind, and I understood exactly what Lucifer had done to him. He'd fucked with my father's mind just as completely as he had done to Valerie.

"Dad?" Tom stepped closer, blocking his glare, and he blinked, his eyes refocusing on Tom as my brother crouched lower just outside the salt ring.

My father's gaze moved between my brother and my mother, trying to reconcile what his eyes were seeing against the hell he endured for the last two years. I had heard Lucifer. I had heard the lies he told my father. That we never existed. That we were as much a figment of his imagination as marrying my mother had been. Lucifer promised him he died in that hellhole, that there had been no miracle.

When his gaze landed on me, his jaw clenched and the pain in his eyes shot through me. I took a step closer, and he flinched, his grip on my mother tightening.

My father never flinched. Ever. And seeing it was like a punch in the gut. The profound effect made me step forward. I had to break whatever Lucifer had done. I had to let him know he wasn't insane, that we weren't figments of his imagination.

I crossed the salt line between Tom, and my mother, and my father shot to his feet. His hand flashed out, grabbing my throat as the fury overrode every sense he had. I didn't stop him.

"I wasn't going to leave you there for...ever," I squeaked out as both my mother and brother tried to break his grasp on my throat.

Tears made my vision wobble, and I blinked. Heat squeezed out of the corners of my eyes and rolled down my cheeks. My father snarled fowl curses, promises to make me pay for what I had done to Jessica.

"Ty!" my mother yelled, pulling his gaze from my face to hers. "Let go of our son!"

The order she issued didn't compute at first and his incessant blinking announced his confusion. His grip loosened but remained clasped on my throat and my chin trembled.

"Dad," I whispered, trying to pull air into my starved lungs.

His gaze dropped to my chest and the ruined jacket before popping back to mine. After a moment, he looked around at where he was and his hand dropped from the grip on my throat to press against my chest like he was testing the boundaries of his sanity.

He glanced at my mother again. "Is..." He stopped and licked his lips with another scan of his surroundings. "Is this real?"

"Yes. Our boy decided a rescue mission was in order," she said and glanced at me. "Despite the waves it caused upstairs."

He stepped back and stared at the ground. Each time he began to speak, he rethought his statements and closed his mouth. Finally, he said, "Paradise Cove?" and looked up at me.

I gave a weak laugh and nodded.

He was slow to respond, but his gaze traveled upward and all around at each one of us before landing on Damian. "I... I think I remember..."

I knew that feeling and when his gaze landed back on me, he bit his lip and covered his mouth. "He really fucked with me," he whispered, and tears shined in his eyes.

"Yeah. Just like he screwed with Valerie," I said, and he blinked as that memory came back to him.

His gaze moved from me to Tom and then to my mother and in the next instance, his arms squeezed all of us together in a tight hug.

"He told me I died in the complex. That everything else was my mind's last-ditch fantasy to deal with Jessie's death. He made me watch her die before the chains tore me to pieces. It never stopped... and it never changed."

His body shook and his sobs layered over us like a blanket of rain. We all held onto him just as tightly as he gripped us. When his shakes subsided, we all let go, and he wiped his face before bringing his gaze to mine.

"I'm not sure what memories are real," he sniffled, and his hands gripped my cheeks as he targeted in on our original plan to send Lucifer back to hell. He searched my eyes and then tears formed in his and he pulled me into a tight hug. "But I hope to God this means what we did worked."

"It did," I whispered.

"How long..." he started before he trailed off.

"Two years," I said and shuddered at the thought. "Lucifer turned you into a hellhound," I whispered, and he pulled away. His gaze dropped to the ground as he searched for the memory, but it didn't surface and he shook his head, trying to clear fact from fiction.

"I got married a couple of months ago," I added and lifted my hand so he could see the wedding band.

He stared at the band surrounding my left ring finger and his brow creased before he glanced at my mother.

"Yes. That's the wedding band I gave you. Valerie is wearing mine," she confirmed with a smile.

His brows arched and his head snapped back in my direction. "You and Valerie?"

I nodded. "It took a while to undo what Lucifer did to her, but yeah, we toughed it out."

He smiled for the first time since the haze cleared from his mind. "Congratulations," he said, and my mother extended her hand to him.

"Come on, babe. We have a lot of catching up to do, and we can't stay here," she said. He took her palm in his and followed as she led him toward the brightly lit water. He stopped at the edge and turned, meeting Tom's stare.

"I'm proud of you," he said directly to my brother, and then his gaze moved to mine. "Both of you." With that, he and my mother faded, becoming one with the mist and I slowly lowered to the ground, wrapping my arms around my knees as the sobs took hold.

Tom's hand squeezed my shoulder and then both he and Damian left me alone in the confines of the cove.

I don't know how long I sat on the frozen moss, crying, but it wasn't until a hand threaded through my hair that I looked up. I expected Valerie, so the grand expanse of white wings before me shocked me into silence. He slowly crouched so our eyes were level.

"I will make sure Heaven takes good care of your father," he said. "Especially given his willingness to sacrifice himself for my children."

"Raphael?" I asked and wiped my face on my sleeve.

He smiled softly and extended his hand. "Yes. The last of the true archangels," he said, and his wings ruffled before they folded neatly on his back. I took his hand and Raphael pulled me to my feet. His dark eyes reminded me of Naomi's and there was something nurturing about him I didn't get from any of the others.

"I am the healer," he said to my train of thought. "Not a warrior unless I am pushed into a corner."

He smiled, and calm settled over me. "I'm a bit more like my brother Gabriel than I am Michael." He winked, and my lips twitched into a smile of my own.

"So... not all archangels are dicks?" I asked, and his laughter floated over the cove, warming my soul.

"My heaven's, no," he said as the laughter wound down. "Some of us have softer hearts than others."

"Can you heal my father's wounds?" I asked, thinking of the scars visible under his tattered clothing.

"I can fix the scars on his skin, but your mother is the only one who can fix his fractured soul." He offered a smile and pulled me to his chest, wrapping his arms and wings around me. His warmth saturated my skin, taking the shake from my cold limbs. "As for you, I can ease your mind and prepare you for your next battle with Lucifer."

He pressed his lips to my forehead and light encompassed me, showing me a litany of visions that brought tears to my eyes and hope to my heart. I glanced into his eyes and his hand covered my heart, pushing in a ball of light. His pristine wings shriveled as his grace filled my form.

He stepped away and gave me a nod, fading the same way my parents had. I turned toward the path and stopped at Valerie's awed stare. I leaned down and picked up one of the fallen feathers, holding it in my hand as I glanced up at the sky.

When I turned my attention back to Valerie, my gaze lowered to her belly, to the tiny miracle that still existed, based on Raphael's vision. I grinned and closed the distance, wrapping my arms around her and delivering a kiss that consumed both of us.

Chapter 28

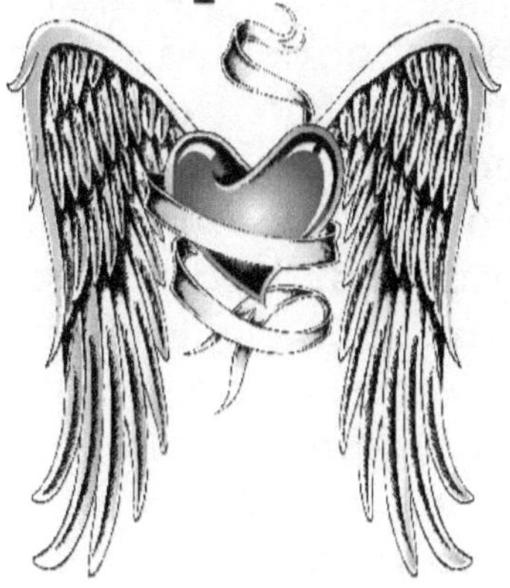

THE KIDS RAN DOWN the beach, enjoying an early summer heat wave. Their little legs pumped, and their laughter floated on the breeze. Damian ran after them, pretending to be a big, bad sand monster, catching each one in his arms and rolling onto his back on the sand. Gracie jumped on his chest and her little fingers found the ticklish spots on his neck as Gabe and Michael yelled for help.

I smiled as I watched Damian. His kids were entertaining, to say the least, and I traded a glance with Valerie. The visions Raphael shared with me intertwined our families for the foreseeable future.

Valerie smiled at me like she knew what I was thinking. She ran her hand down my arm and we laced our fingers. I returned her grin before my gaze dropped to her oversized belly. An unearthly calm settled over me and I leaned forward, planting a kiss on the swollen skin under her beach dress.

"How you feeling?" I asked.

"Good, considering I'm overdue," she said. "I swear this boy just doesn't want to come out."

Tom and Raven chuckled, turning toward the squealing laugh of their three-year-old daughter. Hannah approached, her tiny hands grasping one of Steve's and one of Jennifer's. She planted her feet and then jumped, letting Steve and Jennifer swing her forward. Her giggle tickled all of us and we exchanged glances before returning our gaze to the wild redhead. She broke free and ran to Damian's three kids, sliding to a stop and dropping into the sand next to them.

Steve and Jennifer approached, taking the vacant seats nearest the kids.

"She's a handful," Steve said, lounging back in the chair.

Tom returned his smile, nodding and signing a simple, "Yes."

"Have you settled on a name yet?" Naomi asked, her eyes locked on her children building a sandcastle a few feet away.

"Ty," Valerie said, pulling everyone's gazes to her. "Ty Alexander Ryan."

Damian smiled, scanning the horizon, wondering if my father was finally at peace in heaven.

Grace stood and crossed the distance, trading a glance with me before she focused on her father.

"He is, Daddy," she said, patting his hand, leaving tiny traces of sand with each pat.

A CHILL DRIFTED OVER ALL of us. I knew her minor revelation sent a chill through Damian, and I raised my beer in response. Grace seemed to have a line straight to heaven, one that even I didn't have, and I smiled.

She was going to be a handful when she grew
up. My gaze traveled to Valerie's stomach, and I
sent a silent good luck wish to my son.
After all, Grace would be his handful someday.

The End

Continue THE RYAN CHRONICLES with ANGEL
BLOOD.

About J.E. Taylor

J.E. Taylor is a USA Today bestselling author, a publisher, an editor, a manuscript formatter, a mother, a wife, a business analyst, and a Supernatural fangirl. Not necessarily in that order. She first sat down to seriously write in February of 2007 after her daughter asked:

"Mom, if you could do anything, what would you do?"

From that moment on, she hasn't looked back.

Besides being co-owner of Novel Concept Publishing, Ms. Taylor also moonlights as a Senior Editor of Allegory E-zine, an online venue for Science Fiction, Fantasy and Horror, and co-host of the popular YouTube talk show Spilling Ink.

She lives in New Hampshire with her husband and during the summer months enjoys her weekends on the shore in southern Maine.

Visit her at www.jetaylor75.com to check out her other titles.

If you liked ANGEL WRATH, check out the rest of THE RYAN CHRONICLES:

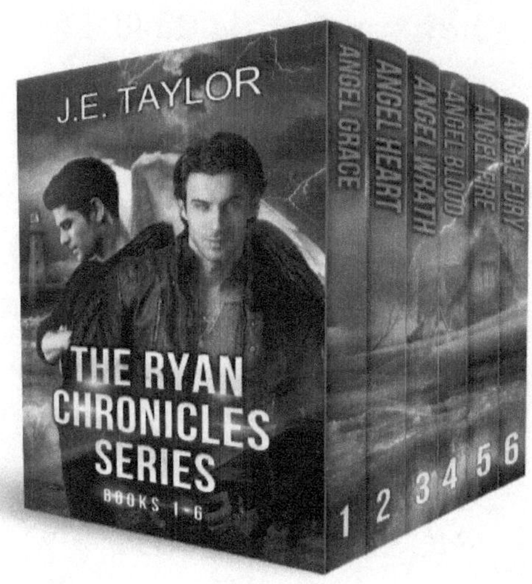

THE RYAN CHRONICLES

**Demons, vampires, angels, and the devil.
What the hell kind of nightmare do I live in?**

CJ Ryan was born with enough psychic power to destroy the earth. And Lucifer wants him to do just that.

Raised with a strong moral compass, CJ won't sacrifice innocent lives to protect his own, and that puts him at odds with the devil.

But if he doesn't give in, he and all he loves will become the target of Lucifer's rage.

When CJ gives his twin brother, Tom, a dose of his powers to keep him safe, it puts Tom directly in Lucifer's crosshairs.

As the final battle draws near, what will they have to sacrifice to keep their loved ones safe?

Can they survive the devil's wrath?

THE RYAN CHRONICLES includes these titles:

CJ's Story:

ANGEL GRACE - Book 1

ANGEL HEART - Book 2

ANGEL WRATH – Book 3

Tom's Story:

ANGEL BLOOD - Book 4

ANGEL FIRE - Book 5

ANGEL FURY – Book 6

Fans of Supernatural and Shadowhunters will enjoy this series.

You might also like the GAMES THRILLER SERIES which highlights CJ and Tom's parents and their unorthodox history together.

GAMES THRILLER SERIES

Intensely disturbing. Beautifully horrific. Indescribably intense.

When Ty Aris kidnaps Jessica Connor for his stepbrother's underground film network, he is not prepared for the impact she has on him.

His obsession with her lights a fire under his ass to get out of the ungodly business with his stepbrother.

But the only way to leave the business is in a body bag.

In the dark plane between life and death, Ty is given a choice: save his soulmate or save his very soul.

The Games Thriller Series includes:

Fallen – A Games Series Prequel

Survival Games

Mind Games

End Game

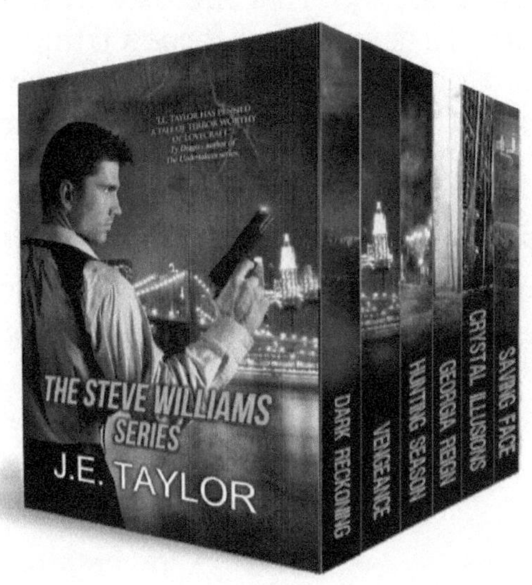

THE STEVE WILLIAMS SERIES

Special Agent Steve Williams excels at his job, catching the most heinous of monsters walking the earth.

Serial killers.

When his job brings him face to face with a psychic, he struggles to accept her gifts in his neat little black and white world. Armed with her visions, along with his skills as an FBI agent, he hunts the worst of the worst, but will he catch the killer before they set their sights on him?

Unstoppable, breath stealing, and terrifying all at once.

Gripping, rich and magnificent!

263

The Steve Williams Series mixes compelling crime thrillers with supernatural forces that will grip the reader from page one. This six-book series takes you through some of Steve Williams' darkest cases in his FBI career.

The STEVE WILLIAMS SERIES includes Dark Reckoning, Vengeance, Hunting Season, Georgia Reign, Crystal Illusions, and Saving Face.

FIRE CURSED TRILOGY

Lucifer's daughter rises.

Faith Kennedy's mother hid the awful truth from her daughter for sixteen years. Until she lay on her deathbed. Only then did she reveal who sired her daughter, and the revelation terrifies Faith.

The devil may have sired her, but he only wants her beating heart ripped out of her chest. After all, that's where her angel grace fueling her fire power is stored, and that will give him what he needs to bring about humanity's fall.

And Lucifer will take down anyone who gets in his way.

When Faith is given an ancient knife that can kill the devil, she faces the toughest challenge of her young life. She must hunt Lucifer and put him down. Otherwise, the world will burn.

But if she succeeds, she may wipe herself, and everyone she loves, out of existence.

This set includes Fire Cursed, Homecoming, and Judgement Day.

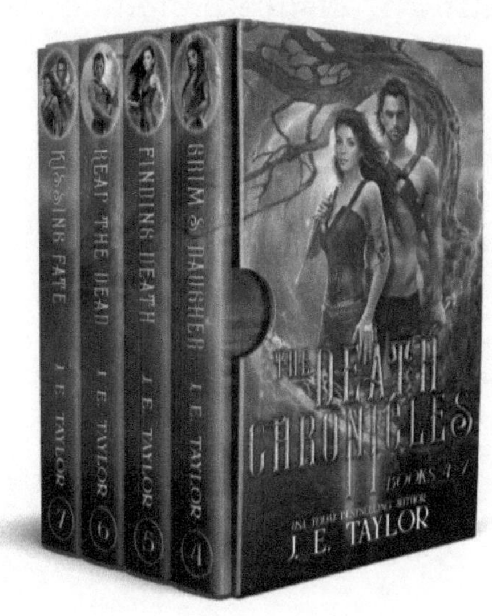

THE DEATH CHRONICLES II

Death is the family business, but not one I want to pursue. Thankfully, it's been passed down from father to son for generations, so it should skip me as Death's daughter. Then I won't have to stop being alive and can actually live my life. Right?

Well, the reapers don't agree. And neither do the angels.

One thinks I'm destined to take over, the other believes I will destroy existence. Both want me dead to match their own agendas.

I have an agenda of my own, and Leviathan who has sworn to protect me. But once my family and friends start being targeted, the family business, while grim, might be the only choice I have to save those I love.

The Death Chronicles *II* includes the following
titles

Grim's Daughter

Finding Death

Reap the Dead

Kissing Fate

Find these titles and other fantasy and suspense
titles on J.E. Taylor's website!

www.JETaylor75.com